Dev

Lords of the Night
Book One

Sandra Sookoo

Adventure. Humor. Inclusion. Romance

New Independence Books

This is a work of fiction. Names, characters, places, and incidents either are the product of the author's imagination or are used fictitiously, and any resemblance to actual persons living or dead, business establishments, events, or locales, is entirely coincidental.

All rights reserved. No portion of this book may be reproduced or transmitted in any form or by any electronic or mechanical means, including photocopying, recording or by any information retrieval and storage system without permission of the author.

DEVIL TAKE THE DUKE © 2021
ISBN: 9798478518721

by Sandra Sookoo
sandrasookoo@yahoo.com
Visit me at www.sandrasookoo.com

Published by New Independence Books
newindependencebooks@gmail.com

Edited by: Angie Eads and Heather Garcia

Book Cover Design by David Sookoo
Couple:–Period Images
Background images: Deposit Photos

First Print Edition: 2019
Second Print Edition: 2021

Dedication

To my husband David. Thank you for your unwavering support and encouragement, on the high days and the low ones. You are now, and always will be, my hero.

Acknowledgements

There is much work that goes into putting out a book, and while the author spends the bulk of that time alone, locked away with their computer and their characters, there are times when it's essential that friends and readers have a bit of input. I'd like to thank the following people and Facebook friends for all their help and input on various topics while this book was in the writing stage:

For help in choosing what sort of paranormals will inhabit my Lords of the Night series:

Gwen Phifer, Resa Haile, JJ Nite, Alexa Dare, Cate Peace, Beth Caudill, Tammie King, Penny Elliott, Evita Perez, Lindsay Downs

For help in picking a title:

Cindy Bartolotta. Lucinda Poette, Michele Miller, Anna McLain, Kay Springsteen Tate, Gail Hart, Beverly Ross, Heather Garcia, Colleen Thompson, Talina Perkins, Mary Dieterich, Penny Elliott, Christine Warner, Amy Valentini, Jennifer Gryner Coleman, Lori Farner Dykes, Donna Antonio, Mary Anne Landers, Angie Eads, Michele Jensen, Jessica Coulter Smith

And finally, to all the staff at Blue Tulip Publishing. You have taken my career to the next level and have opened another avenue for me so I can continue my writing journey, and for that I'm eternally grateful. Thank you.

Blurb

He accepts her but doesn't love her... Donovan James Arthur Sinclair, 8th duke of Manchester, is cursed to roam the Earth as a wolf-shifter. He doesn't mind the beast most days, for the life of a duke is quite splendid, but it is trying if he's honest with himself. When he saves a country miss from an out-of-control carriage in a rural village, it occurs to him that he might be wrong.

She loves him but cannot accept what he truly is... Miss Alice Morrowe, is blind and firmly on the shelf, unloved and unwanted by nearly everyone she's ever met. While she's happy with her life, she wants acceptance for who she is. When she is thrown to the ground in a tangle of limbs by a very naked man amidst a thunder of hooves, she cannot help but wonder if her life is about to change.

A marriage of convenience that's anything but... In her, Donovan sees a way to break his curse if he can seduce her into love. In him, Alice finds solace and the thrill of romance. She's only too happy to wed him and grasp a life she's always wanted, but is her love what he needs to banish the beast within? Emotions run high when things don't turn out the way they've each planned. Only discovering truth and genuine love can bring clarity, hope… and happily ever after.

The Legend of the Cursed Lords

At least a hundred years ago, a handful of irreverent, spoiled lords had their way with female gypsy travelers in the countryside of England. In a fit of spoiled, drunken revelry, they set fire to a wagon and laughed as it burned while the remainder of the caravan fled in terror. That vehicle was owned by an ancient witch, existing through the years from the magic flowing through her veins. She took high exception to the destruction, as well as the uncaring attitudes of those English lords, and under the light of a full moon, the gypsy witch brought forth a powerful curse onto those unfortunate men.

> *From here to eternity, you will never know peace, never live the life of a full human man. You will always be a slave to the shifter, the beast, or anomaly within. All women who look upon your face will turn away in disgust, for in moments of high emotion, they will see the truth; there is no hiding from that. You will be held in terror once your secret is revealed—for tell them you must. And though you might marry, you are destined for the coldness of a*

joyless union, unless you find the very heart and secret of life. You will carry the burden alone, for this curse will only belong to you and cannot be transferred or shared with a mate.

But I am benevolent, men with no hearts, no morals, and less feelings. Every five years, during one full moon each quarter, the curse might be broken, if you are wise enough to come out of the shadows and see the error of your ways. Beneath the light of that one full moon when the kiss of unselfish, pure love crosses your lips, and pride, fear, and ego falls, then you might know the freedom of living as a full human with your affliction broken and your offspring unhindered. For yes, unless the curse lifts, any male children you might have will suffer too.

Tread carefully, accursed ones, else you will forever go through life cold, unloved, feared, and isolated.

To this day, those men are referred to as the Cursed Lords of England—the Lords of the Night—and until they find themselves hopelessly and helplessly in love so deep that they cannot survive without winning the heart of their lady, they are doomed to walk the earth hand in hand with their beastly halves, alone.

CHAPTER ONE

September 11, 1815
Shalford, near Guildford, Surrey, England

The chill of the early autumn ground seeped into his paws while the crisp air ruffled through the thick fur on his back as he ran.

Donovan James Arthur Sinclair, 8th duke of Manchester, crested a small hill and loped to a halt. Illumination from a half moon filtered through the tree leaves, frosting everything on the ground faintly with silver. Each blade of grass, each leaf, each groove in tree trunks was thrown into sharp relief. He threw back his wolf head, filled his canine lungs with air, and then let out a wild howl that echoed throughout the countryside.

As his hackles rose with anticipation, he bounded into movement once more. Every muscle in his body bunched and released as he ran. His claws dug into the soft earth with each footfall. Snout to the ground, he snuffled for the scent of prey through a few dry, fallen leaves and rotting vegetation.

On nights like this he felt at one with his beastly half, and when the freedom of running overtook him, he could ignore the curse that sent him shifting into the wolf every night.

As his tongue lolled out of his slightly gaping jaws, the sharp metallic taste of blood hit his palate. He'd recently killed a deer to assuage his hunger, and though his belly was full, the urge to hunt still raged, for it also amused him, and he hadn't run all the way to Surrey from London for nothing. No doubt there were still a few animals for him to bedevil. A trip that would take a few hours by carriage, he accomplished in nearly sixty minutes.

There's something to be said for becoming the beast within.

His wolf half howled into his mind with a sound he interpreted as laughter. *Let me always be like this. Running free as the beast.*

Donovan uttered a snort. *I beg to differ with you. I rather enjoy my human form.*

As a duke, he was afforded certain privileges that other men of the *ton* didn't possess. At a position just beneath royalty, he maintained a lofty title, had accumulated two fortunes of his own in his lifetime through clever investments and the sweat of hard work, and he had only to arch an eyebrow or crook a finger if he desired a woman's company in his bed. He wanted for nothing; his existence unfettered by demands of a spouse or children.

A twinge moved through his innards. Children that he'd been careful not to father for fear that males would be cursed as well and further besmirch his name through society. If the line stopped with him, so be it, but he refused to have anyone else trapped by shifter blood for something they—or he, or hell, even his grandfather—didn't do.

I'm not that *selfish.*

He snickered. But he was selfish enough to live only for his pleasure. He was a duke, after all, and it was his God-given right. Life was perfect, or it would be if not for the damn curse he'd struggled with every day of his five and thirty years, fought against the whims of the beast within. He narrowed his wolfish eyes. Just like seven dukes of the same title before him, he'd had no choice except to submit to the demands of his beast when the desire to shift came upon him.

But he made damn certain to keep tight control on that aspect of his life. He refused to kill people, and in that, at least the shift remained civilized, for he'd learned much about himself during his stint in fighting Napoleon. In those years, he'd allowed the beast free reign. The wolf had killed many French; it was war after all. Afterward he'd despised himself even more for what he'd done, and he'd vowed to never again let the wolf override his human logic and thinking.

Being cursed was his lot, and he attempted to make the best of it, even if he hated it at times, but he didn't need to reduce himself to a beastly mentality. If he didn't have his wolf, he'd never know the joy of running through the English countryside or the freedom found with escaping the confines of London and the responsibilities that came with the title.

Those that were still valid in the places where he was accepted and not black-listed. Another "benefit" that came with the curse.

He pushed such thoughts from his head. Almost dawn, light had begun to break at the horizon, and those gold and lavender glimmers reminded him that he'd need to turn about soon and return to London if he didn't wish to be seen as the beast, or worse, naked as he reclaimed his human form.

Stay longer. It is good here, nice for me. Quiet. There is the scent of goodness, of nature.

Donovan quelled the urge to roll his eyes. *And London is nice for me. We're going home.* He might be bound to the animal, but that didn't mean he had to live like one. London could be loud, dirty at times, and crowded, but it was his home.

His wolf remained silent, no doubt in high dudgeon. Amused, he continued his run, intent on cutting through the sleepy village of Shalford before turning back toward the capital. Following the River Tillingbourne, he snuffled along the shallow banks as he came into the small village proper. As he trotted past a grain mill with its water wheel, he had to admit the setting was quaint, if one liked that sort of thing, but he couldn't imagine cooling his heels in such rustication. Hell, he rarely visited his own country estate, Kimbolton Castle in Cambridgeshire. What was the point?

Much room to run there.

Yet there is little entertainment, he silently reminded his canine counterpart.

Devil Take the Duke (Lords of the Night #1)

His wolf whined. *There is more to life than that.*

If there was, Donovan didn't wish to know.

Minutes later, he hit a dirt road that led into what would be a bustling area later in the morning. The tiny commerce section left much to be desired and featured a handful of businesses, namely a bakery, a butcher, a sundry shop, a musty-looking bookseller, and a few more he couldn't bring himself to take an interest in. What amusement could such a village offer him that London couldn't top?

Tiring of the pedestrian place, Donovan made his way off the path in favor of following the tree line, and just as he ducked into the foliage, a woman appeared from the direction of the water mill. Bored, but having nothing else to occupy his time, he sat on his haunches while the shrubbery obscured him, and settled in to observe, for a woman was a woman regardless of location.

And he wouldn't be a red-blooded male if he didn't appreciate her form.

Her simple day dress of unappealing lightweight gray wool neither hid nor showcased a figure. The fabric rippled in the breeze and occasionally would outline the length of a leg as she walked. A knitted shawl of ivory concealed her upper half, and for that he uttered a soft whine of annoyance. Such a disappointment, hiding one's bosom with modesty. Those charms were but one asset that made women delightfully delicious. Plus, the rather ugly bonnet trimmed in faded navy ribbons obscured her hair and face.

Damnation. There'd be no fanaticizing this morning. No woolgathering either, for he did adore imagining the slow undress of a woman in his mind. Bedding members of the opposite sex provided entertainment in a world of ennui he'd sunk into, and who was he to turn away the opportunity to slake his desires if the female was willing?

Inside his head, his wolf snorted. *Tiresome females. Bed you out of curiosity, desire your coin, wish the fame of being with you, for you are forbidden.*

The words had the same effect as having a bucket of icy water thrown in the face. *Do shut up.* Yes, his title as well as a handful of other "accursed lords" had been black-listed throughout the *ton* even though they were titles of long-standing. He and his contemporaries were not granted admission to Almack's nor were they given invitations to the most popular events during the Season, for if there was anything the lauded patronesses and sponsors in society liked more than exuding power it was indulging in gossip and rumors.

Not that it mattered, for he and his friends had created a rather tight social network of their own, including an exclusive risqué gentleman's club. The proper circles of the *ton* could go hang for all he cared. *I prefer my women on the scandalous side, and the more experienced with bedsport, the better.*

His wolf chuffed in his mind. *The female is in peril.* It was said in a matter-of-fact tone. *We must help.*

The devil you say. Donovan snapped his full attention back to the ordinary woman on the country lane. From the opposite direction, a curricle raced down the road at breakneck speed. Its driver, still dressed in dark evening clothes that were rather rumpled, held the reins in lax hands, his expression somewhat green about the gills. No doubt a hungover lord driving without care. *Bastard.* Yet, there had been many times he, himself, had acted the same when he'd escaped a married woman's bed minutes ahead of her husband returning home.

No matter that the curricle's wheels crunched and rattled against the ruts and stones in the road, the woman didn't glance up. She kept her gaze on the ground.

Damn it all. Donovan loped from his hiding spot. He headed in her direction at a run, his heart pounding. Why didn't she pay attention?

Inside his head, the wolf whined. *You aren't the hero type.* A certain amount of sarcasm dripped from the comment.

Don't remind me of my shortcomings, and I'm not playing the hero. Even you can agree we cannot stand idly by and let the woman be trampled. Rarely did he concern himself with the affairs of anyone else, and philanthropy or charity wasn't his style. Why should he care when no one showed the same consideration for him? In fact, he'd made rather a habit of remaining aloof and out of the public, for if society didn't accept him, he didn't need them.

When the driver of the curricle shouted as his vehicle quickly raced toward her, she finally lifted her head, but though she looked in the direction of the out-of-control equipage, she still didn't alter her course.

Why won't she bloody move? Regardless that the curricle's driver pulled hard at the reins, his forward momentum wouldn't enable him to stop in time. Donovan pushed himself into a determined sprint. As the carriage bore down upon her location, he jumped, catching her in the midsection with his body. They both tumbled to the side of the road in a blur and tangle of limbs just as the curricle thundered past. The driver flung a string of vulgarities her way but continued his path. Neither did he attempt to inquire as to the woman's health.

What an arse. Even in his capacity as a duke gripped by boredom and apathy, he would have checked on a person he'd nearly run down on a public road. There were manners, after all.

Regardless, such carelessness deserved a sharp dressing down and a severe warning. He grabbed her skirts in his jaw and pulled her into a thicket that lined the side of the lane, and then down a slight embankment. Shrubberies there more or less hid them both from the road and any curious passerby, not that there was such at this early hour. He loosened his jaws, releasing her, but he remained close, waiting to see if she appeared injured.

She lay, apparently stunned, on the grass, her skirts twisted about her legs, hitched up to show the length of her slender calves encased in ivory stockings. "What in the world happened?" The bewilderment in her soft voice betrayed culture and breeding. Despite her plain clothing, this was no country miss.

Intrigued, but no less annoyed, Donovan called forth the shift, and his body contorted. Pain shot through his limbs, ricocheted through each nerve ending as his bones and organs knitted themselves into his normal form. Claws and snout retracted, replaced by nails and human teeth. Fur vanished in favor of his skin and hair, and when the metamorphosis completed its cycle, he collapsed on the ground beside her while she struggled into a sitting position.

Damnation, but that agony sapped at his strength. Never did he grow used to the trauma. As he shook his head to chase away the last vestiges of the transformation, he regarded his unlikely companion. Her bonnet had been knocked askew and hung at an awkward angle to one side of her head. Rich brown hair met his perusal, and in the rays of the dawn, burnished mahogany highlights glimmered. Though she'd landed her gray gaze, wide and confused, upon him, she didn't react to his heroic act nor to the undeniable fact of his naked state. There were no words of gratitude or thanks. Neither did she look upon him with any sort of fascination. His ego twinged slightly, for he wasn't accustomed to being so summarily dismissed.

"Why the deuce didn't you move away from danger? You must be blind to not have seen such a path of destruction meant for you." Every inch of the duke rang in his rebuke as he glared at her.

She put a gloved hand to her forehead. Her eyes narrowed. Anger flashed in those gray depths. "For your information, I *am* blind, but I'm not a simpleton. Though you may be to treat me like you've done." The woman quickly set her bonnet to rights. "I heard commotion but didn't know where it came from."

Rendered speechless, Donovan opened and closed his mouth. What did one say to such an answer? He had no experience with sight impairment. So he took refuge in the annoyance that still swirled hot through his chest. "At least I have enough sense not to let a curricle trample me." He straightened his spine but remained sitting on the grass beside her. How dare this woman think to argue with him.

"I possess manners enough not to shove a lady from the roadway and then proceed to drag her into the brush." Then her eyes rounded and emotions clouded the stormy depths: confusion, terror… and curiosity. She sucked in a breath. "Do you mean to ravish me, then? You saw what you hoped was a vulnerable target and you pounced?" Before he could contradict the statement, she moved her head from side to side, searching with her gaze that didn't hold the typical vacancy or blankness of one without sight. "Yet I was certain what knocked me down wasn't a man at all." One of her hands flexed. "I thought, for a brief moment, I'd felt fur, like that of a dog…"

Dear Lord. Had she seen or suspected he'd shifted from the beast? He yanked himself from his stupor. "Rest assured, it was me who pulled you from the road. After that, I brought you through the thicket and down here." He forced a hard swallow. What kind of woman was she? Any other lady, upon being handled with such rough care and presented with a nude man, would scream the village awake and then succumb to a fainting spell. Yet his companion, though wary, did none of those things. She kept her gaze trained upon his face. "You and I are not finished having words, for I mean to dress you down for such ill-advised—"

"You smell differently from other men," she interrupted as she leaned closer to him.

"I beg your pardon?" His pulse pounded hard in his temples. Surely this odd woman didn't suspect his true nature.

"Your scent, it's wild. Primal." She wrenched off her gloves of worn ivory kid and dropped them to the ground next to her. "May I?" She reached for him. "It's but one of the ways I can see you."

"I... You have my leave." The intrigue deepened, and since he was currently perplexed by her, as well as her lack of taking responsibility for her part in the debacle, he nodded, and then berated himself. If she'd been truthful regarding her blindness, she couldn't see the gesture.

"The way you speak tells me you must be someone of some importance." The woman glanced her fingertips along the planes of his face, his cheekbones, his forehead. Her touch was gentle as she traced his eyebrows, the slope of his nose, the cut of his jaw, his chin.

Awareness rippled over his skin the longer she stayed connected to him. "I'd like to think so," he managed to say, albeit in a whisper. Such closeness, or rather intimacy, demanded matching vocal tones.

"Men always do." She chuckled. The throaty sound skated over him and gathered in his groin, tightening his length. "It is a dangerous way to think." Then she smoothed her palms down the sides of his neck, over his shoulders and sucked in a breath. "You're naked."

"I..." How the devil could he explain away that fact?

"Why are you without clothes?" She scooted closer to him. Their legs touched, her skirts bunched around her knees. Her shawl had slipped revealing a mere hint of the tops of creamy breasts, and still she explored. "However did you manage to go about the village dressed in naught but scandal?"

What an... interesting way of putting it. Some of his acumen returned from the fog that had wrapped about his brain. "You wouldn't believe me if I told you." And there was no way he'd offer the information to her upon this unorthodox meeting. Chances were he'd never see her again.

"Nothing is impossible." Her fingers slipped over his chest, rasping through the heavy mat of hair there. When she gently tugged on a few strands, he gasped. Unbridled lust streaked through his body, building as she smoothed her hands along his torso and then dipped questing fingers lower still, brushing those digits across the flat skin of his abdomen. "Regardless of your improper state, I'm glad. It is a refreshing change and adds a bit of mystery to the meeting." His muscles clenched. When she pushed onward, her palm skating over the wide head of his erect member, he grabbed her hand and held it away from his person.

Donovan sucked in great gulps of air as he willed his body to stop its reaction to her innocent exploration. How gauche it was that he'd grown hard for a woman he didn't know. Desperate for something to take his mind off his baser instincts, he asked, "Are you in the habit of introducing yourself to men like this? For if you are, my next question is why are you allowed out of the house unaccompanied?"

A delighted smile curved her rosy lips, lips he couldn't tear his gaze from with the bottom being slightly fuller than the top, lips he wanted to claim with a kiss, which was the fastest way to Bedlam aside from conversing here while he remained naked. "No, I am not." Then the smile faded and he felt the disappointment deep down in his chest. "In all honesty, men do not seek me out for any sort of meeting."

It was the height of folly to linger here. The longer he did, the greater the chance of being discovered, and no matter who this woman was, he refused to compromise her or have his own life thrust into a situation he didn't want. "I'm sorry to hear that." Her hand in his was soft. She didn't back away and was much too close for his comfort.

"I've learned over the years to accept that my affliction is isolating." The words sounded tired, as if she'd said them time out of hand already.

In this, she and he were in complete agreement. "I understand all too well the sentiment." He peered into her eyes, struck again by how alert she appeared yet didn't see him. In the rapidly lighting dawn, a few silver flecks glinted deep in those depths. The gentleman in him finally rose to the surface. "Forgive me for the rough handling, but it was the only way to prevent disaster and injury."

"Don't trouble yourself. Aside from some aches and what will no doubt be bruises, I am well." Again, a smile curved her lips, and his member renewed its appreciation for her.

"I'm glad." It was absurd, sitting here like this, clinging to her hand, while inside his head, his wolf encouraged him to give into primal instincts. "By the by, I'm Donovan Sinclair, the Duke of Manchester."

And I desperately need to leave before... well before I can do anything that will give away my secret or show her I'm the degenerate rogue I fear I am.

CHAPTER TWO

Miss Alice Morrowe's mind spun from the situation she currently found herself in.

Her chest and ribcage smarted from the impact, and her backside stung, but what held her captive was the completely bizarre fact she sat close to a naked man—and a duke at that. With her skirts in a tangle and her legs on display from the knees down, if someone in the village came upon them, there'd be no doubt in anyone's mind as to what had occurred, even if it was far from the truth.

A naked man who, from all accounts, was interested in her—or at least a specific part of him was—in a base way that he'd no doubt feel for any living, breathing female. Her brief encounter with the tip of his rampant member still tickled her palm. She marveled that she'd been so bold as to touch him there; never had she touched a man, and not *that* part of a man at all. It had been an accident, so caught up in "seeing" him with her fingertips as she was. And yet, she allowed him to keep hold of her hand, and she didn't move away from such sure scandal.

"You're a duke." It wasn't a question. She enjoyed having him so near. In her experience, men, once they were appraised of her incurable eye condition, steered clear of any interaction. Rarely was she sought out. Yes, it was a lonely life, but she'd had no choice except to make the best of it and carve out happiness for herself where she could. Somewhere in the jumbled memories of the events that whisked her from the roadside, she recalled the roughness of animal fur, the strong clench of toothy jaws in the skirt of her dress, the soft snuffle of breath. What had become of the dog? "Why are you here?" Perhaps he'd been on a hunting mission and had gotten separated from his hound.

Yet, the way that animal had slammed into her indicated its weight was significantly larger than a hunting dog.

"Obviously, to rescue you," came his glib reply.

Alice looked directly at him, but she only saw wavy white space. If she glanced over his shoulder, she could make out the general shape of his person, his head, but the image wasn't clear. It was almost as if a thick film had fallen permanently over her eyes, but at least she discerned he possessed light brown hair and that it stuck up in places. The only way to fully see a person was to intimately press herself against them, and that wasn't something she could do at the moment, for he was a stranger.

And a duke.

And naked.

Even though she'd already forgotten herself and hand run her hands over the bulk of him. "Yes, well, there is that." A trace of heat infused her cheeks as her thoughts dwelled on his scandalous state of undress. Each time she went out of the house it was a risk, a gamble she never knew if she'd win. Being blind didn't exactly lend itself to full self-efficiency, though Lord knew she tried her hardest. But the world was also full of people who wished harm to befall its most vulnerable residents. "I meant, why are you here in Shalford?"

Besides upending my world.

"Ah... business. I'd been on my way out of the village, returning to London in fact, when I came upon you." His deep, tenor-pitched voice rumbled in her own chest, and she shivered as gooseflesh sprang on her skin.

"I see. Hunting?"

After a slight pause, he said, "You could say that."

"Where is your hound?"

"I don't have one."

Very curious indeed. Not only did he not have a dog, but there were no hunting weapons, tools or any other accessories nearby. And why was he naked? "Were you successful?"

"More or less." Was that amusement hanging on his voice?

As a member of the gentry, even as a poor relation, she wasn't given much value, and being with a man here and now, one who'd gone out of his way to push her from being run over by a carriage, was interesting and intriguing. He didn't have to concern himself, yet he had. What did he wish for in return? A chill swept up her spine. Cold disappointment coiled in her belly. Was he like all the rest? She wasn't a woman of loose morals, wouldn't lie with him out of desperate loneliness, his boredom, or her own curiosity. Merciful heavens, did that explain his state of undress? He was already prepared to ravage her? "Perhaps you should be on your way now that you've ascertained I'm well. You no doubt have prey to hunt." She pushed at him with her free hand, but instead of shoving him from her, she swept her fingertips over the expanse of his bare chest—his strong, muscled, and hairy chest. The warmth of his torso called to her as did the crispness of the mat of hair she'd currently buried her fingers into.

He is quite manly.

"Excellent suggestion, unless…" he pitched his voice lower until it was a mere caress of sound that flowed over her like honey. The duke tugged on her hand, bringing her closer, so that his features swam into some semblance of view.

"Unless what?" she asked, her own voice a breathless affair. Alice anchored her free hand to his shoulder while peering into his eyes that were the color of brandy. His hair, light brown and longer than current fashion, falling in disarray about his head to curl at his neck, tempted her and she slipped her hand to his nape, where she reveled in its softness as it rasped over her fingers. Stubble shadowed his lower cheeks and jawline. What would that feel like if she rubbed her palm over it?

He chuckled, which sent butterflies waking through her insides. "Unless you were of a mind to tryst here in this sheltered place before I make my exit. Perhaps you shall be my prey." Still holding onto her, he slipped his free hand down her back.

Heated tingles followed in his wake, and when he dared to cup her buttock, a gasp escaped her. "After all, I'm dressed—or undressed as the case may be—for such an activity, and on second glance, you're quite pleasing to the eye."

A haze of untested desire mixed with confusion and inquisitiveness enveloped her. It had long been a dream to catch the attention of a gentleman, one who would look past her blindness and see her for who she truly was, yet... Alice shook her head, scattering the cloud of sensation he'd invoked. His words sank into her addled brain. "...on second glance, you're quite pleasing to the eye." Did that mean when he first spied her, he thought her ugly or unattractive? A trace of hot anger speared through her. "How lovely to know you wouldn't dare bed a woman who didn't possess the requisite look you desire."

The duke removed his hand from her backside, only to cup her cheek. He ran the pad of this thumb along her lower lip. Renewed awareness zipped along her spine. "It wouldn't stop me, for women are women, but I do enjoy slipping a blindfold over their eyes before the deed is done." The warmth of his breath skated over her cheek, and again she caught the wild, primal scent of him she had earlier.

"Why..." She moistened her lips. "Why would you do that? Do you not wish bed partners to look upon you during something so intimate?" He was much different than anyone she'd ever met, and it both frightened and exhilarated her. Obviously, there was so much she didn't know about relations between men and women.

"Ah, such innocence." His voice tickled her ear as he put his lips to the shell of that organ. "The bit of the unknown heightens the act and adds mystery. And I ask again, my sweet country flower, are you of a mind for a tryst?"

She might be rejected by society, but she needn't act the wanton because of it or when a strange man paid the slightest mind to her. "That is rather an improper offer." And one she'd do well to steer clear of unless she wished to pay the consequences, for since he was so high on the instep, it was unlikely he'd do right by her or a child that might result. Yet the need for more information regarding his wont to blindfold mistresses warred with self-preservation.

"So it is." But he didn't release her and neither did she move. "Tempting, all the same, is it not?"

"Perhaps, if it was given to a different woman on a different day in a different life." *Oh, Alice, don't be a widgeon. Don't be what the village expects.* Proper might be boring, but it kept her safe. Too many young girls fell for the charm of men like him and found themselves in situations that left them ostracized. This time when she pushed at his chest, she didn't allow herself the distraction of exploring his hard body. Then she scuttled away, putting much needed distance between them. "I should go. This is highly irregular."

And slightly maddening. No matter how much she longed for romance, she refused to go down this road where love didn't dwell. Still, her heart squeezed from knowing that she wasn't enough for a man of his caliber. He wanted to bed her, not court her.

"As should I." The duke blew out a heavy breath as if finally remembering himself. The flesh-colored blob that represented his form stood. "I've held out a hand for you, should you require assistance up."

At least it was more respect than his last offer. Alice felt around and when her fingers came into contact with his hand, she grasped it, only squealing a little when he hauled her into a standing position without effort. "Thank you, Your Grace." How bizarre it was to converse with one so lofty in society while they were in such a situation. Thank goodness she'd learned the proper manners and deportment as a young lady before being abandoned. Her heart twinged for an entirely different reason. Her only family, distant though they were, didn't want her when it had become apparent she wouldn't "grow out" of the vision affliction. When they'd turned her from their home, the luxury of certain things attached to a barony went with them.

"It has truly been my pleasure." He released her hand with alacrity, yanking her from her tortured musings. "However, despite my duty to escort you to wherever it is you were going, my lack of clothing prevents me from parading through the village." His self-deprecating laugh was a sad affair. What was his life like? "I fear I shall have to leave you here."

Her heart fluttered at the heroic implication, much better than the slight he'd given with a request for a tryst. "Indeed, and you've yet to explain why you're naked to begin with." Then she gasped. Her eyes widened. "You didn't flee from a lady's bed, did you?" Perhaps the woman, or even an angered husband, had tossed him and his clothing from a window. She bit her bottom lip to keep from laughing. Was there a draw for noblemen to seek out liaisons in sleepy English villages?

"I did not." A trace of humor lingered in his voice.

"That is good to know." With haste, she removed her shawl and held it out to him. "Cover yourself, my lord. You're in no danger of my seeing you in the altogether, but others might." Though she'd touched the most shocking part him, and that was scandalous enough.

Oh, dear. Does this mean I've been compromised? Not that it mattered. She had no one in her life to impress or woo with a sterling reputation.

"You're too kind," he murmured, but when he took the garment, their fingers brushed. Pleasant tingles flowed up her arm from the point of contact. He retreated, presumably to wrap the shawl about his waist, but then he scooped up her hand and brought it to his lips. A certain thrill moved down her spine when he kissed the back. "Thank you for the loan. How should I return it? I don't know your name, let alone your address."

And neither shall you.

"It's best that I remain a stranger." Gently, she slipped her hand from his. Never had she been left at sixes and sevens in the presence of a man. It was odd, and every moment she spent in his company left her heartbeat tripping out an excited rhythm.

He snorted. "I'd rather know the identity of the woman I rescued, the woman who makes certain I don't embarrass myself any further than I already have."

Did that mean he felt sorry he'd asked for a tryst or that he'd appeared in the village *sans* clothes? Confliction bounced through her brain. It was unlikely they'd ever meet again, so what did withholding her name matter? "Miss Alice Morrowe. I'm nobody, and by tomorrow, you'll have forgotten all about me. People always do." The muscles of her stomach clenched. What a sad commentary of her life, that she couldn't make a singular impression on anyone. "I've become used to it, so you needn't do the pretty or lie to me." Heat infused her cheeks at the admission. That she'd say such a thing to a relative stranger horrified her.

"That's where you are wrong." Once more he availed himself of her hand. "Today, you *are* someone, for I don't concern myself with people who don't matter."

So says the ego of a duke. Before Alice could form a response, he applied the veriest pressure and tugged her to him. His face came vaguely into view. He had the dearest dimple in his left cheek, and then he brushed his lips against hers in an oh too brief kiss—her first kiss. Finally, she—Alice Minerva Morrowe, firmly on the shelf at the age of thirty—experienced the pleasing press of a man's lips to hers.

The duke pulled away. He released her hand and left the area so quickly she barely noticed he'd departed. Perhaps that was due to standing so still with shock. She cocked her head and listened, but there was no hiss of grass blades bending beneath the soles of his feet, no crunch of dirt or gravel when he gained the road. There was nothing left of him except the lingering warmth on her lips.

Well, this is no longer an ordinary day.

Bemused and somewhat mystified, Alice made her way out of the embankment, skirted around the hedgerow, and then gained the main road. Dawn had broken while she'd tarried with the duke. The growing brightness prickled at her eyes; the heightened sensitivity caused them to narrow and water. Another side effect of her particular form of blindness, and one reason she tried to walk to the shop where she apprenticed before the sun came fully up.

Did her affliction matter to one such as the duke?

She snorted as she hurried along the road. *Stop being a ninny, Alice. He is not for you. You had a chance meeting. That man will never return to Shalford, and you'll not see him again. Be grateful you had an adventure.*

The tiny shop, with its wooden sign hanging from two iron hooks proclaiming, "Shalford Millinery" glimmered, for the rising sun reflected off its plate glass window. The owner, John Sparkes—who also owned the water mill—agree to

Devil Take the Duke (Lords of the Night #1)

let her reside in a cozy, cramped room at the back of his mill if she'd assist his wife, Mary, in her hat shop. No coin was exchanged, for she received room and board, and after all he'd said on more than one occasion, what else could one such as herself wish for in life? No doubt the man assumed he was doing a charitable work in giving her a kindness, but every once in a while, Alice resented being treated by everyone she knew as either a poor relation, an obligation, or a servant. Though she detested on relying on charity, her options were limited, for her only family had tossed her out.

I am none of those things yet I cannot make people see me differently.

Her thoughts caused her to laugh. Funny, that. They refused to see her and she literally couldn't see them. *At least I've kept my sense of humor through life's pitfalls.*

"Alice, there you are!" A brown-colored blob separated itself from the door to the shop. Her only friend in the village grabbed her hand. "I'd wondered what happened to you. You're never late."

"Hello, Fanny." Alice smiled and squeezed the other woman's fingers. "I was run off the road by a fast-moving carriage and only gathered myself enough to come here." It wasn't a lie, but it wasn't the whole truth either.

Fanny Smith was two years younger than she, and the eldest of twelve children. Forced to help provide for an ever-growing family, she'd begun working in the village at the age of fourteen. Now she was one of the most trusted members of

Shalford. The only difference between them: Fanny was engaged to be married to the son of the butcher, who had a shop in the street behind this one. Alice couldn't begrudge her the happiness; she deserved everything life held.

"I'd wondered why you look different today," her friend continued.

"Don't be silly. I'm not different, except for a few grass stains and perhaps bruises," Alice said, brushing off the comment with a shrug. Did one have a certain look who'd just been kissed?

"What a bammer you're telling." Fanny squeezed her hand. "Why are you blushing then? What else happened other than a runaway carriage?" When Alice remained silent, hoping the ground would open up and swallow her whole, her friend pressed onward. "Did you indulge in a midnight tryst with the blacksmith?"

Alice recoiled. "Joe?" She screwed up her face. For the better part of a year, that bear of a man had bothered her, badgered her about taking a walk with him, coming to dinner, or horror of horrors, meeting with him at the back of his smithy for a little slap and tickle. "Absolutely not. I'd rather die than let that man touch me in any way." It was troubling he wouldn't understand that her polite declines of his offers would never change. At this point in her life, her next refusal would be forceful, and she didn't care if he was humiliated in a public setting. She was blind, not beholden.

"You could do worse." Fanny huffed, and the brief breeze ruffled a tendril of escaped hair at Alice's temple.

"True, but I could also do better. There is no need to settle for crude." At the last second, she stopped herself from pressing the fingers of her free hand to her lips where the fleeting brush of the duke's kiss lingered. For one insane second, she allowed herself a silly fancy. What if the duke was so taken with her that he returned to the village merely to see her? Yes, a duke was infinitely better than a sweaty, hulking blacksmith, but it was such an impossibility, she laughed. "Dearest Fanny. You know I'll forever remain an old maid. You also know that I've resigned myself to that fate." Yet her heart constricted. Why couldn't she have her dreams even though her reality was so much different?

"I suppose someone has to be. We all can't marry," was Fanny's practical reply. "But once I do, I shall share with you every detail of what occurs in the marriage bed."

Heat shot through Alice's cheeks. "I..."

Her friend laughed. "You must learn of it some time." Another trill of laughter erupted in the quiet morning. "After work, we shall call upon Mrs. Kelley. You know she's rumored to be."

The heat furiously clung to her cheeks. "A lady of the night." That woman's reputation was legendary through rumors and whispers in the village. It didn't help that she lived above a tavern at the end of the village.

"Yes, and you can ask her all the questions you'd like. I can too. I'm sure I can use that information in a few days." When she was married. She squeezed Alice's hand again. "Don't worry.

You will forever be my children's favorite aunt. My little brothers and sisters already love you as such."

Alice rolled her eyes. It was better than nothing. Gratitude filled her that she had a friend in Fanny. "I would be honored."

"Good." Fanny pushed open the shop's door. No doubt Mrs. Sparkes had already arrived before them. "We'd best start our day before the missus grouses."

"Agreed." But she didn't know how she'd be able to concentrate on checking the handiwork on countless hats when all she wanted to do was woolgather about the duke. There were so many questions about him she'd never see answered. Clipping loose threads or gluing down errant bits of lace wasn't as exciting as it once was now that she'd been offered a glimpse of life beyond what she'd previously known.

CHAPTER THREE

September 14
London

Donovan ordered a bottle of brandy at his club—the exclusive place he and the other Accursed Lords had created as a safe haven of sorts. Bête Noire was what they'd christened the place nigh twenty years ago—rather fitting for the beasts they were—and if a gentleman wished it, he could obtain any sort of scandal, for no one in London knew who the founding members were let alone the owners.

And they worked hard to keep it that way. The club offered sanctuary from the slings and arrows of *ton* society; it was also a way for the Lords of the Night to partake of that same society without needing to immerse themselves in it.

Barely had he settled at his customary table at the rear of the main room, his back to the wall so that he could monitor the comings and goings of guests, when two of his friends and fellow Lords of the Night entered. Upon seeing him, they made their way toward him.

"Fancy seeing you two here tonight," Donovan drawled as the two men took seats at the table.

Rafe Astley, twelfth Earl of Devon, rolled his eyes that flashed briefly red in the low candlelight. He was cursed as a vampire, a true denizen of the night, and if anyone questioned why he was rarely seen abroad in the daylight, they had the good sense not to ask it boldly of him in person. "I could say the same of you, Manchester." His blond hair, waved in a popular style, gleamed. He had the look of a Greek Adonis... except for the fangs that lengthened when the need to feed came upon him and the tendency for his skin to burn if left in the sun too long. "I'd wager you were out running through the countryside, terrorizing all manner of innocents."

"I'm not of a mind for all of that at the moment." As if to enhance the statement, his wolf whined into his mind.

We haven't run for days.

Donovan ignored his canine companion in favor of taking a deep swallow of the smuggled-in brandy.

"I know that look. Have seen it too many times." The other man at the table, Valentine Butler, the Viscount Mountgarret, pointed an elegant finger at him. "You're bedeviled by a woman." The man's red hair tended toward curling despite the cut or the pomade he used to bind it, though when he returned to the sea, he let it grow long. He also maintained a lean, muscular build that had ladies angling after him, but his beastly half didn't walk the land. Instead, he was a slave to the waters as a merman, and a fierce fighter at that. As such, his properties always needed to support a body of water, and his country estate wasn't far from the sea. When he lingered in London, he haunted the docks.

"Do shut up, Mountgarret. Is not Coventry with you?" He glanced past them but the fourth of their set didn't appear.

"The earl is currently playing puppet to his sister. He has taken her to Bath for a week's holiday." Rogue shrugged. "He spoils her."

"So he should. Sisters are interesting creatures and have a tendency toward overprotectiveness." Lord knew his own was, and she was quite protective of him as well. And they lived with the uncursed. A novelty, to be certain. "In any event, I'm hardly bedeviled." Donovan glared at his friends. "Is there anything else you'd say to me? You're both fairly bursting."

The earl exchanged a speaking glance with the viscount. Then a teasing grin curved his lips as he lifted an eyebrow. "Ah, but you *are* thinking about a woman."

"This shouldn't come as a surprise to the two of you," Donovan groused. He didn't wish to talk about Miss Alice Morrowe with his friends, for they'd only make matters worse and she was different enough that he didn't want for her name bandied about a gentleman's club.

"No, but your usual meetings are with the usual sort of women, and you brag about the conquests every chance you have," Mountgarret was quick to remind him. "Now, your very reticence is telling." His brilliant blue eyes, bordering on turquoise, twinkled with mirth. "Have you gone two sheets to the wind over her then?"

"Bastard." Donovan glared. "No. But if you must know—"

"—we must," the Earl of Devon interrupted with a grin of his own.

"—then I'll tell you that I did, in fact, have a run in with a woman. Literally. I was forced to plow into her while in wolf form and save her from being trampled by an out-of-control curricle. That was three days ago."

"Here in Town?" the viscount asked with a healthy dose of skepticism in his voice.

"I was in Surrey at the time. Village of Shalford, actually." Donovan shrugged. "My wolf prefers to exercise in the country. There's more excitement there—for him."

Nowhere to run in the city, his wolf chimed in.

Again, his friends exchanged a glance. The earl frowned. He poured a measure of brandy into his own glass. "Why is this news? Unless she isn't your usual type of skirt."

He refused to tug at his cravat that he swore grew tighter as the conversation went on. "She is, in fact, not. Besides, I assumed the two of you would find the tale interesting. Perhaps I was wrong and you've become too jaded."

Mountgarret snorted. He nodded when the earl offered him a portion of the smuggled spirits. Crystal clinked against crystal to blend with the soft rise and fall of conversation throughout the room. "The question remains: did you bed her?"

Devil Take the Duke (Lords of the Night #1)

Heat rose up the back of Donovan's neck. "No... but I kissed her."

His friends hooted with laughter.

The earl stared, his tumbler paused midway to his mouth. "And?" He made a gesture that meant get on with it.

"And... nothing." Being certain to keep the tale brief, Donovan related more events of the encounter.

"Interesting." Mountgarret stared into the contents of his glass before pinning Donovan with his intense gaze. "Another full moon arrives on the second of next month. It might be the one spoken of in the curse. Perhaps you could make her fall in love with you and thereby break the curse."

"Not this again." Donovan rolled his eyes. All his life—and theirs—breaking the ancient curse had been a topic of conversation. Especially since this year put them in the five-year window where one full moon a quarter could conceivably usher in the events to break or reverse the curse.

And the year was growing short.

"Yes, of course this." The earl, Rafe—or as he preferred contemporaries to call him, Rogue—chuckled. "Isn't it what we're all hoping for?"

"Perhaps." Donovan conceded the point. "What makes you think this woman will be any different than the others I've had into my bed?"

Inside his head, his wolf snorted in annoyance. *She's different.*

Mountgarret grinned. "None of them were in love with you."

"Neither is this particular woman," he returned, his voice taking on a particularly grouchy tone. He shook his head, not convinced breaking the curse was even possible. "She isn't in my usual style, as you both have said."

"Yet, you've set the stage," Rogue pressed as he leaned forward. Faint red rimmed his pupils. "I mean, how often can a story of courtship say it started with a collision and a man *sans* clothing?"

"*And* from your own admission, you let her put her hands on you," Mountgarret inserted. "She felt various portions of your anatomy, old boy, and she didn't run away screaming or rave about a wolf. That must count for something." He pinned Donovan with a knowing look. "Did she set your prick to dancing?"

"I'm surprised you didn't indulge in a bit of slap and tickle," the earl said with a laugh. "It's taken far more drink and less effort for you in the past."

"This meeting didn't have that end in mind." Donovan shook his head. "And—"

"And nothing," Rogue interrupted with a grin that matched the viscount's in cunning. "What's the harm of pursuing her to see if there's a spark?"

"Oh, any number of things, actually." He slammed his empty brandy tumbler onto the polished wooden tabletop with more force than necessary. Lingering amber droplets sprayed onto his hand and the piece of furniture. "Take your pick."

His wolf snorted. *These men are foolish romantics. Love doesn't happen on the spur of the moment.*

And it certainly doesn't happen to any of us who suffer the curse.

The earl sobered. He dropped his voice. "Fear that you'll fall for her without her returning the sentiment?"

There was always that danger, but as of yet, he'd never thought deeply enough of a woman that he risked losing his heart. "No. I fear it's false hope, this breaking the curse business, and even if it was possible, what happens to her? I've made my peace with what I am—mostly. I'm comfortable with my circumstances and have worked hard not to let trading lives with the beast embitter me." *Liar.* "Why should I ruin hers with a courtship she neither wants nor welcomes?" For the fact remained, he'd had but a chance meeting with Miss Alice Morrowe and that was all.

"Ah, so that's the extent of your reach, saving the girl from certain death or injury? You've done your duty, did a good deed and now you don't care that you could possibly come close to breaking the curse?" Rogue's eyebrows rose to his hairline. "Impressive, Manchester. I never thought you'd willingly toss away the chance for a normal existence."

"Yes," Mountgarret nodded with enthusiasm. "If such a thing had happened to either of us," he gestured between himself and the earl, "we would play up a romance to the hilt." He sobered. "This year grows short and none of us have come close to perhaps breaking the curse."

The earl nodded. "If it were me, I'd only need one chance..."

Botheration. Donovan blew out a breath. "Perhaps that is because the both of you nodcocks wish to find yourselves leg-shackled." He glared at his friends. Marriage wasn't for everyone. Hell, his parents had had a terrible go of it. Was it due to his father's curse or the fact they'd had nothing in common when they'd wed? Would things have been different if they'd loved each other? Unlikely. "I'll ask again: what does the woman gain from such a union if I indeed wished to proceed on such a fool's errand?"

Rogue rolled his eyes. He leaned back in his chair. "She'll be a duchess. Don't all women aspire to such heights and titles within the *ton*?"

"I have no idea what she wants, but if she is angling for a title, she'll find herself sorely disappointed in mine." This time a trace of bitterness flowed through Donovan's words.

He'd never taken an interest in the deeper thoughts of any of the women he'd bedded. Beyond the mutual physical release and pleasure, he'd simply not cared. And to let any female grasp the coveted title of duchess meant he'd give up his freedom, his way of life... as well as his beastly secret. The last time he'd asked a woman to marry him—and perhaps that blasted question was the key to blurting out the tale of the curse—she'd thrown the ring back in his face, hurled a few choice words at him, and then had run screaming from the house.

I refuse to repeat that bit of embarrassment if I can at all help it—or lose my heart.

Both had been extremely painful life lessons, and he wouldn't go through either again.

Mountgarret softly cleared his throat. "Look, Donovan, it's the best chance you've had in years. And if she's truly a lonely country miss, you can easily secure her affections with a brief flirtation. It won't take much to turn her head."

The earl took up the cause. "Absolutely. Once you've done the pretty, poured on enough of your charm, kiss her under the full moon and enjoy your human existence." He beamed. "What could go wrong? It's a straightforward plan, and one that will solve a few of your problems in one fell swoop."

"Now I have more problems than just the curse?" What sort of friends were these?

"Of course you do." His vampire companion flashed a smile. There was only a hint of elongated fangs, but they were no less impressive. "Do your duty by the title, get off an heir, etcetera."

"Spare me the list of my obligations," Donovan said. He poured out another measure of brandy, but for the first time in his life, he could imagine what it might feel like to have the curse broken and usher in the life of a full human. No more talks with his wolf. No more running as the beast through the countryside. No more killing for the thrill of it. No more excruciating shifts that broke bones and stretched muscles. "I am well aware of what the future wants from me, but what will I do without the constant companion of my wolf in my head?"

The viscount shrugged. "Same as the rest of us. Celebrate. Live life. And in your case, chase after skirts with a new confidence?"

Rogue snorted. "Bed them without a blindfold so that you might actually share the most intimate of acts with them by peering into their souls?"

This whole conversation prompted too much thinking on his part, when the bulk of what he'd been doing the past three days had been just that. For whatever reason, Miss Alice Morrowe wouldn't leave his mind, and he wanted to know why. He cleared his throat. "You both have valid points. Yet, if I did happen to charm her enough to make her fall, you think I should also marry her in order to fulfil the needs of my title? Would not securing her affections without wedlock be enough to appease the curse?"

His friends stared at him with speculation and askance. Finally, the earl sighed. "Only you can decide that. As will we all when—or if—our time comes."

Indeed, but damnation, what a coil either decision could become. "If I married her, what then? Send a wife I don't want to my country estate?" For, at the moment, he most definitely did not require a duchess, but if it was the only way of having the girl?

Stuff and bother.

Inside his head, his wolf snuffled. *Rut with her and be done with it.*

Perhaps it might be that easy, yet would such an event break the curse?

Mountgarret shrugged. He fiddled with his half-empty brandy glass. "It's the lesser of the two evils, Donovan."

"Mayhap." He nodded. "And I'll be free."

Rogue laughed, which caused the others to do the same. "To a point. Trading one demon for another with an unwanted marriage."

"Yet it will leave her a virtual prisoner." Donovan sobered. He downed the remainder of his brandy in one gulp and then twirled his tumbler between his thumb and forefinger. The glint of candlelight turned the etched crystal into sparks of light.

"Not necessarily," the earl continued. "Give her babes. She'll have all she's ever wanted, could ever aspire to from such humble country roots. You both win and you can both move forward in your lives."

Without love to muck the whole thing up. Donovan rested his glass on the tabletop. "That's a rather cold outlook, Rogue." What the devil was the point in taking a wife if one whisked her off and hid her, never to spent time with her? A wife wasn't like a painting or a piece of décor one could pack off to a garret when one had no more use for it, yet many titled gentlemen of the *ton* did just that.

"That's the reality men like us face," the earl answered in a low voice. "Perhaps we were never meant to have everything we'd like, for eventually, we all must answer and pay homage to the curse, and it's oftentimes a cruel taskmaster." Bitterness flooded those words.

Mountgarret nodded. All traces of mirth had vanished from his expression. "On the other hand, you might find that you suit. Love and romance are a novel concept for you, I'm sure, but stranger things have happened."

Donovan snorted. Love. Romance. Those things only occurred inside fairy stories. Real life had no room for them, and not especially for men like him. "We have nothing in common, she and I."

"Such gammon," Rogue replied. He flicked the side of his drink glass, and the crystal resonated a clear tone. "You feel lust for her, do you not?"

He pinned his friend with a glare. "That isn't the same as love, and well you know it." Just the remembrance of Alice's exploratory touch had his member hardening.

The earl continued with a wicked grin. "How did she act when you kissed her? Is there a chance she'd return that interest? It would make the flirtation go more smoothly."

"To be honest, she was rather stunned, and I left without waiting around to see what would happen next." Donovan slumped in his leather-bound chair. The situation was impossible no matter what angle he looked at it. And there was the rub—sight. "Also, she's blind. She cannot see, so already a courtship will prove difficult, for if I can't use my looks to help charm her, my suit is doomed."

"What difference does that make?" the earl asked in a tone that suggested Donovan was a

Devil Take the Duke (Lords of the Night #1)

bacon-brained idiot. "A man doesn't need another pair of eyes, does he?"

But her eyes were a most interesting shade of stormy gray with silver flecks…

"You have the use of your words, the gift of your touch," his friend continued. "Those are powerful tools in your arsenal." He leaned forward in his chair while the viscount nodded. "If it's marriage that's souring the deal, forget about it. As long as you can get your rocks off and bed her, go ahead and seduce her. Make her love you. No doubt a gel like her has been shunned by male company. Probably won't take much coaxing on your part. Coat your truth in so much sugar, her head spins with desire and confusion. Then your task will be completed, the deed will be done, and your new life starts."

Not much of a challenge there, his wolf complained. *Don't want a woman we don't have to chase.*

He couldn't agree with his beast more.

Mountgarret added, "You've wanted this your whole life, Donovan. Hell, we all have. You have the best chance in front of you. Why not take the opportunity and see where it leads?"

Donovan remained silent. He stroked his chin as he stared at his friends. When a buxom blonde drifted close to the table, her skirts dampened and clinging to her lower limbs, he waved her attentions away. She left with a pout, for he usually would invite her onto his lap and fondle her ample charms. Tonight he couldn't summon interest for such distractions. In fact, he hadn't visited perfumed sheets or had plump flesh in his bed since he'd met a certain sweet country flower…

Damn and blast. I must ponder this new possibility.

Rogue elbowed the viscount with a chuckle. "When a man falls into the danger of thinking about a woman…"

"Do shut up, Devon. I do not need your ribbing." But there was no bite in the command.

CHAPTER FOUR

September 15, 1815
Shalford, near Guildford, Surrey

Alice nearly fainted dead away when the duke came to call that afternoon at the milliner's shop.

It had been four days since the chance encounter with him, and in that intervening time, she'd assumed he'd gone on with his life and had forgotten about her. After all, dukes didn't visit country misses, and they certainly didn't call upon poor relations who'd been firmly put on the shelf for years.

So, when the austere man strode through the shop door and the tiny tin bell announced his arrival and he announced in his deep tenor, "Good afternoon, ladies. I'm the Duke of Manchester, looking for a Miss Alice Morrowe," she gasped and turned toward him, no doubt just as all the other females occupying the store did.

Mrs. Sparkes told the duke she would fetch Alice for him, and before Alice could puzzle out why the man had popped in for a visit, her boss had wrapped a hand about her upper arm. "There is a gentleman here to see you, a duke, and I'm sure I don't need to tell you how important such an event is." She guided Alice through the maze of tables containing hat stands and hats that appeared as colorful blobs to her vision. "Don't muck this up, for he might bring the women in his life here for head gear."

It was on the tip of Alice's tongue to argue and say that no doubt the women floating through the duke's life were probably not the quality of female Mrs. Sparkes would wish for clientele, but that good lady brought her to a jarring halt, and a dark shapeless form she assumed belonged to the duke loomed before her.

"Ah, Miss Morrowe, there you are," he said in a cheerful tone. Then he turned away to address Mrs. Sparkes, who lingered. "Thank you. I did so need to speak with Miss Morrowe."

"It's a pleasure to have you in my shop, Your Grace." With ingratiating voice, her boss continued. "I can bring you tea if you require it."

"I won't stay long, so it's not necessary."

By shifting her vision over his shoulder, Alice caught his movements as he turned toward her and took a step closer. His scent wafted in a cloud around him, and she surreptitiously inhaled. Lemon, bergamot, mandarin and cardamom top notes combined with clary sage, sandalwood and cedar with a hint of musk bottom notes. It was a heady, complex blend, much like the man himself, and much different than he'd smelled that first meeting. Sure she had his attention, but acutely conscious that Mrs. Sparkes, Fanny, and the two other girls who worked in the shop stared, Alice clasped her hands before her. "What are you doing

Devil Take the Duke (Lords of the Night #1)

here, Your Grace? Do you attend another hunt in the area?" It wasn't outside of realm of possibility, for the autumn presented many opportunities for hunting of all kinds.

"After a fashion. Why are *you* here?"

She wished she could see his form. No doubt it would be as dashing and intriguing as his voice sounded, and she also wished she could feel his clothing, to "see" for herself how he'd chosen to outfit his body… the body she knew only when he'd been naked. A rush of heat infused her cheeks and as he waited for an answer. "I…" Alice sputtered, aware of the eyes on her. Silence reigned in the shop. She cleared her throat. "I am employed here, in exchange for my room and board at the mill."

"I beg your pardon. You reside… in a water mill?" Heavy bewilderment ran through his tone.

Embarrassed heat poured into her person. "It's, ah… complicated." Oh, why wouldn't he just go and leave her alone? She hated that so much attention was directed to her.

"Alice, don't talk in such vagaries to a duke," Mrs. Sparkes admonished, which only served to further heighten the mortification. "My husband and I felt sorry for her when she wandered into the village years ago without funds or recourse. So I let her work here and my husband graciously gave her a room, and we provide her meals. Doing our part for a charity case, Your Grace."

Oh, dear Lord, why won't the floor swallow me up?

"In London, one doesn't speak of such things openly, for charitable works shouldn't be done for the attention, Mrs. Sparkes." A certain reproach wove through his tone. Then he apparently decided to switch tactics, for his tone softened with the same charm he'd treated her to that memorable night of their first meeting. "Surely you can appreciate how awkward this is, for all of us, Mrs. Sparkes."

"Of course, of course," the woman said, bobbing her head, and looking much like a giant, blurry chicken blob.

"Ah. It would make me more comfortable if I could converse privately with Miss Morrowe, so if you could find it in your heart to let her leave her shift early?"

"You absolutely may, Your Grace," came Mrs. Sparkes' answer. She even went so far as to sink into a curtsey. "I suppose the rest of us can manage without her, and we hope you might find the shop pleasing enough you'll return."

Alice tamped down on the urge to roll her eyes.

"Excellent. I'd like to take Miss Morrowe driving. I shall have her back soon." The duke slipped a hand about Alice's upper arm with a sure, strong grip. "If you'll consent to accompany me, Miss Morrowe?" he asked, and his voice rumbled through her chest with thrilling accuracy.

"It doesn't seem you're leaving me much of a choice," she whispered as he propelled them into motion.

"Yes, well, I *am* a duke, after all."

As if that made him more important a person than anyone else. Certainly, in the hierarchy of the *ton*, this was true, but to her way of thinking, a man's actions told his story, not his title, and respect was earned. Alice blew out a frustrated breath that ruffled the curls on her forehead. "You could have asked nicely."

"I believe that I did."

"Except you didn't wait for a response."

An unexpected chuckle escaped him, and the sound flowed over her like warm honey. "The answer would have been the same, don't you agree?"

"Yes." Drat the man's eyes. She was too curious about the reason for his call to refuse. All too soon they reached the shop's front door, and he whisked her from the establishment to the tinkle of the tin bell. Outside, as soon as the panel swung closed behind them, she grumbled. "You realize the whole village will be abuzz about this within the hour, and I don't relish that sort of attention. I've lived my whole life on the perimeter."

Yet warmth flowed through her. Yes, she was flattered he'd sought her out. If only he hadn't done so in such a spectacular manner.

"People everywhere adore gossip. It matters not how I arrived; the results will be the same. Perhaps it's time people noticed you, my sweet country flower." He guided her along the street. "Besides, I needed to return your shawl."

She scoffed. "You could have sent a courier or utilized the post."

The duke put his lips to the shell of her ear. "I wanted to see you." His breath skated over her cheek. "What better excuse did I have?"

Delicious tremors fell down her spine. "Why?" Alice squeaked in alarm and surprise when he moved his hands to her waist and easily lifted—tossed essentially—her onto a bench. When she settled herself, she gasped again. The man drove a high perch phaeton. How exciting! She'd never been in such a vehicle before, much less been driving with a gentleman. Most males assumed—if they'd deigned to take an interest in her—that because she was blind, she wouldn't enjoy the other aspects of such an activity. "Oh my." It was scandalous how much she reveled in having his hands on her person, even more so when flutters erupted low in her belly. Such a novel experience.

"Why?" he asked in answer to her question. "You intrigue me and I'd like to know just how much." He swung up beside her. The carriage rocked from the shift in weight. Then he gathered the reins and with a flick of his wrists and a click of his tongue, he set the equipage into motion.

Something brushed against her ankle, and when she bent to investigate what it was, her fingertips encountered the wool of the shawl she'd loaned him. He'd been telling the truth. When she straightened into her seat once more, leaving the garment where it was, her right side pressed into his left. Heat trailed through her insides. "I don't know what to say. About any of it." A duke, here in Shalford, to see her.

It was too outrageous to think about. Yet it was happening, and everyone would know by dinnertime.

"The world is full of small wonders and miracles and things unexplained, Miss Morrowe. Best start believing." He chuckled, but he didn't say anything else, merely guided the carriage along the main thoroughfare of the village.

Eventually, the sounds of vehicles rumbling over the hard-packed earth, the hum of people laughing and talking, and the general din of a Shalford afternoon faded as they moved farther away. Then the bleating of sheep and the occasional moo of a cow and the cheery chirp of birds wove through the backdrop. Anxiety crawled through Alice's insides. What did one say to a duke, or to a naked man she'd touched, for that matter? They had nothing in common, he and she, for he moved in circles too far removed for her to even imagine, while she toiled for her very existence and remained largely ignored by the world.

Before she had a chance to wrack her brain for the answers, the duke cleared his throat. "How long have you suffered from your affliction, your blindness?"

She gasped in surprise. Either people ignored her, or they treated her like a leper. No one in recent memory had ever asked her about her vision or attempted to understand it. "All of my life." She clasped her hands together in her lap to still their shaking. "When I was small, I didn't realize I was different. I was loved. My parents never treated me differently than anyone else of their acquaintance."

"What happened?" Polite interest wove through his voice. "Why are you not still with your family? Love helps to build the bridge of acceptance into many places."

A lump of emotion formed in her throat. She swallowed around it. "My parents died of a fever that went through our hamlet. I was nineteen, so I was subsequently shuffled off to my father's third cousin, Baron Weatherly, who resides on the other side of Surrey, in Horley." Where she was little more than a servant, more or less given the task of looking after the baron's growing brood, that no self-respecting governess would since the children were such hooligans. More often than not, the oldest ones took advantage of her and locked her in various rooms around the manor house.

"You are not with the baron and his family why?"

The *clip clop* of the horse's hooves on the earthen road held a soothing edge and calmed her nerves. Alice sighed. "Those people turned me out two years later. In their eyes, my blindness negated my worth." She shrugged. Some of the sting had left her history now that she told it to him. "I couldn't catch a decent husband or make important connections, let alone watch over their offspring with any sort of authority, so I was therefore considered a burden."

Something akin to a growl emanated from him, but he said nothing.

Thus encouraged, Alice continued. "The baron and his wife made plans to send me to an institution in London, a place where sight-challenged people are put when they cease to make themselves useful." She clutched her fingers tighter. "I refused—loudly—so out I went. It was either go to the institution where I'd no doubt be treated little better than an experiment or trust my luck on the streets and citizens of Surrey." Her chin trembled as she remembered those early days when she slept in barns or other places that could provide shelter before she came to Shalford. "I have been looking after myself since then."

"What a horrible story." The duke sounded properly shocked. And rightly so. No one should be made to feel unwanted simply due to events they couldn't control. "I'm sorry to hear of your ill-luck and your family's treatment, but it doesn't surprise me." A hard edge had entered his voice. "The *ton*, even its rusticating members, craves an impossible image of perfection. Those who do not fit are given the Cut Direct and discarded like refuse."

Alice turned her head. She focused her gaze over his shoulder, caught the lift of a few strands of his hair as the breeze ruffled them. "Do you have first-hand experience, Your Grace?"

"Unfortunately, I do." A long stretch of silence followed. "Tell me how you see the world around you."

"Is it something you truly wish to know about, or are you merely asking to pass the time?" It was odd, this having someone take an interest in her.

He leaned his head toward hers. "I genuinely want to know... for me." The warmth of his breath caressed her face.

"All right." She glanced away, for fear of what he might glimpse in her eyes, and she certainly didn't want him to spy her confusion or budding regard. "As you are aware, I use my fingers to feel an object or a person. Touch gives me a good start."

"Can you see anything or is the world around you dark?"

"If I look straight at someone or something, my vision presents as white with fuzziness running through it, but if I focus my gaze over a shoulder—or slightly to the left or right of a person—I can see better. Not clearly, mind you, but I can discern outlines, colors. It's blurry, like looking through cloudy glass smeared with water." Again, she turned toward him. "However, if I move something very near my face, like when I read, my vision is nearly flawless." A self-deprecating laugh broke from her throat. "Though it's the height of improper to press myself against a person in order to read the emotions in their face or eyes. Not that I need worry; most folks don't bother with knowing me at all."

Eventually, the duke guided the phaeton beneath a grouping of oak trees that overhung the side of the road. He pulled the brake and then presumably let the horse forage on the grass. "The people who don't wish to know you are the ones who don't deserve your attention. It's they who will eventually regret that they cast you aside."

Her heart squeezed. Warmth flowed inside her chest. "Thank you. Not even my friend, Fanny, has given me such sound advice."

"Then you need to seek out a better circle of acquaintances."

She snorted. "Easier said than done, Your Grace."

"Donovan."

"I beg your pardon?" At such closeness, when she peered upward, she discerned the brown hair that curled at his collar and just over his ear. For a duke so high on the instep, he apparently didn't care about fashion. It was endearing and made him all that more approachable.

When he chuckled, a thrill ran down her spine. The sapphire stickpin in his pristine cravat sparkled in the sunlight. "My name is Donovan. Please make use of it, for I grow weary of formality in most of my relationships."

"Oh." She tumbled his name through her mind a couple of times before speaking it aloud. "Donovan. It's quite a commanding, respectable name." His sleeve brushed her arm when he shifted into a better position so that he more fully faced her. Tingles lingered in its wake. "Please, address me as Alice."

"Thank you." He glanced his knuckles along the side of her face, and she mourned the fact that he wore gloves, and she couldn't feel his skin against hers.

Before she could ask him a question of her own, he spoke once more. "Do you enjoy your life as it is, Alice? Or do you yearn for more, have goals you want to reach in the coming years?"

She sucked in a breath of surprise. His line of inquiry went beyond polite interest. "I am happy, of course. Why should I spend my life in anger or bitterness? That seems a waste of the time I've been given. I'm blind, not broken." Would he think her too bold?

"Is your condition reversible?"

Once more, his question put her at sixes and sevens. "I… don't assume so. I have never seen a doctor, and it's been my experience that the eye isn't an organ the medical profession is rushing to study." Oh, she'd asked when she lived with the baron, but was told that she might grow out of it, so there was no need for the expense of traveling to London.

"If there should come a time in the future when such a professional could be procured, would you see him?" The tone was low, intimate, much more than a relative stranger would employ.

"I wouldn't say no, of course, but I cannot fathom how or why such an occurrence would find its way to me." She trembled with the possibility, but then in the next breath, she dismissed it. He wasn't offering, merely speculating. "As for my goals, it's always been a particular dream of mine to open a school for children who suffer from similar ailments as me, teach them that they still have value to society and that they aren't throwaways destined only to toil in shops or trades because someone told them 'that's the only thing they can do'. I want those children to know there is hope." Her eyebrows rose. Never had she shared those dreams with anyone, so why him, why now?

"Noble plans, to be sure," Donovan said with a smile evident in his voice. Did the dimple in his cheek wink? "I commend you on your vision."

Alice snickered. "Is that a joke?"

He joined in on her mirth. "Not intentionally."

A grin curved her lips. When he wasn't in the persona of the duke, he was an enjoyable companion, and though she was flattered by his interest, she warned herself to remain wary. She might be innocent, but she wasn't naïve. "What of you? Are you a newly minted duke?" Not that she would know, for she'd never before concerned herself with the upper ten thousand.

"No." His chuckle sent gooseflesh racing along her arms. "Father died ten years ago, when I was a cocky young man of five and twenty. Suddenly, in the middle of my Grand Tour, I was summoned home with the news that my father lay dying of complications from when his heart attacked him."

"I'm sorry for your loss." She nudged his side with her shoulder. "It's never easy losing a parent."

"This is true. Mother died while attempting to birth my younger brother years before that. My sister and I were left to our own devices much of the time, for I don't believe Father actually thought he'd ever die. In his mind, fate wouldn't dare interfere in his life." A sigh sailed from him. "He gave me very little training."

"Such an impressive responsibility. Do *you* enjoy your life?" She couldn't fathom the weight of everything he must carry on his shoulders.

"It has its moments." Donovan took her hand in his. Again, she wished he was as gloveless as she, for of course she hadn't been given the proper time to grab hers or even her bonnet. "I've found the obligations vastly outweigh the pleasures though." Was that regret twisting through his voice?

"You seem to find amusement anyway." His fingers were warm and strong as he held her hand. She felt comfortable in his presence, and that in itself was odd. Surely such a thing would take time.

Donovan laughed and lowered his voice. "I have large appetites and live for only the best indulgences."

A different sort of shiver raced down her spine to throb deep in her core. "For yourself." He was a decadent lord she had no business associating with, for it could only mean trouble.

"Perhaps." Companionable silence brewed between them, broken only by the snap of the grass tearing as the horse took his lunch. Overhead, birds chattered in the boughs.

"And you are here with me why?" She had to know, for she would not be made a fool.

He brought his face close to hers, went so far as to layer his forehead to hers. Alice met his gaze, fell into the brandy-hued pools of his eyes. "Perhaps I have a craving for a sweet country flower, one of such rarity that I cannot find it's like in London."

"I see." She drew in a shuddering breath. With every word they uttered, their lips brushed. Did he mean to do that or was it happy serendipity? "Well then." What else was there to say? Except, a million questions bounced about her mind like soap bubbles. "You are interested in me... for me, or do you find me an oddity, a puzzle to be solved?" It was best to discover his exact intent now before her heart became too far engaged. At the moment, that organ was in danger of making the jump to affection from his attentions.

"Are we not all puzzles to be solved by someone?" Donovan squeezed her hand and then pulled away, moving farther and farther out of focus until his form vanished behind the fuzzy shield of white. "But yes, I am interested in you alone. Everything else is like icing on the finest of cakes."

"Oh." Her heart skipped a beat and she smiled. "That is good to know." Perhaps he was different after all.

He threw the brake on the vehicle, and grabbing the reins, he set the phaeton into motion once more. "Shall we take tea together in Guildford? I'm rather famished, and cake sounds wonderful. I don't fancy returning to Shalford so soon."

As a matter of fact, neither did she. "That would be lovely." For the moment, she'd enjoy being in his company, and she deserved to live as all the other women her age.

CHAPTER FIVE

September 17, 1815

Alice grows more intriguing by the day. Donovan's wolf snuffled in his mind. *She is merely a woman.*

No, she's different from any woman I've ever known. Which was odd, for that very reason. Being a duke brought him into contact with many of the more delicate beings of the species. So why, then, did this one stand out? Perhaps it was the novelty of her sight condition that drew him to her, perhaps it was her air of innocent curiosity, yet it felt more than that. She was strong instead of helpless; she remained optimistic over bitter from her circumstances. How did she manage it?

I need to know. For mayhap she could help him through his own.

And her dream was selfless and flawless. It didn't benefit her at all. That made him yearn to understand her mindset. Did she ever do anything for her own selfish pleasure or gain? Doubtful. That wasn't Alice's style, but what was? Did she want pretty gowns or valuable jewels or anything a typical woman would wish for? Did she yearn for a husband and children, or was there something else she held close to her heart?

Devil Take the Duke (Lords of the Night #1)

She is not like the women you draw to your bed, his wolf finally agreed. *She is... good, pure of heart.*

Donovan didn't answer as he ran through the countryside in his wolf form. He didn't go to Shalford, for if he did, he'd want to see her again, and another chance meeting while in the nude would draw more suspicion than it already had. She'd ask questions he wasn't ready to answer for fear those words would run her off. Yet all of his thoughts revolved around Alice, and that was disturbing. Already he'd spent more time with her than he had any of the other women of his acquaintance... and he didn't have a bedding to show for his efforts. So why, then, did he still persist in seeing her when there were other, easier ways to gain release?

Is she our mate?

The tentative question echoed softly through his mind and shattered his thoughts. *I don't know.* Mate? As in a wolf mate, a partner, a helpmeet. Wolves mated for life, so such a thing was equivalent to marriage. And asking a woman to marry him meant a lifelong commitment, speaking sacred vows and giving a promise he wasn't certain he could keep. Would uttering such a weighty question to Alice mean he was one step closer to breaking the age-old curse?

What will become of me, human? Once the curse is no more, will I also cease to be?

Donovan kept his head down as he ran. What a coil. He couldn't ignore those very real questions, nor could he banish the trace of fear that echoed in the inquiries. *I don't have those answers.* Did he want them? How could he live with himself or enjoy being fully human if that meant essentially killing the beast within?

A life for a life. It didn't seem right, and how could he be the judge on something so weighty?

On the other hand, even if he could make Alice fall in love with him in order to have a chance at breaking the curse, at the moment, he had no plans to return that lauded and dangerous state. Yes, he was intrigued by her, interested in her as a person, lusted after her body, but he liked his life and didn't wish for changes. Merely contemplating doing away with his wolf was enough to send chills down his spine even though breaking the curse and living free had featured into his long-term goals all his life. Adding the complication of a female to the mix was enough to fit him for Bedlam.

She'll want you to change… for the better, his wolf was quick to remind him. *She'll demand your fidelity and your time.*

I have no wish to change my ways. Yet, he hadn't bedded a woman since meeting Alice. That in and of itself was disconcerting, for it meant he'd already changed without knowing it.

The woman is under your skin. Inside his head, his wolf howled with laughter.

Not at all, he countered as he jumped over a collection of bushes and shrubbery. *My ultimate goal is still the same.*

Rut with her.

Yes, and seduce her enough that she falls in love with me long enough to break the curse. Once he did that, this weird obsession with her would fade, he'd kiss her beneath the full moon in two weeks' time, and he'd continue to enjoy her body for as long as she'd let him. Though, once she saw through his plan, he doubted she'd remain in his company.

And he'd be alone once more... but fully as a human. Thanks to Alice and her noble sacrifice.

What does she want with you?

Donovan didn't know, refused to contemplate that at the moment, for the answer, he had a feeling, would be terrifying.

Why?

What the deuce was his beast on about with the continuing questions?

He snorted through his wolf's snout. Did Alice possess guile enough to play him for a fool? Perhaps she wanted the title of duchess after all, and it wouldn't matter to her whether there was real emotion at play behind his actions. A woman like Alice could do many good works with the prestige that came from his name as well as his reach. Perfectly understandable from her perspective, yet... His gut clenched and he snapped his jaws at a rabbit who'd just emerged from beneath a bush. The animal darted away. Donovan let him go. His heart was in the hunt no longer.

You want more with her even if you won't admit it. His wolf cut into his musings.

More. How much more? Marriage meant bedding her for a purpose, to set up his nursery, beget an heir and a spare. Conversely, if the curse wasn't broken and those children were male, they, too, would grow up with the same affliction he had. *Nonsense. Haven't I already seen that love offers nothing but heartbreak and strife?*

It will be different with you, for the choice is always yours, his wolf reminded him. *If your children are lucky enough to have beasts of their own, they will have lifelong companions. Is that such a bad thing?*

Bah! He lunged into the tree line and changed directions. Going back to London was what he needed to do right now. *I've had enough of this conversation.* It did him no good and didn't help him out of the mire in which he currently resided. The thought of debating the merits or not of housing a wolf within was beyond his ken at the moment.

How the hell had one woman featured so heavily in his thoughts after such a short amount of time?

Yes, bedding her was the answer, and only after that could he attend to other matters with a clear head and conscience.

The sun had been up two hours by the time he roused himself from the bath, dressed with the help of his valet, Burroughs, and then made his way to the morning room, where he'd fallen into the habit of taking breakfast of late. It was one of the only rooms in the townhouse that had full use of the autumn sun, and it was cozy enough that he could remain by himself without the feeling of being alone swamping him.

He'd barely seated himself at a round table that sat four, when a frustrated huff sounded at the doorway. "I know that sound," he said by way of greeting as he accepted a filled plate from a footman.

Lady Elizabeth Sinclair popped her hands upon her hips and glared at him from her position. She wore her hair down this morning, tied back with a blue ribbon, and the caramel tresses gleamed in the morning sun streaming in from floor-to-ceiling windows. "Where have you taken yourself this week without a word?"

Donovan rolled his eyes. "Anywhere the wolf wants to go." He tucked into his breakfast with gusto, for morning runs consumed much of his energy. Around a mouthful of eggs and hamsteak, he asked, "Why do you want to know?"

Four years his junior, Elizabeth had made herself his protector. She despised how horribly he and his friends were treated within the *ton* and worked tirelessly to smooth the way for him with the pillars of society. Each year a few more invitations trickled in, largely in part to her efforts, but not even his sister's charm could gain access to hallowed halls or coveted invitations.

"How can I continue as your moral conscience if I don't have a blessed clue where you are, or if you've tumbled yourself into danger?" She advanced into the morning room, and when she flounced into a chair next to him in a cloud of blue skirting, she heaved another sigh.

"I never asked you to, and I don't tell you things because you'll worry." Inside his head, his wolf laid down and covered his eyes with his paws. Donovan grinned. Teasing her was one of the things that brought him pleasure. "Please, share this meal with me. It's rare that you're in residence the same time I am."

His sister harrumphed again but accepted a plate from the footman. When Donovan jerked his head, the young man hastened from the room. Yes, the whole of his staff knew of his affliction, and they'd gone through a rigorous vetting process to ascertain their secrecy and loyalty, but there were some things he didn't wish discussed before them. They doted on him, but he refused to let them know how gruesome his beast could be when tearing through livestock or fighting for survival while in the woods.

"Donovan." Elizabeth softened her gaze and landed it on him. "Are any of these places where *you* wish to go? Becoming the wolf is one thing, and you cannot help it, but eventually you need to do that which makes you happy. You need to come to terms with what your life is—darkness and all."

"I rather think that I have." When she cocked an eyebrow, he sighed. "I haven't killed anyone, if that's what you'll ask."

"That's good to know, but for how long? If you beast wishes it, would you do it?"

He laid his hand over hers, choosing not to answer her. "Why concern yourself with me? You have your own life." Though, because his title had been black listed long ago, the likelihood of her making an advantageous match was more of a challenge than for other duke's sisters. The weight of that responsibility lay heavy on his shoulders. "Or, I should say, you have a life of your own making, no thanks to me." Besides her self-appointed title of being his protector and social secretary, Elizabeth did charitable works in some of the lowliest and economically depressed sections of the city. Her most recent cause was bringing bread to the children who had the misfortune of living in or near the Dials.

And she did it with full confidence, for if she fell into trouble or was molested, her brother would rain down vengeance while in wolf form. She knew what it would cost him if he opted to sink his teeth into human flesh. Once it happened, resisting that call would break him, and he worked too hard to prevent such an occurrence.

"Pish posh, brother." She squeezed his fingers. "Why my concern? It's been too long since you've smiled. You're two shakes away from brooding, and that simply cannot be allowed, for it is gloomy enough around here."

"I apologize. Life hasn't exactly turned out the way I'd hoped for you." His sister rattled about the townhouse to remain with him, sacrificing her time to keep him out of trouble.

"It's never too late to think circumstances might change." Then she turned her big brown eyes upon him and really looked at him. "There's a different air about you today, though. You have a new glint of hope at the backs of your gaze. Why?"

Interest sprang into her expression as she waited on his answer.

"Ah, Elizabeth." His champion, even if he didn't wish it. After throwing his linen napkin onto the tabletop, Donovan pushed away and rose to his feet. "I don't wish to have this discussion right now." The last thing he needed was his sister to make his love life her next project.

"And I do. You have too many secrets as it is." She sprang from her seat and swiftly pushed him back into his with a hand on his shoulder. "Is it about the curse? You haven't attempted to reverse it for a while, and Lord knows the women you have through here don't exactly fit the parameters of how to break it."

A trace of heat climbed the back of his neck. "That isn't something you'll need to worry about in the future." He loved his sister, and perhaps her insight would help him unravel the knots of his thoughts. Donovan waved her into her seat. "Mayhap this is about the curse, but it's a mess of confusion."

"Ah, it *is* about a woman!" Elizabeth shoved her mostly untouched breakfast plate away. She planted her elbows on the table and dropped her chin in her hands, her eyes wide. "What's special about this one?"

Would that I knew. He shrugged. "I don't know, other than she's an innocent."

Elizabeth erupted into laughter. "The virgin who lured the beast."

"Yes." Donovan gritted his teeth while the heat on his neck intensified. "No. Perhaps, but she might accept me—curse and all—for she's carrying her own affliction."

"Cursed?" She gasped.

"No." He shook his head. "She's blind."

"Donovan Sinclair, how dare you?" Again, his sister jumped to her feet, and again, she popped her hands on her hips as she glared. "You'll hurt her, ruin her, toy with her affections, and all for the damned curse? That is beyond cruel, even for you."

His jaws parted slightly while he gaped at her. Then he remembered himself and his manners. "I understand how you feel; however, for a chance to grasp humanity without being cursed as the beast..."

"Then be human with your actions." She shook her head so vigorously that her hair flared about her shoulders. "If you mean to break the curse by using another person in such a manner, you deserve to remain beneath your affliction for the rest of your days." His sister closed the distance between them as he stood. She drilled a forefinger into his chest. "Be a better man... now. Find a different way." Then her voice softened. "You aren't that heartless. And you are desperate to live as other men. Perhaps that will happen; perhaps it won't, but don't throw away what humanity you do have by trifling with a woman's affections."

He grabbed her hand and then kissed the back of it. "Only time will tell, dearest of all sisters, if I'm heartless or not." But he appreciated her chastisement. It kept him honest, if he wished it.

She huffed, but she smiled. "In other news, I directed the butler to throw out things leftover from your last mistress. If she was so careless of her belongings, she doesn't deserve them, and quite frankly, I don't wish her to return for them."

Donovan rolled his eyes. Elizabeth had never liked any of his paramours. "It's for the best." And reminded him that he needed to formally break things off with the Lady Celia. One more thing to add to the mounting pile of responsibilities that he didn't care to tackle, for Alice dominated his thoughts. "I'm off to visit Miss Morrowe."

"Please think about what I said." But Elizabeth stood aside to let him pass. "There's always room for improvement no matter how a person struggles."

"I'll bear that in mind." With a wink, he escaped the morning room, but his mind remained conflicted, perhaps more so than before.

Donovan arrived in Shalford too late to escort Alice to church, so he boldly walked to the water mill and then rapped upon the door to her room.

As the panel opened and Alice stood in the frame, she gasped, and he remained perplexed at how she knew it was him there. "Your Grace, er, I mean, Donovan." Twin spots of rosy color bloomed on her cheeks. "What are you doing here?"

"Calling upon you." He flashed her a grin that had won him the regard of ladies before her. "May I come in?"

"It's the height of scandal, my lord. I have no chaperone."

"We have not had such at any of our previous meetings, but I promise to behave." He winked. "Now might I come in?"

Emotions crossed her face in quick succession: doubt, interest, curiosity, pleasure. Finally, she nodded. "Very well." Alice stood aside, and he made certain his arm grazed her breast as he went past. A tiny gasp was the only indication she acknowledged the brief touch, and it made him grin.

Then shock cycled through him as he glanced about the tiny room she resided in. A narrow bed occupied one wall with a simple nightstand beside it. A tidy quilt of faded patchwork lay over the bunk, with a straight-backed wooden chair waiting at the foot of the bed. Dainty, lace-edged ivory curtains of muslin hung at the single window. A battered wingback chair of maroon brocade rested in one corner with a small, round, rose-inlaid table. In another corner, a stand containing a basin and pitcher waited, with clean lengths of folded fabric waiting for daily ablutions. A faintly clouded oval mirror hung on the wall above, and he wondered at it, for she wouldn't make use of such a thing.

How the devil did she manage to live in such tight quarters, even if she did keep her lodgings neat, orderly, and feminine?

"You're wondering how I could possibly live in such a place." The dulcet tones of Alice's voice brought him out of his thoughts.

"You either know me too well, or you've heard the question before." He remained close to her, and the light, flirty scents of apricot with the warm, sweet aroma of vanilla wafted to his nose. Why, she smelled positively delicious, like the finest French pastry. His hunger for her grew exponentially. Perhaps today was the perfect time for a seduction.

"It is a little of both." Her lips curved with a smile, and he couldn't stop gazing at those plump pieces of flesh. "Let me say that I wasn't given a choice, but this room has grown on me. It's the only spot in the world that belongs just to me, and it's more than some in my position have." A quiet sort of desperation clung to the statement.

"No need to explain." He raked his gaze over her person. The simple day gown of mint green, though a few years out of style, clung to her curves in all the right ways. She tempted him merely by moving naturally. His groin tightened. "I'd meant to arrive earlier, perhaps escort you to church, for I assume you attend?"

"I do, for it's expected when one lives in a small village such as this one." Her smile remained in place. "Also, I firmly believe in thanking God whenever I can for the life I lead. It could always be worse."

His respect for her rose and he took possession of her hand, cursing the fact that once again he wasn't touching her skin to skin. "You are a marvel, Alice, and that fascinates me." How many times in the course of his life had he cursed and railed at the heavens for his own life circumstances?

She squeezed his fingers. "The Creator only gives us what we can bear, and perhaps to show others the particular mountain He has assigned can be conquered." She lifted her face and smiled, her gaze finding his without seeing. "Why should I go about with a woeful attitude when I could be encouraging others with optimism?"

"Why indeed?" *Teach me how.* Not for worlds would he utter those words aloud, for he didn't wish to appear weak in front of her. He brought her hand to his lips and placed a lingering kiss to the inside of her wrist where her pulse hammered.

A soft inhalation of breath followed, but she didn't pull away. "You shouldn't be here. Already the village is talking about you, and consequently me. Not all of it is flattering."

He rolled his eyes. "Society, any society, will always gossip about those they consider different, and about me especially."

"Why?"

"Like you, I suffer from an affliction of sorts." His jaw worked as he sought appropriate words that wouldn't reveal too much too soon. "At times it is… isolating." How often did he hide himself away in his townhouse, avoiding human interaction, for what was the point when the curse would eventually make itself known and frighten away everyone he cared about?

"Donovan." Alice slid out of his grasp only to run her fingertips along one side of his face. The sweetest of tingles followed in her wake and he briefly closed his eyes against the novelty of her touch. "Will you tell me what you struggle with?"

"Would that I could." Unaccountably, he nuzzled into her palm, reveling in her warmth. Women didn't voluntarily treat him with tenderness. Of course, he used them as playthings, for physical release, to ward off bouts of loneliness, but the curse was an exacting task master, and once the deed was done, he was always compelled to tell them of his alter-ego. Which started the process all over again in an endless loop. He placed his hand over hers and pressed a kiss to her palm. "Perhaps another time."

Alice stepped closer to him, framing his face between her hands, their noses touching. She peered into his eyes, while the strangest sensation washed over him. Her eyes, so clear, so trusting, cut through to his soul even if she couldn't see him fully. It was intimate and he craved more. "Are you a good man despite your affliction?"

Was he? Not according to his history as seen through her perspective. Suddenly, he hated what had become of his life and strove to conduct himself better. "Only time will tell…"

…and if the curse is lifted.

Inside his head, his wolf whined but didn't comment.

She smiled, and his gaze once more dropped to her mouth. He wanted to kiss her, taste her, drink from her until the fount of joy she seemed to sip from transferred to him. "It's never too late to change."

It was uncanny how she seemed to follow his thoughts, or even those that his sister had said. "You don't know…" He cleared his throat. "I don't know if it is possible now." To prevent her from asking more questions or probing too deeply, he cupped a hand around her neck, pulled her to him and then kissed her. He gently explored, nibbling at the corners, asking permission, searching for answers he anxiously wished to find. There was no pressure, no demands as he softly tasted her plush lips. When she shivered and a sigh shuddered from her, he pulled away with a grin. Oh yes, she would fall, and soon. He fit her hand to his crooked elbow. "Let us walk and perhaps remove ourselves from temptation."

And me from doing something that will jeopardize this seduction.

Alice nodded, but bemusement twinkled in her gray eyes.

Not far out of the village proper, a hulking man wearing a blacksmith's apron intercepted them. He stood in the middle of the path and glared at her.

"What game do you play, Miss Morrowe? You refused my bed, but chose his?" He sneered and spit in Donovan's direction. "I never took you for a whore, but then I ain't high on the instep like a duke, eh?" He narrowed his gaze on her, and when he raked his hot gaze along her body, Donovan stiffened. "Does he pay you well while you're on your back?"

When Alice gasped, Donovan drew himself up to his full height. He slipped an arm about her waist while strong protective instincts grew. Inside his head, his wolf snapped to attention, his hackles raised, a warning growl in his throat, his teeth bared.

"If you know what's good for you, you'll cease babbling nonsense and let the lady and I pass." Every inch of the duke rang in his tone.

"What, the doxies in London don't satisfy you anymore?" the man continued as he swung his angry, deep-set gaze to Donovan.

"Enough, sir. I won't ask you again to cease and desist." Warning rumbled in his voice.

"Mayhap I'll throw a punch and see how brave you are after that," the man taunted instead.

Before Donovan could reply, Alice stepped forward, her cheeks red, anger flashing silver in her eyes. "Stop your lies this minute, Joe. What you say is horrible enough, but to nearly assault a duke? Threaten him? Even you have to know how dangerous that is." She curled a hand into a fist. Would she fly at him with fists raised if she had the opportunity? Donovan appreciated her instinct to defend him.

The giant man with the shaggy mop of blond hair grunted and flicked his attention to Donovan. He completely ignored Alice. "Best watch your step. Even nobs can have accidents in the country. One little slip, a turn of the ankle on unfamiliar land, and down they go." Then he shoved his way past them, knocking Donovan's shoulder as he passed. And in a low voice, he added, "Best remember to leave your wolf home if you come calling again."

Devil Take the Duke (Lords of the Night #1)

What the devil? Did he know about the beast within, and if so, how? "I'll remember that next time I'm here on a visit," he couldn't help responding. He chuckled when the big man didn't respond.

A sigh of relief escaped her. "I apologize for him. It seems he had a temper and has no understanding of rejection."

"Has he threatened you before?" Every instinct screamed at him to shift into the wolf and run after the man, tear into him for daring to act with vulgarity and insinuation against her. But he remained by Alice's side, his arm still about her waist, shielding her with his larger body—protecting her.

She is ours, his wolf insisted in his mind. *He'll be trouble.*

He absolutely ignored his beast. Now was not the time to speculate.

"He has acted… ugly a time or two when I turn down his advances." She angled her head toward him with a frown. "It's his assumption I can do no better than him, and that he's doing me a favor by paying me attention."

Donovan turned them both about and set them into motion. "If he does so again, tell me and I will respond with the fullest extent of my reach." He glared even as his wolf urged action. "I will make certain his life is miserable."

Alice huffed, with annoyance or something else, he couldn't say. "I am capable of handling my own problems. You needn't concern yourself."

"No doubt you are, but if it bothers you, it bothers me. For my own peace of mind, do me this courtesy." When she gave him a curt nod, he relaxed, but only a fraction. "I'm escorting you back now, but will you be of a mind for another call soon?"

The worry clouding her face cleared with her smile, and his own outlook brightened from it. "I would enjoy that, and perhaps we shall have more time together then."

"I shall do my level best." And he knew one other thing with certainty: tonight while in wolf form, he'd stand guard near her door in an effort to keep the blacksmith away.

CHAPTER SIX

September 19, 1815
Shalford, Surrey

It had been two days since Alice had seen the duke. Two days since he sent her head spinning and her heart trembling. Two times since their first meeting had he deliberately sought her out, and what was more, he didn't seem bothered or even concerned by her blindness.

Merciful heavens, what does this mean?

She didn't know, but the tingling warmth of seeing him wouldn't altogether fade, and even now, heat flirted with her cheeks when she allowed herself a little glimmer of a dream.

The duke would have to wait until another time, for today was a special day in its own right. Her best friend Fanny would wed her beau today, and Alice, not exactly standing up with her, would be in the front row and watching with dutiful adoration.

Is there anything more thrilling and romantic than a wedding?

Because of that, Alice dressed with more care than usual, and donned her best day gown, one of sprigged muslin in robin egg blue. A petticoat and shift of fine lawn—leftover from her days of living with the baron and hidden away, saved and safe, for a special occasion—slid against her skin each time she moved. It was so much better than the scratchy garment she usually wore. She'd been given the gown through a friend of a friend, who'd snagged it from a charity pile of one of the genteel homes in the Surrey area. With a few alterations, the three-year-old gown fit as if made exclusively for her. And she'd embellished it with leftover seed pearls, glass beads and bits of lace from the hat shop. A matching bonnet, designed by her, completed the ensemble.

Alice stood at a full-length cheval mirror in her room and looked critically at herself as far as she could see. "I'm sure I'm not fit for presentation to the King, but I'm passable for Shalford."

After gathering a reticule that she also saved for special occasions and donning slippers she'd received with the gown, Alice left her room at the water mill. Fanny would marry in the small church in the village square, and a celebration dinner would follow at her parents' cottage a mile away. The crisp afternoon air gave her a new spring to her step, and though she wished for her shawl to keep the chill at bay, she hated to cover such a lovely gown. Once she was among people, she'd warm.

As she walked through the business district, she approached a grouping of men who clustered on the steps of the pub. The sound of angry voices grew with intensity to join excited exclamations. Joe, the blacksmith's son was one of them.

"I swear I saw one," a man inserted.

"Saw what?" another asked, and since Alice's natural curiosity wanted to know as well, she was glad someone asked the question.

"A wolf. I saw a damned wolf. Big, brown fur, menacing teeth. Slinking through the fields as if on the hunt," said the first speaker in a stronger voice.

Alice's heartbeat pumped faster. A wolf? In Shalford? There hadn't been wolves in England for over a hundred years. *How interesting.* Was that the animal who'd bumped into her and threw her from the public road the first time she'd met the duke?

"I saw it too," another man backed up the first claim. "I'd come home from this pub and I saw him. With the fresh kill of a sheep in his jaws."

"My sheep!" An older man Alice recognized as a farmer inserted himself into the conversation as she drew closer. "I'm down three in the last week, and I know for a fact it's been killing other livestock on neighboring farms."

Yet another man spoke. "Next, that beast will come for our children in the night. It'll snatch them from their beds and eat them up."

She nearly bit her tongue stopping herself from commenting. *I rather doubt a hungry wolf, presented with fat sheep and more than enough cows, would start prowling through the village and attempting to open doors and windows to get at children.* Their fears sounded like something out of fairy stories instead of grounded in logic and reality.

"We ain't never had wolves here afore, and then that duke fellow come to Shalford. He brought 'im. You'll see," said yet another man who sounded suspiciously like the blacksmith.

Gooseflesh raced over Alice's skin and chilled her. Did he know how insane he sounded? It was the height of folly to even suggest something of the sort. Dukes didn't command such beasts, neither did they consort with them.

The conversation turned ugly and heated after that, and while Alice found the information both curious and disturbing, she continued on her way. None of the men paid her attention, except Joe, who called her name, but she ignored him. As more men gathered and raised their voices, Alice hurried past.

Angry men in a mob didn't bode well. And especially these who promoted action before thoughts, and she especially didn't wish to find herself cornered by the blacksmith.

After a while, she arrived at Fanny's cottage, and things were frantic with preparations. Alice greeted some of Fanny's many siblings, who ushered her into her friend's tiny room that she shared with three sisters.

"Alice! Can you believe I'll be married soon?" Fanny rushed over the floor and engulfed her in a hug that smelled like orange blossoms. "My dress is gorgeous. A butter yellow organdy with a veil trimmed with Brussels lace Mother sent away for."

"I'm sure you look radiant, just as a bride should." Alice ran her gaze along the yellow blob that was her friend. She came close and dropped a kiss to Fanny's cheek, felt the softness of the veil as it brushed the side of her face, ran her fingers along

Devil Take the Duke (Lords of the Night #1)

the puffed, satin-like sleeve of the wedding dress, and she sighed. "Yes, I'm quite certain that you do." She pulled back and smiled. "I wish you a happy life and all that you've ever wanted."

"Thank you." Fanny sighed with such joy that Alice suffered a twinge of envy. "A married woman. Me." She giggled and Alice joined in on the mirth as her friend picked up a small bouquet of yellow and white daises. Even with her blurry vision, Alice identified the flowers as well as their fresh, clean scent.

"You'll make a fine wife," Alice assured her. And she meant the sentiment even as her heart squeezed for her friend. Fanny was entering a part of life Alice never dreamed would happen to her. What would it be like to have the title of wife, to share daily life with a man, feel the love of that same man both in and out of the marriage bed, to one day feel the swell of a pregnant belly or hear the squall of a newborn babe? "Your Rupert is a lucky man indeed."

Will I ever have that in my own life?

Then Fanny's mother bustled in. Young ladies—Fanny's siblings—surged around them, all babbling at once, and Alice was buoyed along in the excited tide, out the door. While Fanny and her mother were given the luxury of being taken to the church in someone's carriage, the rest of the party walked, Alice among them.

At the church, Fanny clustered with her mother and sisters, while Alice found an open seat on the front pew. The buzz of anticipation flowed through the room. Talking bounced about in low currents, punctuated by laughter.

Then the atmosphere changed so perceptively that the hairs on the back of Alice's nape quivered. Whispers started, and like a fire, they swept through the church. She turned her head in an effort to catch a snippet, and then quickly wished she hadn't.

"…it's that duke fellow Miss Morrowe knows…"

"…her reputation is being ruined each day…"

"…such a pretty lady he's with. Lovely caramel hair and flawless skin…"

"…must be done with Alice if he's with a new one…"

"…perhaps it's his wife…"

A sick feeling circled through Alice's stomach. *What is happening?* She swallowed a few times to ward off the urge to retch. Why was Donovan here, and accompanying a different woman? Then she reminded herself that she had no claim to the duke, nor he on her. Theirs was an unlikely friendship, nothing more. Except the kisses they'd shared seemed cheap and tawdry now, and not the tender and gentle explorations they'd been. The heat of mortification blazed in her cheeks. She pressed a hand to one of them while her heartbeat hammered. The urge to run, to hide, filled her. Why had he come? Could he not see how humiliated she was?

The woman next to her on the pew clicked her tongue. She patted Alice's hand. A cloud of heavy rose perfume enveloped her. "It's for the best, my dear. Obviously, he's a womanizer of the worst order. Thank the Lord you never let him tupp you." She shook her head. "It's scandalous how men carry on these days, especially toward defenseless women who don't know better."

Oh, please, stop talking.

A fog of cold disappointment wrapped about her. She tuned out anything else the woman said. Surely he wouldn't be so cruel. But then, what did she know of him anyway? Next to nothing, that's what. He was a duke, and he'd made no secret of his vices in the short amount of time that she had spent with him. Her chin trembled while her chest constricted. How could she have been so stupid? Her breath came in labored pants as Alice struggled to maintain a calm she didn't feel. She'd let him turn her head with pretty words and fancy gestures and fleeting kisses that had made her long for more from her life.

Made her forget that she might manage to strive for something else than her lot.

Forget who I am.

Still, she'd had those silly dreams of a future different from what she'd been given; it was inevitable. And now here she was being made the fool yet again in front of the whole village. Alice bowed her head lest the people around her spy the tears gathering in her eyes, threatening to choke her. As Fanny's ceremony began, Alice prayed if—when—she did break into sobbing, the people around her assumed the excess of emotion stemmed from happiness for her friend.

Instead of from a heart twisted and the murder of budding hopes.

Fanny said her vows and received them from her groom. The affection and devotion in their faces further worked to send tears crowding into Alice's throat. How beautiful it was to find that one man above all others who made a woman cleave from everything she'd ever known in order to walk by his side and build a life together. Surreptitiously, she sniffled until she had to root about in her reticule for a delicate, lace-edged handkerchief she'd fashioned herself from a leftover scrap at the shop.

Inevitably, the end of the ceremony came, quickly, for officially wedding one's life-mate took very little time, and the minister announced them both husband and wife. Fanny and her groom hastened to sign the registry and then they swept down the aisle and out of the church. As people followed them out, a chorus of clapping and well-wishes resounded.

While the people around Alice stood and made their way outside to presumably greet the newly married couple, she remained in her spot, waiting for the crowds to thin and also wishing the duke to the devil. Perhaps he'd exit and she wouldn't need to see him. Perhaps the floor would open and swallow her whole. Perhaps she'd find some balm to make this betrayal more tolerable.

Oh, would that I were elsewhere so I could give into these stupid tears.

The decision was taken from her when she felt a hand on her shoulder, noted *his* scent long before he spoke as he joined her at the front of the church. "Miss Morrowe... Alice." The way he released her name from his lips in such an intimate fashion sent thrills down her spine. "It had been my hope to arrive well in time to sit next to you, but alas, I was unaccountably delayed." Humor rode through the statement.

And it sent her anger to the boiling point. "Yes, well, no doubt waiting upon the whims of your newest fancy piece does take a toll on your time." She shook off his hand and then stood, slowly, and faced him, hoping her expression conveyed the proper amount of ire. She didn't care that the minister lingered or that a few of the village-folk clustered about the door, either stuck in foot traffic or so gauche that they wished to overhear.

It was time for her to grow bold and defend herself. She'd been docile enough throughout her life and let everyone else dictate her fate. No more.

"I... I beg your pardon?" Surprise hung on his voice, and the woman accompanying him had the audacity to laugh. She *laughed*! "I don't have a clue to what you're referring."

Heat sprang into Alice's cheeks. She stared past his left shoulder, noted the deep burgundy color of his frock coat, caught a glimpse of a pink-colored blob she assumed was the gown of his latest mistake, and she launched into the rest of what she would say to him. "How dare you, my lord?" As best she could, she ignored his companion. "Not only have you shown up here, to an event where you were not invited, but you've also brought a mistress," her voice wavered upon the word, "after you spent time publicly seeking me out?" So angry was she that she shook from the force of her emotion. Not even when the baron—her own relation—turned her from her home had she been as incensed as she was now. "That is outside of enough, even for you. Now, if you'll excuse me? I find I have somewhere else to be that doesn't include dancing attendance upon you."

It sent her ire ratcheting up another notch when he chuckled. "I must say, it's quite refreshing to be so thoroughly dressed down, and in a church no less."

Alice narrowed her eyes. Is that how all members of the *ton* behaved, as if everyone on the Earth were there to amuse them? "Please leave, Your Grace. I am quite finished with you." She crossed her arms beneath her breasts and waited for him to comply. The joy had faded from the day.

"Oh, I'd wager that's not true at all," he said in a lowered voice that smacked of sin and slid over her person like the finest silk. He laughed again, as did his companion, and when Alice opened her mouth to tell them both off, Donovan slid his hand around her upper arm in a gentle hold. "Before you fly into the boughs again, let me explain. This woman, contrary to what you believe, is not my fancy piece. In fact, I believe she took offense at your statement, for she thinks it already a trial she resides in the same residence as me."

Alice gasped. "Shares your home?"

He continued as if she hadn't spoken. "She is, in fact, my sister—Lady Elizabeth Sinclair."

Oh, merciful heavens. I've just taken a duke and his sister to task. "I…" Her words drifted off, for nothing she could say would make right the discretion.

The duke fit his lips to the shell of her ear and whispered, "Elizabeth insisted she play chaperone, for she's worried I'll ruin you with continued calls if I come by myself."

Heat of a different kind than anger or mortification swamped Alice. She trembled the longer he remained near, but hope crept into her heart once more. He must be serious in his intent if this was the result. Perhaps she was a fool for continuing to believe in the dream.

"In addition, Elizabeth rather thinks she's my protector," he continued.

"Protecting you from what or whom?"

He laughed, and a trace of bitterness clung to the sound. "That is a story for another time."

A heavy sigh escaped her. "I apologize for my assumption and my words," she mumbled, and when she attempted to move from him, he released her only to slide his arm about her waist.

Then his sister took both her hands in her own and tugged her away from Donovan. She kissed Alice on the cheek, which allowed Alice to see her face, albeit blurrily. Caramel hair upswept and held with jeweled combs, frank brown eyes and features similar to her brother's. "Good afternoon, Miss Morrowe. I'm Lady Elizabeth, but please do call me Elizabeth." She laughed and the sound was no longer mocking. "I have a feeling you and I will spend much time together." Then she linked an arm with Alice's and led her down the church aisle.

"My brother doesn't understand the finer points of courtship."

Alice gasped. "He is truly courting me?" Tingles of pleasure played down her spine. It would be nice to have that confirmation.

"In his own way, yes." Elizabeth patted her hand while she guided them out of the church. The warmth of the late afternoon sun beat upon Alice's arms and chest. "Shall we adjourn to the party? Weddings make me famished, and I do so enjoy fancy food."

"Don't mind me. I'll just be walking by myself back here instead of talking with the woman I came to see," Donovan said in a sing-song voice, much to the amusement of his sister. Even Alice couldn't help but laugh, so light was her heart now that the misunderstanding had cleared.

"Time enough for all of that, brother dear," Elizabeth replied and kept her arm linked with Alice's. "I have a few questions for her… or perhaps I'll reveal a few secrets."

"You wouldn't dare," he whispered, and a certain warning hardened the words.

Alice wondered at the interplay between them, but since Elizabeth remained silent, she didn't question it. What secrets did the duke keep he didn't want her to know?

Once at the cottage, where people milled about the grounds, laughter and conversation buzzing around her, Fanny tugged her a bit away from Elizabeth, but Donovan hovered, not quite close but not far.

Devil Take the Duke (Lords of the Night #1)

"Why did you bring *him*?" Fanny hissed into her ear as she tightened her grip on Alice's arm. "People are talking about the duke and not me." Her huff of frustration ruffled the curls on Alice's forehead. "It's my wedding day!"

The joy Alice found at having Donovan with her again faded in the face of Fanny's discontent. "I didn't *bring* him. He showed up. I do not dictate his movements." The very idea of manipulating a duke made her giggle, which further annoyed her friend.

Fanny let go Alice's arm. "I never thought you'd wish to steal the attention from me—the bride. How cruel you've shown yourself to be, Alice. I thought I knew you, but now this day will forever be ruined in my memory. You have changed, and not for the better. Have you always been so jealous?" Then she presented her back to Alice.

"Fanny, I…" How many more bewildering emotions would assault her this day? Alice stood with a tight chest and tears in her eyes for a different reason. "I didn't… I would never," she whispered, but Fanny stalked away. She set off to follow her friend.

"Alice." Donovan gained her side and drew her hand into the crook of his elbow. "Perhaps it's best to give her some time. If she's truly a friend, she'll realize you didn't do what she's accused you of." Kindness threaded through his tone, and her eyes once more filled with tears. "Come. Walk with me back into the village proper."

"Where is Elizabeth?" Alice asked as she let him guide her away from the festive activity around them.

"It's her turn to trail behind." He released her only to clasp his hands behind his back as they walked the dusty, hard-packed road.

Silence brewed between them for long moments. Finally, Alice couldn't stand the void, and with a fair amount of annoyance behind her words, she asked, "I wish to know what your plans are, for you have put, and continue to put me, on precarious ground in Shalford. My reputation is being cut to ribbons, and I do not appreciate it." Even if she remained flattered by his attention.

"My plans?" A certain note of wariness crept into his voice.

"With me. For me." That was as plain as she could say it. If he couldn't understand, then he didn't deserve her continued time.

"I'm not certain yet." Nothing except honesty hung on the reply.

At least there was that. "Are you only amusing yourself until I give you whatever it is you want?" From behind them, Elizabeth snorted with apparent hilarity. Alice ignored her. "I won't be best pleased with you if so. My condition does not give you leave to trifle with my affections."

"I well understand that." Donovan drew to a halt, which forced Alice to do the same. She faced him, planted her gaze on him even though she couldn't see him. Let him look into her eyes and discern the very real emotions there. "*Do* I feature into your affections, Alice?" he asked in a low voice.

The heat of embarrassment blazed in her cheeks while butterflies tickled through her insides. "I'm not sure."

"Ah." But he chuckled and the sound sent awareness of him sailing over her. "What will it take on my part to secure such feelings?"

She gaped, stunned. Was he serious or was it part of a game? Emboldened by her earlier words in the church, Alice closed the distance between them and traced his face without waiting for permission or even asking it. There was nothing in his expression to indicate he made jest of her. Lines of somberness framed his mouth and the corners of his eyes, but he stood still as she explored. Satisfied, she stepped away. "Show me you are different than other men. Show me that you care."

Another swath of silence lengthened between them. Finally, he cleared his throat and took her hand. "I can do that." He pressed a kiss into her palm and the warmth of his lips seeped through the fine lace of her fingerless gloves. "I promise to do just that in the coming days." Then he drew her hand through the crook of his elbow. "Allow me to take you back to your room. It is not my intention to cause you further embarrassment."

But what exactly is your intention, my lord?

She didn't know, but perhaps now wasn't the time to question it, for he'd been nothing but a gentleman so far... except their first meeting when he was nude. Or the fact that he'd stolen a few kisses. For the moment she'd remain thankful he was here. The puzzle of why could wait.

CHAPTER SEVEN

September 21, 1815
London

Donovan returned home from a run well after midnight. He slipped into the townhouse, completely nude, for unless he made the decision to undress ahead of the shift, once the ancient magic took hold, his clothing was shredded and disintegrated with the change.

Oftentimes, he didn't waste time with such things, which was good that his staff knew to not to question his choice of dress or undress, as the case might be.

The night had been cathartic. As the beast, he'd feasted upon a sheep, bedeviled another one until it became lodged in a thicket of thorny hedges, chased a handful of rabbits and then ran until he'd worked out all the knots from his muscles and smoothed the questions from his mind.

And through it all, thoughts of Alice continued to plague him. He'd even visited Shalford and stood guard near her door for long hours. What the deuce was he to do about his sweet, innocent country flower? She wished him to show himself as different. He snorted as he lowered himself into the copper bathtub his butler, Griggs, had arranged for him upon his arrival. If she only knew how different he truly was.

He'd just begun to lather himself with the fine-milled French soap that smelled of sandalwood and various citrus fruits and spices, when Griggs appeared at his door.

"I apologize for the interruption, Your Grace. However, the Earl of Devon is here to see you." The older gentleman with salt-and-pepper hair averted his gaze. "Where shall I show him?"

Why come to call so bloody late? Donovan closed his eyes. He blew out a breath before pushing the soapy lather over his face. "Show him in here. I'm much too tired for formality tonight."

"Very well, my lord."

While the butler was gone, Donovan continued his ablutions and had just washed the dirt, grime and blood from his hair when the earl appeared in the room. Literally appeared, for one of the man's attributes of being a vampire was his ability to move at quicker than human speeds.

"Do you not have women to feed from at his hour, Devon?" Donovan complained as he slicked the hair back from his forehead. Water ran down his face and neck. His mood hadn't improved after his extended run, and that annoyed him more.

The earl wasn't perturbed. Instead, still dressed in immaculate evening clothing, he leaned a shoulder against the doorframe and crossed his arms at his chest. "Don't you have livestock to terrorize or virgins to debase?" he countered with a jaunty grin.

"Well played." Donovan shared a laugh with his best friend. Then he finished with his bath, and after grabbing a towel from the floor beside the tub, he stood and wrapped the cloth about his waist. "What do you want?" He eyed the man as he climbed out of the bath. "Looking like you've come from a *ton* event."

"I have, in fact, come from the Earl of Coventry's rout. He's apparently indulging his sister in allowing her to mix with society in the hopes that—"

"Yes, yes." Donovan impatiently waved a hand. "In the hopes that she'll manage to snag a husband despite the rumors attached to his name." He rolled his eyes. "I have one of those myself, except mine is hell bent on protecting me from the nest of vipers we refer to as Polite Society."

"There is that." The earl pushed off the doorframe and followed Donovan into his dressing room where Burroughs waited. "How have you kept yourself these last couple of days? I haven't seen you about Town."

Donovan shrugged. "I've stuck close to home when I'm not running the countryside as the wolf." He allowed his valet to suggest clothing more appropriate to making an afternoon call over sleeping like most men did at such an early morning hour.

His friend snorted. "You're brooding, which essentially means you're closeting yourself in your study, oftentimes in the dark, staring out the window in contemplation, overthinking your existence."

It didn't escape Donovan's notice that his valet shared a knowing smirk with the earl. "I'm not. What concerns me at the present time requires a bit of handling with metaphorical kid gloves." All of which centered around Alice and how the devil he was to show her he wasn't the lecherous man she thought. Not to mention how to charm her enough that she'd fall quickly for him. Time was rapidly running out.

"Ah." The vampire moved about the room so that he remained in eye contact with Donovan. "Then you are mooning about the female currently turning your life to sixes and sevens."

"Also not true."

"I see."

It was unfortunate that his friend knew him so well. "Why do you bedevil me, Rogue?"

"Because it's so easy." The earl grinned and the faint red ring around his pupils glowed brighter for an instant. "Why did you not come to the club last night? You never miss our card evenings. Hell, Coventry was even there and commented upon it."

Donovan rolled his eyes. He waved away the help of his valet in favor of folding and tying his cravat by himself. "There is much on my mind at present. I didn't need additional cluttering by spending hours at a table playing cards with you fellows or listening to you categorizing the charms of the new female in your life." And he certainly didn't want to share anything about Alice with his chums, for such talk would cheapen her, and she was much more than fodder over a table of drinks at a gentleman's club.

Do you hear yourself? Inside his head, his wolf howled with laughter. *How can you tell this man you're above all of that when you cannot manage to banish thoughts of the woman from your mind?*

He gritted his teeth against the truth his beast dredged up. *It means nothing.*

It means everything, human.

"Would that I had a female in my life." Rogue narrowed his eyes and contemplated him with speculation lining his handsome face. "For the hell of it, let's assume what's uppermost in your mind is the curse, since obviously the next full moon comes due soon."

"Yes." The word was clipped and terse. He summarily dismissed his valet as soon as he donned a jacket of navy superfine that matched the embroidery on his gray waistcoat—a color that seemed dull and lifeless when he remembered the glint of silver in Alice's eyes.

Damn it all to hell and back.

His wolf, thankfully, didn't comment.

"You're not happy your days of being a slave to your beast are almost over?" Rogue frowned. He looked truly surprised. "This is a good thing, yes? It's what we all are striving for. After all, we have, the four of us, failed in that on more than one occasion."

Donovan's shrug only lifted one shoulder. He flung himself into a maroon-and-navy brocade wingback chair and slumped into the interior. "It's... bittersweet. More of an ethical dilemma, actually." He waved a hand and then let it fall into his lap. "How can I end his life while embracing mine?"

His wolf whined in agreement.

Rogue nodded. "Understandable, and a unique problem I do not need to wrestle with." He cocked his head to one side as he stared at Donovan. "What of the woman you mentioned the other day?"

Alice, and the unique pull she had upon him. And the spirit she showed at the rustic wedding. That had impressed him more than it should have. "I'm going slowly." Even though every time he was with her, his wolf urged him to throw her down and claim her. There were limits, after all, and he had his.

"Have you told her yet of any part of your life, the curse, your secret?"

"No." Donovan rubbed a hand along his jaw. Day old stubble rasped against his palm but he was disinclined to shave. "That level of trust isn't quite there between us yet. As it is, Miss Morrowe battles for her place within village life. My presence isn't helping her cause."

"And this makes you wary?" Rogue clasped his hands behind his back. He paced the confines of the dressing room, his gaze never leaving Donovan's face.

"If she's on the outskirts of a village society, how the deuce will she fit into *ton* life?" He held up a hand before his friend could catch the slip. "That is, *if* I choose to go forward with my seduction, and *if* I wish to bring her to London to deepen our relationship."

Devil Take the Duke (Lords of the Night #1)

The earl's lips twitched. Amusement danced in his eyes and the red ring glowed stronger. "Do you wish for her to integrate into a society where you yourself aren't fully welcome?"

"I'm not certain." He raised his gaze to Rogue's. "On anything at this point."

Silence brewed between them while the earl continued to pace. Finally, he came to a halt near a window and faced Donovan. "Do you care for her? That's the only reason I can find for your unaccountable confliction. You've never been so before."

This was true. In all of his dealings through life, he'd never second-guessed himself. Until now. "No." He shook his head. "What I feel for her is protection, interest, empathy—"

"—lust," Rogue interrupted with a slightly crooked smile.

Donovan couldn't hold one of his own back. "Certainly." He drummed his fingers on the armrests of the chair. "Her curves tempt me beyond reason each time I see her."

"Yet you've done nothing about it. Interesting." The earl cocked a blond eyebrow. "What else? There must be another reason for your regard."

"She has challenged me to do something different, something no other man has done for her, something that shows her I care." He frowned. "An impossible task, I sometimes think."

"And one you desperately wish to fulfill." Rogue nodded, a thoughtful expression on his face. Then he laughed. "She's coming to understand you.

Perhaps you are well-matched and that is what bothers you."

Donovan rolled his eyes. He made a vulgar gesture at his friend, to which the earl laughed harder.

"You wonder if you'll change your mind about the seduction and wish for other things from life," Rogue continued, ever the devil's advocate.

"Perhaps." Donovan stared at his friend. Why wouldn't he give over solid advice? Of course, if the roles were reversed, what would he say to the earl to help the confliction of mind? Nothing, for this problem was unique to the man, and no one could make the decision for him. "We shall see what occurs after my secret is revealed."

"When you bed her."

"Yes." For that's what always happened. It was a part of the curse. As soon as he found release and his heartbeat returned to normal, the truth burst forth from him no matter how hard he attempted to fight the urge. Some women lasted one night more after that fantastical revelation; most dressed and ran from the house with mumbled excuses. If they bandied the tale about London, he didn't know, for rumors about him had always abounded.

Neither did he care. *This is who I am, and if they will not accept me for that... I don't need them.*

His wolf snuffled into his mind. *Will Miss Morrowe accept you? Will she accept me?*

Anxiety clawed at the pit of his stomach. *It's critical she do exactly that.*

Devil Take the Duke (Lords of the Night #1)

The fact she showed such jealousy regarding Elizabeth was encouraging. Yet…

Rogue softly cleared his throat, which brought Donovan's wandering attention back to him. "Are you seeing her today?"

"Yes. I plan to catch her unawares early this morning." He lowered his voice. "And while Elizabeth, Alice's self-appointed chaperone, is still abed." Donovan grinned at the earl's knowing look.

"Dear God. Your sister will flay the skin from your bones once she's aware of your plans." Rogue's joke held the sting of truth, for Elizabeth had made herself and her strong personality known already to his small circle of friends. At one time he'd fondly thought that perhaps Rogue might have courted her, but romance hadn't bloomed. "Perhaps it's time to truly seduce Miss Morrowe, to accelerate her tumble into love."

"Good luck." A smirk curved his friend's lips. "It is a razor's edge you walk. In every way."

"Indeed it is, but isn't that part of the challenge?" And when he finally coupled with Alice, the act would be all the sweeter for the chase.

By the time Donovan reached Shalford—for he and Rogue had continued to talk for some time, then they'd raided the kitchens while the staff still slumbered—dawn was an hour or so off. Somewhat fitting, for the first time he'd met Alice, dawn had not yet crested.

He'd parked his curricle in the woods and then accessed the village on foot. What the gossiping tabbies didn't see, they couldn't circulate, and for the time being, he didn't wish for this visit to have witnesses.

His heartbeat raced as he softly knocked upon Alice's door. Yes, it was the height of scandal to do such a thing, but time was of the essence, and he wished for her to remain at sixes and sevens to better coax her into his arms. When he raised his hand to knock again, she cracked open the door.

"Donovan?" Surprise propelled the word into the air. Pleasure widened her eyes.

"How did you know it was me?" He marveled at the seemingly sixth sense she possessed around him. Inside his mind, his wolf took notice.

Her throaty chuckle, so early in the morning, sent awareness skittering through his body. Was that what she'd sound like if he woke her up in the wee hours to satisfy their mutual need? His member tightened. "I recognized your scent. It's unique and sets you apart from other men."

"That is good to know." He had the blend special ordered from a shop on St. James Street. "Will you let me in? I'd rather not conduct this conversation at your door in the event someone wanders the village early."

"Of course." She opened the door wider, revealing a nightdress of plain lawn so thin her healthy peach skin showed through, but adorned with a row of pearl buttons and trimmed with lace.

"Except, your alternative is the height of improper."

"I'm nothing if not consistent." As he passed her, he smiled at the blatant delight in her stormy eyes. How encouraging. When she'd closed the door behind him, he tugged off his gloves and tossed them to the foot of her narrow bed, with its freshly rumpled sheets and counterpane. Her pillow showed the indent from her head; obviously he'd roused her from slumber. She'd not yet risen for the day. The intimacy of it all further worked to fan the flames of his desire.

"Why are you here so early?" she asked as she fluttered a hand between her cheek and her throat, where the placket of her nightdress was unbuttoned. He adored her state of dishabille, but what would she look like covered in satins and silks with perhaps a string of pearls around her neck or that pale skin decorated with diamond choker? Riches that he'd peel off layer by layer to reveal the pale skin beneath?

He wrenched his gaze away from the tempting flesh, even though she couldn't see the action. "I wanted to spend time with you, away from my sister, away from the judgment of the village." Donovan glanced about the small quarters, but her apricot-scented presence filled the space and reminded him she was there. So innocent. Waiting to be plucked. "I'm quite selfish that way."

"To my way of thinking, you are selfish in every way, my lord." She flashed a smile, and in the darkness of the room, he swore the gesture lit the shadows. "You've chosen scandal once more then."

"Is that such a bad thing?" When he matched her smile, realized she couldn't see, he caught her hand and then pressed her palm to his lips so that she could feel their curve. "I'm familiar with it, so why rout it now?" As he continued to grin, he darted out his tongue and licked her skin. Finally, they were both without the barrier of gloves.

Alice sucked in a breath. She raised her eyes to his. Confusion and surprise lit those depths, but her pupils widened. "What am I to do with you?" Breathlessness infused her whisper.

Damnation. Did she not realize the fetching, tempting picture she presented? He cupped her cheek while she did the same to him. "Anything you wish." He traced her lower lip with the pad of his thumb. "Do you have any ideas?" Oh, but he could think of quite a few things. Both his wolf and his thickening length agreed with them all.

Her gray eyes, so wide and still dreamy with the last vestiges of slumber, invited him to jump in and drown. Trust shimmered there with the silver flecks, trust and infatuation. "I could make you a cup of tea. There's a hearth inside the mill…"

"Hmm." He brushed his fingertips along the side of her throat, and when she sharply inhaled, he smiled. "I have a different idea." What better way to help a seduction along than offering to dance with a lady? Dancing meant holding her close and that could lead to all sorts of delicious activities. He fingered the long braid resting over her shoulder. "Perhaps you'll share a dance with me?" As he spoke, he drew his hand downward, following the slope of her shoulder, along her bare arm to her hand. Oh, but he wanted to skim his palms over her breasts where even now the rosy tips of her hardened nipples thrust against her night clothes.

"Are you insane?" She moistened her lips, and he moved his gaze to her kissable mouth. "Here? In my tiny room? We'll trip over each other."

"Not a bad thing either." With a bit of luck, he could tumble her onto that bed. It was just waiting to be of use... His wolf urged him to do exactly that, but Donovan held back. Slowly. *It's an art.* "Unless you'd rather adjourn to the mill?" No doubt there'd be more floor space, and dance with her he would before he plied her with kisses.

"Oh, I haven't had a proper dance in years." Longing wove through her voice and she trembled.

Donovan grasped her hand. "Even more of a reason for us to indulge." Quickly, before she changed her mind, he escorted her from the room, being certain to close the door. With her delighted laughter ringing in his ears, he pulled her around to the mill's door, and when he found it not locked, he chuckled. "So much trust in Shalford over London."

"We have nothing to fear." Anticipation threaded through her voice.

Oh, but they did—she did. He pushed the thought from his mind as he ushered her inside. The comforting scents of flour and grain met his nose. So easily could he imagine the bread those things would be used for once ground. "Now is not the time for fear, my sweet country flower." Then, without further conversation, he swept her into his arms and immediately moved them into the steps of a waltz.

Bloody hell. He'd thought she'd be the one enchanted by the tactile necessity of the dance, but it was he who felt as if he drowned in her presence. The heat of her seeped through her thin night dress and transferred to his hands, his body as he pressed her closer. The bakery-like scent of her wafted through his nose and fed his hunger. Though she stumbled through the steps until she found her rhythm, he didn't care, for each misstep meant he could hold her to him, guide her through the turns, murmur instructions to keep her steady, until he wished they were in a ballroom with her skirts swirling about them, and alternately he imagined her *sans* clothing as their bodies fit and moved together in a different sort of dance.

Once they drifted to a natural halt, Alice rested a hand on his chest while the other she'd wrapped about his neck. She stared into his face with such trust and bemusement that he caught his breath, but it was the need that twinkled at the backs of her eyes that spurred him onward.

"Ah, Alice," he whispered, and since she couldn't see him, he set out to tantalize her other senses. "How you tempt me." Donovan took her hand, pulled it away from his person. He caressed his fingers along the inside of her arm, traced her palm, glanced them along the side of her neck. "So beautiful." Then he gave the same treatment to her other arm and hand until she trembled in his hold and her breathing accelerated.

"You are quite proficient in this," she whispered and then glided her fingers over his face leaving tingles of need in her wake.

"Perhaps, but the lady makes the difference." And that was the truth. Then he bent his head, kissed the hollow of her throat where her pulse rapidly fluttered, feathered a kiss to the inside of her wrist, licked at the life force that surged through her veins, and when she gasped, he moved to her lips, kissing her without pressure, just teasing little nips.

"Have I…" A sigh shuddered from her as she lifted on tip toe to return his kisses. "Have I made a difference with you?"

"Uncommonly so." Perhaps more than any woman he'd ever known. Donovan kissed her lips with more gusto. Alice was hesitant in returning the overture at first, but when he remained patient, merely nibbling at the corners of her mouth, moving over her lips as if he had all the time in the world, she followed his lead, and he continued with more insistence.

"I'm glad. I think it's a good thing for you to be with someone different, someone you can learn from." With every word she uttered, her lips brushed his, and she pulled him closer with gentle pressure of her hand at his nape.

Then he was lost. Donovan walked her across the dusty floor until her back connected with a wall. He groaned. How could she be so innocent yet such a siren at the same time? His hardened member pressed insistently against the front of his breeches, and he pushed her arms over her head.

When she murmured a protest, he quickly caught both of her wrists in one hand while with the other, he cupped a breast, teasing the beaded nipple with his thumb.

"Oh!" A surprised moan followed the breathy exclamation, and when he kissed her lips, she sighed. The mewling sounds she made at the back of her throat when he continued his fondling tugged at him, fueling the flames of his own need.

"You were made for pleasure, Alice." His pleasure, hers—theirs together. Finally, he released her wrists and he cupped both breasts. The plump globes tempted him, her body called out to his, and while his wolf paced about his mind in high anxiety for the act that would surely come, Donovan blocked those impulses in favor of flooding the woman in his arms with sensations she wouldn't soon forget.

He dipped his head and took a tight bud into his mouth, teased it with his tongue. The scrape of the fabric provided an interesting texture and added another layer of heat to the desire circling through his body. She furrowed her fingers through his hair, holding him to her breast as she wriggled from his attention.

"Donovan." His name uttered from her lips sounded like the most pleasing invocation. "I never knew I could feel such things. It's... freeing, exciting." She kissed him. "Teach me."

Damnation. It would be so easy to coerce her into the act, to bury his aching length in her honeyed heat, but he hesitated.

Rut with her! Claim her, his wolf urged. *Show her what it can be like to lie with a man the first time.*

The words froze him and cooled some of his ardor. *But there is the rub. It will be her first time, and shouldn't be a quick, dirty tryst hidden in a mill.*

"My sweet Alice. You have so much to learn." As his pulse thundered in his temples, he rested his forehead against hers. When he stared into her eyes and saw the glimmers of adoration there, he smiled. "Perhaps we should talk while passion dies, else I'll embarrass myself." He left the explanation at that, taking the blame to further endear him to her. He cringed because it was such a cold, calculated plan.

And she didn't deserve it.

"That is rather a good idea, for the way I'm feeling right now…" She broke off with a laugh that only served to re-fire his blood. "I might just give you what you want." Alice clung to him, and he wrapped his arms around her.

Dear girl, how you tempt me.

His wolf whined when he didn't make further inroads into the seduction.

They remained locked together while a comfortable silence wove around them. Then she broke the mood, and her words chilled him.

"There are rumors in the village about wolves killing the livestock. Some of the men have claimed to see one of the animals. Can you believe that? Such things haven't been in England for over a hundred years." She laughed, as if the topic were absurd.

Donovan gently eased away from her. Cold sweat plastered his shirt to his back. "I believe it more than you can know." He'd been careless if he was seen. Too much time spent in the Surrey countryside. The remainder of his passion died. If she laughed away the stories, how would she react when he had to tell her the truth? With his existence known, he'd need to conduct his visits with more attention.

Time was truly critical now.

CHAPTER EIGHT

September 22, 1815
Shalford

Alice lifted her face to the afternoon sun and reveled in the autumn warmth. Soon the seasons would turn with the tree leaves. The comforting scents of bonfires would pervade the air, bringing with it a crispness where the world prepared to wrap itself in glory before preparing for its winter's nap.

At present, she couldn't help but think that the winds of change were about to enter her life, and she didn't know how she felt about that. While excitement buzzed at the base of her spine, trepidation churned in her belly. What would happen between her and the duke?

Perhaps nothing. Their relationship was bizarre, yet she couldn't shake the feeling of hope that bloomed in her chest each time she thought of him.

"Alice, you're wool-gathering," Fanny accused as she touched Alice's shoulder. "Here I've been telling you how sorry I was for my snappish words at my wedding, and you've not paid attention." A trace of annoyance ran through her words.

"I apologize." She'd met her friend at their special spot up the river beyond the water mill. A large boulder rested on the bank and Alice liked to perch upon it, pretending, dreaming, wondering. It allowed her time away from the village where she could listen to the moving water and find balance. "My thoughts have been scattered of late."

"So have mine," Fanny replied with a secret smile that Alice couldn't understand. "Lying with a man is quite... different than anything I've ever known."

"How so?" Alice thrust thoughts of Donovan away in order to better concentrate on her friend.

Fanny chuckled. The sound held a note of smugness and experience. "It is hard to describe except that it can be wonderful once in a while." She sighed. "Most times, though, it's more of a chore than anything else. Lovemaking seems to benefit Rupert the most."

"Oh?" Though Alice knew the basics of what occurred between a man and a woman, she couldn't begin to even guess at the rest.

"After he climbs on top of me, touches me, he grunts as we... you know. He hits release and then sleeps after without caring if I reach the same heights." She shrugged. "Mum says that's how it goes most times, but it must be enjoyable for the woman more often than not; otherwise, I wouldn't have so many siblings, right?"

"Oh, Fanny, perhaps you only need give it time. I doubt many couples learn such things perfectly the first few times." But Alice laughed along with her friend. "There are many women in the village who say relations are awkward."

"And short." Fanny patted her shoulder. "For all the talk about the dirty deed, Lord it's too short to really enjoy."

Alice smiled. "You have a lifetime ahead to find a rhythm." Conflicting thoughts circled through head. "Didn't Rupert give you chills of excitement or anticipation before you indulged each other physically?" When she remembered what she'd felt when Donovan kissed or caressed her, tendrils of heat twisted up her spine. Merely hearing the tone of his voice set butterflies loose in her belly. Did Fanny not experience such things?

"I don't know what that means." Fanny moved away to sit beside Alice on the boulder. "I wanted a husband and babies. He wished for a place to stick his prick." Her laugh this time didn't ring as bright. "Of course, I wouldn't give it to him until he agreed to the wedding, but I guess we get on all right." She bumped Alice's shoulder. "It's the living with him that'll take some patience. Men are quite different in that regard, too."

"I can only imagine." *Yet, how... disappointing.* Alice's smile faded. She was of a mind there should be more from intimacy than the raw coldness of what happened in the marriage bed. More than a perfunctory joining resulting in pregnancy. Surely there were emotions involved that enhanced such things, a sharing of souls with love making. Did not love take precedence, or at the very least fondness?

Perhaps that was also a silly dream. *Despite my advanced age, I'm regrettably ignorant.*

Fanny prodded Alice in the ribs with her elbow. "But you should already know all of this, yes? Now that you have experience in the carnal world." She snickered. "The world of sin, some would say."

That brought Alice out of her thoughts with alacrity. She turned her head toward Fanny and leaned close enough that she could peer into her friend's face. The smug expression and mocking light in her eyes sent cold chills of anxiety curling through her insides. "What do you mean?"

Fanny snorted. She raised an eyebrow. "You're bedding that duke who keeps coming around, sniffing at your skirts. Everyone in the village is talking about it. Some of the men have put down wagers on when you'll get with child." Her laugh took on a wicked note. "Mum says it's scandalous the way you're behaving and that I should limit my time with you, but I think it's interesting. I wouldn't have thought you'd have it in you to be *that sort* of woman."

Heat slapped Alice's cheeks as hotter annoyance rose in her chest. "It is gossip, nothing more, for none of it is true." It must be out of hand if even her best friend believed the talk over what Alice had told her.

"Aw, don't be like that." Fanny grabbed one of her hands and clasped it between her own. "You can tell me all the dirty secrets."

"What is there to tell?" She shook her head, still fuming with her ire. "It's certainly not what you and the others think." Pausing, she searched her mind for the appropriate words. "The duke has come to see me a few times. That's all." The heat in her cheeks blazed more furiously than before. "He took me out on a drive and a walk. We didn't even stay long at your wedding celebration before he escorted me home." Her friend didn't need to know about the early morning visit a couple of days ago that resulted in lovely kisses and hot caresses in the mill or the gentlemanly way he gave into honor instead of pushing for relations.

Fanny put her nose to Alice's while she searched her face. "You're blushing. Either there's more to your story or you're lying."

Perhaps there were some things that didn't need cheapening by telling them to a girlfriend, especially since Fanny was prone to gossip. If Alice revealed all about the duke, her friend would run with that information to everyone else, and Alice wished to keep such special moments between her and Donovan. She shrugged and gently removed her hand from Fanny's. "We have exchanged a few kisses. That is all."

"And?" Fanny poked her in the ribs. "There must more. I mean, if I was kissed by such a dashing man, I wouldn't stop there."

If Alice's cheeks flared any hotter, she'd burn to a crisp right there. "Truly, he and I have not gone any further." Yet, a smile curved her lips as she thought about him. "He is… nice, mysterious as if he's keeping big secrets, and I have yet to discover why he's interested in me, when he could have his pick of any woman in London." Was she guilty of over-thinking the issue? Did he truly think there was something in her he couldn't live without? He'd said a few times that she intrigued him, buy why? It was maddening to contemplate.

"Don't be such a widgeon, Alice." Fanny sighed. "He wants to tupp you. That is all. It's what men want from women the world over. The end."

"I'm not convinced. He seems quite polite and everything lovely."

"Men lie."

Alice let silence roll over her. Was that the truth? Was he like all the rest, like Joe the blacksmith, in that he only wanted what was between her thighs? Disappointment chilled her. She sighed as a trace of tears filled her eyes. "If that is what he truly thinks, then I shall have to cut ties with him. I'm worth more than that."

Was she, though? A poor relation of a baron who'd been cast off, and blind to boot, working in a milliner's shop. What did she have to offer a man like the duke besides a quick roll in the sheets?

"That is a sensible answer." Fanny slipped off the boulder. "You know how the upper crust is. They never care about folks like us and are always living for pleasure or entertainment."

"Perhaps..." Yet Alice still wasn't convinced that was true for all of them. "There must be good folks among the *ton*, just like there are bad ones in the lower classes."

"Who can say?" Her friend briefly touched Alice's shoulder. "Besides, it's unlikely you would bring a duke up to scratch."

Devil Take the Duke (Lords of the Night #1)

"Why would you say such a thing?" Again, her cheeks blazed but with anger this time. "Isn't it possible he could fall in love with me?" There was always that dream and Alice was of the opinion that everyone in the world deserved such an emotion.

"It might be possible, but I doubt it will happen. You're blind. Even you know that sets you apart from every other woman, makes you less. You couldn't enjoy anything that might occur between you, let alone conduct yourself as a proper duchess." Fanny snorted. "Have you ever heard of a duke taking a woman who is less than perfect to wife?" She chuckled as she warmed to her subject. "A blind duchess? It's simply not done, and if it was, the *ton* would tear you apart."

"You cannot know that."

"I have a fair idea," her friend responded with a firmness Alice didn't understand. "You let life happen to you. You're not a fighter and are too good. Without a backbone, London will destroy you."

How dare Fanny? It mattered not that her marrying a duke was naught but a fairytale or that it would never happen to her life. Her friend shouldn't have said such hurtful words, and even if Alice aspired to the title of duchess—which she did not but there were dreams, after all—Fanny should have supported that dream. The anger building inside Alice hit the boiling point. She struggled off the boulder and fairly quivered with indignation.

"I would rather not have my sight and think everyone deserves acceptance wherever they go, to follow my dreams no matter how silly they might sound to you, than have sight yet remain prejudiced to each person's abilities."

"I'm only looking out for you," Fanny protested.

Alice's breath came in fast pants. She clenched her hands into fists. "Everyone regardless of their affliction or handicap, has something to bring to the world, something exclusively theirs, and if given the opportunity can do much good with that." With every sentence she uttered, her voice rose. She narrowed her gaze as she looked at the brown blob of Fanny's form. "Regardless of people like you who would hide them from the world... for their own good."

Fanny gasped. "I didn't mean to set you off, I merely said what I did to help keep you grounded. Such a life isn't for you."

"You cannot know that." Not that Donovan had made an overture that would usher in marriage, but his presence in her life as well as his sister's words indicated he was indeed courting her—for a purpose. "Perhaps the life I lead now isn't for me. There's no way of knowing." She sucked in a breath, but peace wouldn't come. Just like the time she gave the duke and his sister a dressing down, the same urge overcame her. "This conversation is finished, and until you can support me in the way I most need it, I have nothing else to say to you."

"Alice, come back!" Fanny called after her. "Where are you going?"

"I need some air and exercise. Go home and don't worry about me, not that you do anyway."

"You shouldn't go out alone and so close to the river," Fanny continued.

"When will you understand that I can do everything you can with the same conviction and authority?" Yes, her vision was compromised, but that didn't mean she wasn't a living person who had plans for her life.

With anger still coursing through her body, she shook from it, felt it even to the roots of her hair. *I am more than people expect of me.* She followed the river. The call and chirp of birds in the trees not far away invited further exploration. Not even the gentle ebb and flow of the water could promote calm in her being, neither could the autumn sun on her face, for she'd left her bonnet on the boulder in her haste to leave Fanny's presence.

She walked and walked. Thankfully, Fanny didn't follow. Alice didn't care. She needed friends in her life who supported her regardless of the absurdity of the dreams she held deep in her heart. If she was ever fortunate to brush shoulders with members of the *ton*, those connections and the reach could help her wish of opening a school. Now more than ever vision compromised children needed to know blindness wasn't the end of their life; it was only the beginning of achieving greatness.

We all must touch the lives of others in a different way than sighted people.

Then her thoughts circled back to Donovan and how she felt while in his presence. She'd asked him to show her how different he was from other men. Would he do so? Oh, how she prayed and hoped that he was, for already her heart had been engaged. Perhaps it was folly to care for a man she hardly knew, but he treated her blindness with respect, had taken her words into account and conversed with her accordingly. Memories of him coming close to her face or pressing her hand to his face so that she might "see" his expressions brought a smile. That said volumes about his character.

And if the only thing he'd wanted from her was a chance to rut between her thighs, he could have taken advantage in the mill, for she'd been oh so willing. A hint of heat curled through her lower belly. The man was potent when plying her with kisses.

But he hadn't forced the issue or taken advantage. Again, he'd shown himself as different than other men by controlling his urges.

He's everything noble and good.

"It ain't often I have you all to myself."

Alice gasped as a hulking blob moved toward her from the opposite direction. "Leave me alone, Joe. I have nothing to say to you." Each day that went by, it seemed as if someone in the village worked to aggravate her.

"Say what you want, but I'm not finished with you." The closer he came, the more anxiety clawed at her insides.

She stopped walking, her body tensed to run. "Go away." How long had she wandered while lost in thought? No longer could she hear the noise from the water mill or the constant grinding from the huge stones within the building itself. There was nothing nearby except for the river and the woods that separated Shalford from the next village. If she screamed, no one would hear her.

"Not likely. I want to say my piece." The blob that represented Joe dominated her compromised vision and he grabbed her upper arm in a bruising grip. "You gave that duke your time. You can do the same with me."

"Let me go." Alice struggled against his hold. "You're hurting me." Pain radiated beneath his beefy hand. "This is not the way to ensure I'll speak with you."

His huff blew onion-scented breath across her face. "You put on too many airs, Miss Morrowe, when you're nothing but a woman the village throws charity at."

"That's not true." No matter how much she pulled and tugged at his hand with hers, he remained attached to her. Perhaps it was best to appease him, for her strength would never match his. She stilled. "What do you want?" Why didn't the people of Shalford give her respect? Having a handicap didn't reduce her worth.

"A kiss. It's only fair you let me show you what a real man would give you."

"Absolutely not." Alice squirmed but he tightened his grip on her upper arm. "How many times must I tell you I am not interested in you that way?"

"Don't believe you." He stuck his face close to hers and she recoiled. Fervor glittered in his dark eyes; anticipation lined his expression. "You're friendly with that duke; I want the same."

"Have you gone mad?" Alice couldn't tug herself away from him, and when he wrapped his other hand around the back of her head and slammed his mouth upon hers, cold fingers of fear played up her spine. She wrenched away, and when she did, she delivered a resounding slap to his broad cheek. "Leave me alone." His lips against hers felt nothing like Donovan's and left her with nothing except revulsion. She spat in an effort to remove the sour taste of him.

"Being with that duke has addled your mind. You got lofty ideas about your place in this world," he ground out. "I want what's mine, and I'll forgive you for whoring yourself out to that nob when you become my wife."

"Over my dead body." Marrying one such as Joe meant a prison sentence that had no end. He wouldn't appreciate her and what she could bring to the world regardless of her blindness. No, a man of Joe's ilk only wished for a wife to serve him. With strength born of desperation, she yanked away from him. "Never will I consent to that." She'd taken a few steps from him when he snaked a thick arm around her waist and tossed her to the grass. Alice landed hard on her back, the wind temporarily knocked from her lungs.

He followed her down, covering her body with his, his forearm pressed across her throat and restricting proper breathing. "You'll change your mind once you feel my prick. I'll wager it's bigger than that London duke's."

"Please..." She gasped for breath, and when he rucked up her skirts and the autumn chilly air kissed her legs, icy panic slid down her spine. "Don't... do... this." No amount of clawing at his arm removed it.

"You won't say that soon." He fumbled with the buttons at the front of his trousers. "Since you like a tumble, I'll get you with child and you'll have no choice but to marry me."

"No." Tears squeezed from her eyes and slid down her cheeks. Alice continued to pluck at his arm. She beat her fists against his shoulder and the side of his head to no avail. He didn't loosen his grip, and when Joe jammed a knee between her thighs, forcing them apart, she screamed as best she could, but without enough air to fill her lungs, it was a pitiful sound.

Why is this happening? Why do people assume I'm a throwaway, only valued for what I can give them?

Or worse, what they feel they could take.

She kicked her feet, tried to buck him off. He was too heavy. His labored breathing rasped in her ear, his weight sank into her form, further cutting off her air. She rammed a heel into the back of his leg to no avail. "Help me!" But the normal sounds of the area snatched at the plea she'd forced from her constricted throat.

Then, a blur of brown plowed into both her and Joe. A low, menacing, feral growl broke through the silence. *A wolf!* Oh, the afternoon rapidly turned worse. As she uttered another feeble scream, the large animal pulled her attacker off. Joe turned his wrath to the animal.

Alice quickly flipped to her stomach. She struggled to all fours and dragged in a few deep lungsful of breath. All the while, the blacksmith fought with the beast. They rolled about the grass in a tangle, blurry heap. Curses and yelling came from him while the wolf uttered yelps and growls guttural enough to send gooseflesh sailing over her skin. Though she stared in the direction that the sounds of a horrible fight came from, all she saw was two huge blobs locked together in combat.

It was a chilling scenario.

That wolf would kill Joe if she didn't do something. The man didn't deserve death, but she hoped this incident would scare him enough that he'd leave her alone. He'd probably attempt to molest her, yet not out in the open. Still, she heaved to her feet and stood on unsteady legs, staggering toward the writhing mass.

"Stop!" She threw out both of her hands, unsure of what to do next but needing to break the terrible fight. "Joe, stop. The animal will kill you, don't you see?" Terror cramped her stomach, and she took another step forward. Perhaps she'd address the wolf, as insane as it sounded. Joe was too stupid to listen to reason. "Don't eat him. He's too foul for even you."

The brown blob of the wolf pressed its front paws to the chest of Joe's darker brown blob as the fighting slowed. The blacksmith wheezed for air, for no doubt the wolf was quite heavy.

"Get off!" Joe threw a punch that connected with the beast's head.

Devil Take the Duke (Lords of the Night #1)

"Please," Alice whispered, crooned to the wolf. "He isn't worth the fight or the kill. Be better."

With a whine, the wolf sprang away from Joe's blob.

"You're mad." Joe grunted as he regained his feet. He came close to Alice despite a warning growl from the wolf. He shook his fist in her face. The sharp, pungent scent of sweat wafted to her nose. "Talking to wolves, commanding them, lying with a duke who brings the beasts to Shalford. This isn't over." He shoved past her, crashing his shoulder into her body so that she stumbled back a few steps. "I'll have my revenge, and you. See if I don't."

"Take this as a lesson. Leave me in peace." Alice's heartbeat pounded so hard she feared the whole village must hear her fear. As Joe ran off, she turned her face to the brown blob of the wolf. The animal hadn't moved. Fascination fell over her. To be in the presence of such a fearsome beast. What must he look like? Yet at the same time, terror twisted her spine and chilled her blood. Would it spring at her? Kill her instead? The brown blob who'd crashed into her the morning she'd met the duke took hold in her mind's eye. This animal reminded her of that time. Was it the same beast? When the animal whined yet again, she said, "How did you come to be here?"

Silly Alice, as if an animal will answer. She took a few more steps toward the beast. He panted hard, and she extended a hand, compelled to touch him. *I need to feel him.*

With a yelp, the wolf bounded away so quickly she couldn't catch his direction.

Alone once again, Alice wrapped her arms about herself as shock poured over her. It was all too much, and on the heels of her argument with Fanny. Her chin trembled. Tears spilled onto her cheeks. Why did such things happen to her, when all she wanted was acceptance, perhaps even love, in a world gone hard? Her chest ached with the need to cry. Her trust had been abused and her faith in humanity shaken. Consistently, the only person who brought her a modicum of peace was the duke. Where was he when she needed his strong arms around her?

"Alice!"

She jerked her head around at the sound of her voice upon the duke's lips. "Donovan?" How was it possible? She'd barely wished for him and now here he was. The crunch of grass beneath his boots reached her. "I saw what happened. Couldn't reach you in time." Concern threaded through his voice. Then he cupped her face, smoothed his palms along her shoulders, her arms until he clutched her hands with his. His breathing sounded labored as if he'd run from a long distance, and his scent was different, wild and raw once more, as it had been the first time she'd met him. "Are you all right?"

Tears fell to her cheeks in earnest as relief flooded her. Everything was wonderful now that he arrived. "I am fine, but oh so glad to see you." Without further thought, she threw herself into his waiting arms and clung to him as if he'd vanish with her next breath.

CHAPTER NINE

Donovan held Alice close as his mind spun with the implications of the scene he'd come upon. The blacksmith had proved a greater problem than he'd anticipated, even more so now that he spouted nonsensical theories linking him to a wolf. She trembled in his arms, clung tight to his neck while sobbing against his shoulder, and brought his thoughts skittering into a different direction.

He'd driven his carriage to Shalford, accompanied by his sister, for he wished to take dinner with Alice, and he'd come the long way, preferring the path through the woods instead of the main road. He'd cleared the trees just as the blacksmith—the same man who'd taunted her and exchanged words with him days before—had thrown her to the ground and pounced. Donovan hadn't thought, hadn't let cool logic guide his actions, for he'd shed his clothing, ignored the warning from his sister and called forth the shift.

The second he had spied another man touching what he considered his, he'd lost his mind. His wolf had been only too glad to comply, for he'd raced from the trees and across the grass toward the river and Alice. He had attacked, sank his teeth into the man's leg and pulled until the beefy offender had removed himself from Alice.

If she hadn't interfered, hadn't implored him to leave off, the blacksmith would have been dead, torn limb from limb by the wolf's powerful jaws. It had been like the battlefields all over again. Though his beast had protested the urge to stay, it had listened, and Donovan had stood with Alice, her hand outstretched, so close to revealing the truth. Oh, how he'd desperately wished for the touch of her hand while he'd been in wolf form, to feel her fingers in his fur and her heat, if only to show her there was nothing to fear from him, but he'd bolted into the trees, terrified that she'd reject him prematurely.

Now, the soft sounds of her sobbing brought him back to the moment and he held her closer still. His heart pounded as if it wished to break free from his chest. In the aftermath of such a traumatic event, he remained stunned that he'd curbed the wolf's desire to kill with merely a word, a heartfelt plea from this woman. Things were changing and he had no idea how to stop the slide. "Alice?" Donovan pulled slightly away, put a finger beneath her chin and tilted it up so their gazes connected. At such close quarters, she would see the very real concern in his face. *I hope that's all she sees.* "Are you hurt, injured? Did that man," he forced a swallow into his dry throat, "touch you, molest you in any way?" For if he did, the blacksmith's time on this Earth was limited.

"No. He tried, but I fought." Silvery tracks of tears marred her cheeks as she stared at him. Her

Devil Take the Duke (Lords of the Night #1)

impossibly long eyelashes spiked with moisture and gave her a dewy-eyed innocence he couldn't ignore. "I'm mostly shaken." The delicate tendons of her neck worked with a swallow. "First Fanny's horrible words, then Joe's attack, and now knowing beyond doubt there's a wolf in Shalford, so close I almost touched it." Awe resonated in her voice, and that both pleased and frightened him.

"Shh." He gathered her close once more, holding her head to his shoulder, and rocked her in his arms. "It's all right now. It's over." The urge to protect her and keep her always safe grew strong, nearly overwhelming with its need. He continued to murmur soothing words while stroking his hands up and down her back. "You'll never know worry when I am near." That was God's honest truth, for he would stand guard over her for as long as it took until she fell for him and the curse broke.

If he hadn't come when he did...

Inside his head, his wolf rolled his eyes. *You would have lost her and would need to start over with a seduction on someone else.*

Yes. No. Anxiety clawed at his belly. Confusion twirled through his mind. *It's more than wanting the curse broken. Alice's life was in danger and I—*

Canine laughter barked into his mind. *Careful, Donovan. You might find you're beginning to care for her, and then what will happen to your plans?*

He didn't wish to contemplate the ramifications of such a thing. Not now, not when being free from the curse was so close.

"Donovan?" Alice lifted her head and sought out his gaze. Stark desire and something softer he didn't dare hope to identify clouded the depths of her gray eyes.

"Yes?" He could barely force out the word from his tight throat.

"Thank you for coming at the exact moment I needed you. You truly are the hero I've longed for." The softly uttered words skittered through his consciousness and bounced against the wall he'd built around his heart. Thread-fine cracks appeared in that barrier.

I'm the farthest thing from a hero. When she waited for a reply, he stroked his fingertips along the side of her face. Her sigh went straight to his soul. "Perhaps you and I share a connection that transcends time." *Gah! What gammon that is*, and he, who was quite proficient at lying to women, hated the words he'd spoken.

"I'm glad you feel it too." And her lips curved with a brilliant smile that had him cursing his own name.

"Aw, damnation," he whispered seconds before he covered her lips with his. He kissed her for his own peace of mind, to remind himself that he had no business mucking about in soft feelings and the messiness of emotions, for he'd allowed this woman into his life for one reason and one reason only: breaking the curse.

In no way did he wish for her to mean anything more to him. That wasn't the plan, and he'd do well to remember it. A man with attachments made himself a target for others who wished him ill, and love was a finicky emotion at best—easy to fall in and easier still to fall out.

Yet when Alice kissed him back with an eagerness that had his length hardening, his thoughts scattered. Perhaps there were two reasons he'd allowed her into his life, and one of them demanded he bed her now in order to stake his claim and mark her as his, make her believe he cared for her enough to grasp that elusive happily ever after.

And break the damn curse. There'd be plenty of time after he was fully human to hate himself for what he'd done without the ever-present consciousness of his wolf in his head.

"Ah, Alice, what am I to do with you?" Donovan moved over her mouth with enough insistent pressure she could have no doubt as to his intent. He nibbled the corners and when he drew the tip of his tongue along the seam of her lips, asking, suggesting, Alice gasped. He easily slipped that organ inside to fence with hers.

Her eyes popped wide open from the new level of intimacy. Then with a sweet sigh, she slowly closed them, held him tighter about his neck and proceeded to mimic his every movement. Silk slid along satin, warmth tangled with heat, and soon enough passion befuddled his brain, his thinking, his body.

I want this woman.

Take her. She's ours. She belongs to us, his wolf agreed with gaping jaws that resembled the most primal of grins.

Breaking the kiss to sweep Alice into his arms, he chuckled at her mewl of protest. "Trust me, this is only a brief delay," he murmured, and then he proceeded to carry her into the wooded area, being sure to avoid the section where he'd parked his carriage. It wouldn't do to have his sister bear witness to this moment.

Once in a spot sufficiently hidden from all, Donovan set her on her feet, nestled her between a wide tree trunk and his chest, and renewed his claim to her petal-soft lips. "Please tell me you want the same thing I do," he whispered against her mouth as he ran his palms up her sides to cup her breasts through the lightweight wool of her dress. His engorged length pressed against the front of his breeches, aching to penetrate her heat.

"I've never felt the things I do right now." Alice moaned, but she opened her eyes and looked at him with those gray depths drugged with passion, her kiss-swollen lips slightly parted and her face flushed pink, and she was the most beautiful woman he'd ever seen. With a tiny start, she planted her palms on his chest and held him away from her. "But doing this now, being here with you isn't proper. It's not right." Regret clouded her eyes, and she caressed her fingers down one side of his neck that added further fire to the infernos blazing inside him. "As much as I care for you, Donovan, I refuse to be yet another conquest."

The words were the equivalent of ice water thrown in his face. "You won't be."

"Hush, Your Grace." Alice gently rested her fingertips against his lips. Her sweet breath skated over his jaw and cheek, for she remained close to him. Though she smiled, her eyes reflected sadness. "I will. Once I give you what you want—what we both want—you'll leave me and Shalford. I'll never see you again." Her voice wavered on the last word.

Hot embarrassment crept up the back of his neck. "No."

His wolf chose that moment to argue with him, of course. *Ah, but wasn't that your first plan, human? To bed her and leave her wanting?*

It was, but then things matured, and I need her to break the curse. Which, when volleyed about with the beast in his head, didn't sound any better than the other.

"Oh, my gallant duke, you may be many things, but you are not a very good liar," Alice rejoined, and her dulcet tones brought him out of his thoughts.

And only served to plunge him back down the cliff of self-loathing, for he was first and foremost a liar, a rake of darkness, and his every action with her had been borne from that vein. Yet time ran short, and if he were to break the curse—perhaps with the next full moon—he had no choice.

"Alice, I—"

"Shh, it's quite all right." Her smile faded, and he died a thousand deaths that he put such grief into her expression. "What you and I have already shared... I never imagined I'd ever drive a man to passion." Her self-deprecating laugh shredded him.

"I'm thankful for what you made me feel, but if we share intimacy, you won't value it the same as I will, and for that reason, I must refuse."

Do something, human! She is going to walk out of our lives. Inside his head, his wolf paced in high anxiety.

The wolf wanted Alice for a much different reason than Donovan needed her for, but the result would be the same if she demanded that he leave her in peace. In light of what had happened between her and the blacksmith, the last thing he wanted to do was remove from Shalford without securing her protection.

She belongs with me no matter what.

With the fear that she'd go away without helping to lift the curse coursing down his spine, Donovan dropped to his knees before her. He caught one of her hands in his. "There is only one solution to our mutual problem."

Her hand shook, and he attempted to quell the tremors by holding her fingers between both of his hands. "I'm listening."

His pulse pounded loud in his ears, thundered through his temples. The last time he'd uttered the words sitting on the tip of his tongue, his whole world had gone wrong. He cleared his throat and silently berated himself for apparently losing his mind over this one woman. "Marry me."

"I beg your pardon?" Her tinkling laughter rang through the noisy woodland sounds and blended so well she could have been a bird. She cupped his cheek with her free hand, and he fought the urge to nuzzle into her touch. "We are not in love, Your Grace. At least, you are not in love with me."

Why would she not make use of his given name any longer? He wanted to hear that word on her lips. "Such an emotion is not required to wed." When she frowned, he rushed on, determined to try again and win her, at least physically. "Despite that, I feel we will suit. You are brave, strong, intelligent, beautiful—everything a duchess should be."

She snorted. "Except possessed of sight."

"That matters not to me, my sweet country flower." It was one of the only truths he'd said to her thus far. "Your integrity and bravery will more than make up for your eyes." Another truth, and he couldn't wait to see her installed as his duchess, clad in rich fabrics and glittering jewels, playing as his hostess. "I want to look after you, Alice, to protect you and keep you from harm, remove you from this village and the begrudging charity you've been shown, give you everything good in life that you should have had all along." That wasn't a lie either.

What the hell is wrong with me?

"Oh, Donovan." Tears welled in her eyes. They rolled down her cheeks with her next blink and one splashed upon his upturned face. She wiped it away with the sweep of her thumb. "I don't know what to say." He'd be a nodcock not to catch the stars of infatuation in her eyes or the twinkle of the silver flecks in her irises that only happened when she was gripped with high emotion.

That was all to the good, so he pressed his suit as he squeezed her fingers. "Be my duchess. I promise you will want for nothing."

"Except your love." She blew out a breath that ruffled the baby-fine curls on her forehead. "I'm not certain I can—"

"Who knows?" he interrupted her. "We have only just met. Love might indeed come once we understand each other better." He forced out the lie from between stiff lips, knowing all along such a thing wouldn't happen. A duke—or even a wolf—was dead if he became vulnerable as a man would once love came to call.

Such a thing happened to his father, and his mother died because of it.

"What is there to understand? You and I are from different worlds, and I'm not certain those were ever meant to mesh." Another tear fell. "No matter how much I might care for you already," she said in a soft whisper he had to strain to hear.

Had it occurred so easily he hadn't been aware she'd fallen? His heart gave a mighty thud, perhaps it even stopped but then started again with a lurch. Inside his head, his wolf whined, and Donovan persisted. "Marry me, Alice. Make me the happiest of men."

With a chance of breaking the curse.

And her heart, his wolf was quick to remind him. Now his beast whined for a whole different reason, and Donovan blocked the sound from his mind.

"I'm confident we can work through any obstacles facing us," he added on in a whisper. "Together."

Finally, she nodded. Her hand shook in his. "Yes." A laugh full of surprise escaped her. "Oh, yes. I can hardly believe this is happening. I'd dreamed of a husband for so long…" The proverbial knife twisted deep in his gut as Alice dropped to her knees in front of him, leaning close to peer into his face. "I promise to be everything you'll ever need." She clutched at his hand as if it were a lifeline. "Yes, I'll marry you."

Donovan froze in shock. He hated himself for the way he manipulated her, ignored his wolf's urging to reveal all before it was too late. He couldn't do it, not now when his connection with Alice was so tenuous. Pushing aside his thoughts, he removed the signet ring from his pinky finger and slid it onto the fourth finger of her left hand. It was slightly large and spun a bit as she held it up. He forced down a swallow. Seeing his ring on her slim digit sent clouds of confusion swirling through his brain. "I will replace this trinket with a more appropriate ring once the ceremony is complete."

"It matters not, for I'll have the man at that point." She traced his face with the fingers of both hands, searching for what in his expression he couldn't say, but his heart pounded faster all the same. He forced himself to smile and appear happy with his proposal. "I'll strive to please you, my lord."

The heat she imparted as she continued to touch his face and the absolute trust reflected in her eyes plowed into him like a blow. He swallowed, ignored the insistent throbbing of his member and the clenching of his stomach at his deception. "Please yourself," he forced out in a ragged whisper. "You've already made me proud." Another truth. The way she stood up to him in the church, coupled with how she'd fought against the blacksmith's attack kept knocking him on his arse.

I'm not worthy of her for so many reasons.

"You are the most romantic man I've ever known." She leaned into him and pressed her lips to his.

Donovan was lost as the heady sensations of lust and desire rose up to meet him. He wrapped her into his arms, plied her with deep, drugging kisses designed to cement her agreement and keep her bundled into feelings so she wouldn't suspect his betrayal, that even now threatened to poison him. He had everything he'd set out to win—the promise of enjoying her body as well as securing her love.

So why didn't the victory feel as sweet as he'd hoped?

When their breathing grew labored and need demanded he lay her down on the mossy forest floor, he put space between them. Her murmured protest nearly undid him, so he scrambled to his feet and pulled her up with him.

"I'll petition for a special license as soon as I return to London." *Good heavens, I'm truly about to wed this creature.*

Devil Take the Duke (Lords of the Night #1)

Alice linked her arm with his. Pleasure flushed her cheeks and sparkled in her eyes. "May we marry here in Shalford?"

The request brought him up short. "We can, but why?"

A smile curved her kiss-reddened lips. "It is petty, I know, but I want to shut up all those tabbies with this victory of mine. Let them talk from the truth this time."

"Ah, my girl, you are a marvel." He gave into a genuine grin while his wolf howled with amusement into his mind. "You may have anything you wish. I live to serve."

And he'd give her everything she could ever desire if she would stay long enough to break the damned curse.

They walked back to the village proper hand in hand. He let her chatter on about the upcoming nuptials while the lump of self-loathing in his belly grew. At her door, he saw her into her room with the caveat that she remain vigilant.

"I promise to return as soon as that license is procured. Do what you need to prepare." And because she looked so fetching in high color and with possibilities sparkling in her eyes, he drew her close, kissing her on the forehead. "Think of me until I return."

Donovan couldn't leave the village fast enough, but the enormity of what had transpired didn't lessen by the time he gained his carriage. *What the deuce have I done?*

His wolf laughed and laughed, kept howling with amusement. *You have come to care for the woman.*

I have not. I'm doing her a kindness. Rescued her, really. I'm merely nervous of how she'll be received as my wife in that viper's nest of society.

The beast snorted. *You will break her heart.*

His own heart suffered a twinge. *It's inevitable, but there's nothing I can do about that.* In a bad humor, he swung himself up into his curricle beside his sister.

"What kept you so long? I was ready to come searching for you." She frowned. "Where is Alice? I thought you wished to take her to dinner?"

Dear God, he hadn't the patience to argue with his sibling just now. "She's safely in her room after I was obliged to rescue her from an attacker." He took up his reins and slapped them against the horse's back with more firmness than he'd intended.

"What else has happened? You are keeping something from me. I can see it in your face. You're... shocked."

Of course his sister was too observant for her own good. He blew out a breath in frustration. "I've apparently lost my mind and asked Alice to marry me."

Elizabeth laughed and laughed, much like his wolf had done. She kept on and the sound crashed around him, and she doubled over on the bench next to him so great was her mirth. When she finally came up for air, she turned to him and grinned with false sincerity, while wiping tears from her eyes. "You are truly in the drink now, brother, and I, for one, cannot wait to see the results of this Drury Lane production." She snickered. "I hope she makes your life hell for this little stunt."

"My life is already hell most times." He kept his gaze straight ahead. "Unless you offer support, do shut up."

May God, and all of them, forgive me.

CHAPTER TEN

September 26, 1815
Shalford, Surrey

For the first time in Miss Alice Morrowe's life, she did something completely in her own interest—she dressed for her wedding ceremony.

The duke had sent word yesterday he'd been able to procure the special license he promised—the day after his surprising proposal came. He also said in the missive that he would arrive in Shalford the next day to marry her.

She dressed by herself in the tiny room she'd no longer need to occupy. Where she'd assumed Fanny would be all too happy to assist, her friend—as well as the women she'd worked with at the milliner's shop—refused to bear witness to her ceremony. Their defection wounded her, but she tucked the hurt away in light of joy this day brought her.

In less than an hour, she would leave Shalford as the Duchess of Manchester, and that was, no doubt, the reason the women in the village wouldn't attend the nuptial ceremony. Of course, by the time she'd returned home late afternoon with the duke's ring on her finger and his promise in her heart, news of her rejection of the blacksmith had circulated. Confronted with it yesterday when she went to the hat shop to give notice that she'd no longer work there, Fanny uttered sharp words to her, to the effect that Joe would have been a perfectly fine husband and she shouldn't think more of herself by landing a duke.

Alice had cried herself to sleep that night after spending countless hours sewing to alter the best dress she owned. There was no shoulder to cry on, no sympathetic listener to pour out her worries, but soon she'd have Donovan, and she'd walk through life at his side. Shalford would be only a memory. She'd wanted to wear the dress she had at Fanny's wedding, for she thought the gown looked better, but after her friend's defection, she left the gown folded in the trunk at the foot of her bed. It held bad memories, and she wanted to fill this day—her day—with fresh ones, happy ones.

Brighter days were ahead.

Still, as she donned the reworked gown of light pink trimmed with lace and seed pearls, Alice frowned. Nerves beset her, tightening her stomach and chest. If nearly everyone in the village was against the union, should she go through with it? On the other hand, the residents of Shalford had never had her best interests at heart. They considered her a charity case at best, destined only for what they handed her.

A knock sounded at her door and her heartbeat accelerated. *It's too early for him!* What if he'd sent word backing out of the engagement? When she opened the panel, a feminine hand on her arm calmed the worst of her fears.

"It's Elizabeth." The duke's sister swept inside. Once the panel closed, she gave Alice a brief hug. "Do not worry. Donovan came with me. He's walking to the church as we speak. I'm to make certain your luggage is loaded into the carriage as well as help you dress."

"I'm afraid I don't have many possessions." Alice pointed to a worn valise on the foot of the bed. "A couple of day dresses, two pairs of shoes, a few hair ribbons, my night dress, a set of undergarments, and two bonnets." She glanced at the yellow-hued blob of her soon to be sister-in-law. Her chin quivered as it became more obvious than ever how different she was in station from the duke. "Not even a trousseau or dowry."

What must he think of me?

"Pish posh. He is not marrying you for material things, I can tell you that for a fact." Elizabeth closed the distance and folded Alice in a hug. "No tears. Not today, for you don't wish to meet your bridegroom with puffy eyes and a splotchy face."

Alice drew from the other woman's strength. "Thank you." She pulled back. "I still need to do my hair and put the flowers into it." She pointed to a few sprays of wildflowers that grew close to the riverbank that were her favorites. The yellow and white blooms would look pretty against her hair.

Not that anyone would see them except Donovan and Elizabeth and the clergyman.

Then a floral fragrance met her nose. "You've brought flowers, too." Creamy pink and white blobs met Alice's vision.

"Yes." The smile in Elizabeth's voice was unmistakable. She pushed a small bouquet into Alice's hands. "Donovan said they were for his 'sweet country flower' or something to that affect, and that he looks forward to you becoming his 'redeeming city blossom'." She chuckled. "Forgive him. Such things are not his strong suit."

"Oh." Heat infused her cheeks as she brought the posy to her nose and inhaled the sharp unmistakable aroma of roses. Two of each with a few fronds of ferns to offset their glory. The stems and thorns were wrapped with white satin ribbon and tied with a simple bow. "How pretty." Both the gift and the words.

And they matched her gown. How had he known?

"Come," Elizabeth said with a guiding hand to Alice's shoulder. "Sit on your bed and let me do your hair. The ceremony will be soon."

In next to no time, Elizabeth braided Alice's hair and pinned it into a coronet about the back of her head. When she reached for the sprays of wildflowers, Alice belayed her and instead asked that she thread the roses Donovan had sent into her hair instead. Elizabeth agreed, and the heady scent of the flowers wafted around her as the other woman fitted the cut stems into the lower curve of the coronet.

Then she thrust a pair of lace gloves into Alice's hands. "Put these on. After I give the coachman your bag, I'll escort you to the church."

"Thank you." As she pulled on the accessories, she said, "I'm looking forward to having a sister." It would be nice with another woman to talk to and help her when in London. "I... I won't feel so much alone in a world so vastly different from Shalford." What if she faltered or wasn't as elegant or regal as Donovan had hoped?

"I quite agree," Elizabeth said with an obvious smile in her voice. "Between the two of us, Donovan will have to stay alert and remain ready for anything." She laughed and Alice smiled at the happy sound. There was such hope on the horizon. "We shall have a merry time of it, I think, before my bacon-brained brother mucks it all up."

Alice frowned. "Why would he do that?" What did Elizabeth know that she didn't tell?

"Oh, forgive me. I'm speaking out of turn. Sibling rivalry and all that." She linked their arms. "We need to go. He is waiting." As she swung open the door to Alice's room, she directed the coachman where to find Alice's bag, and then she moved into the road.

A thrill twisted down Alice's spine. *He is waiting... for me.* Oh, she was fortunate indeed that soon she'd marry a duke.

In the narthex of the small church, Alice sucked in a quick breath when the black blob that was Donovan—her soon-to-be husband—filled her vision. "Is he all that is handsome?" she whispered to Elizabeth.

"Oh, quite." The other woman gave her a nudge. "See for yourself. No one will begrudge you the trespass. I'll let you know when the minister beckons." The tap of her heels indicated she moved away to give them a modicum of privacy.

"I knew you would be lovely on this day," Donovan whispered as he took her hand and tugged her close. "And you've worn the flowers I sent. All the more special." He put his lips to the shell of her ear. "I could eat you up, my dear." His tone quickened her pulse.

Tingles of anticipation played her spine and circled through her lower belly. Surely it was ridiculous to feel such things at her advanced age, but she enjoyed it just the same. "Thank you for the compliment. You give so many, I don't know what to do with such attention." Alice kept her voice to a whisper as well as she traced her gloved fingertips over his face. She swept her touch along his hair. He'd attempted to tame his tresses, but it still curled about his temples and collar. "I'm glad you didn't cut your hair. I… I like it with a touch of wild about you."

"Ah, Alice you have no idea."

Confusion bubbled through her mind. What did that mean? "Tell me how you've dressed yourself."

"Since the occasion is so grand, I've chosen to wear the requisite dark clothing one would wear for an evening event, complete with a tailcoat. White cravat tied in an intricate design, emerald stick pin." He cupped her cheek, and the smooth kid of his glove molded to her skin. "Burroughs insisted that my waistcoat reflect the somberness of the occasion though, but I insisted on the gray with silver and black embroidery, for it reminds me of your eyes."

Tears blurred her already fuzzy vision. "How sweet." It was providential she'd enticed the duke enough that he wished to marry her. She smiled. *Mayhap everything will work out splendidly between us.*

A gentle tap on her shoulder brought her out of the moment, and in a quiet voice Elizabeth said, "It is eleven o'clock. It's time."

Nerves fluttered in Alice's stomach that calmed somewhat when Donovan took her hand and threaded it through his crooked elbow. He would walk her down the aisle in lieu of her having no one else in her life.

Then he set them into motion, and they entered the church where she'd attended every Sunday since arriving in Shalford. Unlike Fanny's wedding ceremony, only a handful of people waited to see Alice married, and they were most likely there to shred what was left of her reputation. But she didn't care. Donovan was beside her, and she was so happy she nearly floated up to the minister's white-colored blob at the end of the aisle.

The minister didn't waste any time, and as Elizabeth sat in the front pew nearby, greeting a man she apparently knew closely, a man who smelled like cedarwood and cinnamon, he said,

"Dearly beloved, we are gathered together here in the sight of God, and in the face of this congregation, to join together this Man and this Woman in holy Matrimony; which is an honorable estate, instituted of God in the time of man's innocency, signifying unto us the mystical union that is betwixt Christ and his Church…"

Alice clung to Donovan's arm, wrapped up in his scent, his strength, her nerves, for her life would change the moment she stepped outside the church. It wasn't until he discreetly and softly cleared his throat that she ceased her wool-gathering and attended to what the minister said as he addressed the duke.

"Wilt thou have this Woman to thy wedded Wife, to live together after God's ordinance in the holy estate of Matrimony? Wilt thou love her, comfort her, honor, and keep her in sickness and in health; and, forsaking all others, keep thee only unto her, so long as ye both shall live?"

Alice trembled, her breath held in anticipation. Did he truly understand the severity of those words?

In a clear voice, Donovan answered, "I will."

Her head spun and the jitters increased, as the minister addressed her.

"Wilt thou have this Man to thy wedded Husband, to live together after God's ordinance in the holy estate of Matrimony? Wilt thou obey him, and serve him, love, honor, and keep him in sickness and in health; and, forsaking all others, keep thee only unto him, so long as ye both shall live?"

She squeezed her hand upon Donovan's arm. "I will." Her answer came out breathless and in a whisper, for tears crowded in her throat.

The duke was instructed to take her right hand in his right hand, and hers shook so badly that he gently squeezed her fingers. He went so far as to put his lips to her ear and whisper, "It will be all right, love. I promise this is not a prison sentence."

Alice smiled lest he think she looked upon the ceremony with dread. This was the grandest thing she'd ever done in her life and she did so hope that she would make him proud that he wedded her. "I'm just so happy," she whispered back.

Whereupon the minister cleared his throat and continued. "Your Grace, repeat after me…" He intoned words that Alice scarcely heard until Donovan said them to her.

"I, Donovan James Arthur Sinclair, 8th duke of Manchester, take thee Alice Minerva Morrowe to my wedded Wife, to have and to hold from this day forward, for better for worse, for richer for poorer, in sickness and in health, to love and to cherish, 'till death us do part, according to God's holy ordinance; and thereto I plight thee my troth."

They were directed to release hands, and Alice was told to then hold Donovan's right hand with her right hand. "Ahem." The minister addressed her. "Miss Morrowe, repeat after me." He gave her the words, and she prayed she would say them all in the proper order.

"I, Alice Minerva Morrowe, take thee Donovan James Arthur Sinclair, 8th duke of Manchester to my wedded Husband." She paused to swallow and squeeze his hand. "To have and to hold from this day forward, for better for worse, for richer for poorer, in sickness and in health, to love, cherish, and to obey, 'till death us do part, according to God's holy ordinance." She lowered her voice to a whisper. "And thereto I give thee my troth." How wonderful and slightly terrifying such a thing was.

Please let me show him—and myself—this isn't a mistake.

They were instructed to again release their hands. Donovan proffered a ring to the minister, who then laid it upon his open Common Book of Prayer along with what she assumed was a form of payment to the minister and his clerk. She'd remember to ask Donovan about it later. Then the minister returned the ring to the duke, who slipped it onto the fourth finger of her left hand, replacing the signet ring. While he did, the minister directed him to repeat another set of words.

"With this Ring I thee wed, with my Body I thee worship, and with all my worldly Goods I thee endow. In the Name of the Father, and of the Son, and of the Holy Ghost. Amen."

Oh, dear Lord, we are truly wed. Alice kneeled when Donovan did, still clutching his hand while the minister invited all in attendance to pray.

As the words of a prayer droned on, Alice closed her eyes and set up a simpler prayer of her own, conveying gratitude and thankfulness and asking for strength to survive what would surely be a difficult adjustment to a brand-new life.

When she and Donovan stood, the minister intoned, "I now pronounce thee husband and wife."

And then it was over. No longer was she plain and overlooked Alice Morrowe, milliner's assistant. She was now the Duchess of Manchester. Unable to help it, she fingered the ring he'd slipped upon her finger. From the corner of her eye, she caught the red flash of a ruby. Rainbows refracted through other stones she assumed were diamonds but couldn't confirm at the moment. The piece must cost a fortune, but then, he was a duke. A sick feeling rose in her throat. What if she lost the bauble? Or what if— The pressure of his hand on hers once more sent the worries flying out of her head.

She and her husband were ushered to a long table where they both signed the registry, which made the union official. Afterward, Elizabeth joined them, taking Alice's arm and leading her down the aisle while Donovan stopped to talk with the man Elizabeth had sat beside.

As she passed the handful of witnesses, whispers drifted to her ears.

"…thinks she's better'n us now…"

"…wed in haste, repent in leisure. You watch, he'll throw her over for a mistress soon…"

"…why'd he choose her when there are others more suited…"

"…London won't take to a blind duchess. The gossips will flay her alive…"

"…she's not good enough for the likes of him…"

With every word, Alice died a little more inside. Instead of the joyous occasion, the day brought instead a murky future and the want to cry silly tears for fear she'd made a mistake. Why had Donovan chosen to marry her when she was vastly unsuited for the position of not only his duchess but his wife?

Elizabeth nudged her gently in the ribs with her elbow. "Don't listen to those great cows. Jealousy abounds, and if you cannot show a stiff upper lip to country folk, the tabbies in London will indeed eat you alive." She patted Alice's hand to soften the frank blow. "I know you're made of sterner stuff than all of that. Donovan wouldn't have picked you otherwise. Never let them see their words wound. It's the first rule of being a duchess."

"I shall try my best," Alice whispered, and then the warm autumn sunshine was upon her face and fresh air filled her lungs as she took big, gulping breaths to stave off tears.

Donovan caught them up. He replaced Elizabeth at her side and slipped an arm about her waist. "Shall we away to London? My sister tells me a small wedding luncheon will be waiting for some of my close friends, since I rather doubt you want to tarry here where all of Shalford is glaring, and the blacksmith looks ready to plant me a facer."

Merciful heavens, Joe had shown up? She took a shuddering breath as nerves once more beset her. "That sounds splendid." Ready to put her days in Shalford past her, she pasted a smile onto her face, hoping she seemed more confident than she felt.

"Excellent." Then he placed his hands at her waist and lifted her into a carriage, this one closed. As he settled into the squabbed bench beside her and Elizabeth joined them, perching on the bench opposite, the duke took Alice's left hand and held it between both of his. "Are you glad, wife?"

Tremors of delight fell down her spine at the use of that word. "I am, actually. It's been quite the morning... husband." Then she giggled. Elizabeth snickered and even Donovan chuckled.

The carriage door closed. The conveyance dipped as the driver took his place, and seconds later the vehicle lurched into motion.

They were London-bound and moving toward a new life.

"Now that the official business of the wedding has been accomplished, there are a few things I'll need to discuss with Alice, decisions made, until she's well-established," Elizabeth began, and she proceeded to tick the items off on her fingers. "Having clothes commissioned, accessories, and not to mention a ball gown, for you'll be introduced to polite society at a ball a week hence." Her new sister-in-law continued, but Alice tuned out the words as worry crowded into her brain.

Perhaps it wasn't the fairy story she'd dreamed of, this being married, but more of a business arrangement. How... disappointing.

Donovan patted her hand. "There is time enough for all of that, Elizabeth. We should let Alice acclimate herself to the changes first." Then he leaned close, and into her ear he whispered, "You will do smashing, so please don't fret, but before all of that, there is the wedding night, and I intend to make love to you until the dawn."

Heat sprang into her cheeks at the thought of finally experiencing the physical relationship between a man and a woman. Striving for some decorum in front of his sister, Alice pushed at his shoulder. "Behave yourself."

But awareness danced along her nerve endings, and she smiled. She would conquer this new life with the same determination that she had everything else.

With him by her side, it would go more smoothly.

CHAPTER ELEVEN

Everything felt as if it were a dream.

"Welcome to your new home. You are now a resident of St. James Place."

Alice smiled at her husband as he assisted her from the carriage. When he lingered his hands upon her waist well after she'd reached solid ground, heat threaded through her insides. "Thank you. I cannot wait to explore."

Never had she been to London, and she strained to hear as much of it as she could before he led her inside.

The low ebb of conversation buzzed in the background as people strolled the Mayfair streets. Birds chirped as they flitted from tree to tree, but the cheerful sound was somehow different here than in the country—more frantic and intense. The *clip clop* of horse's hooves against the hard-packed dirt of the street rang through her head, closely followed by the scrape of carriage wheels against rocks and other obstacles. The air even smelled differently here in the city. It wasn't as fresh or as clear. And through it all a vitality pulsed and caught her up in its flow.

What would it be like to walk the city and discover its secrets? To take in the sights with her new husband by her side?

Devil Take the Duke (Lords of the Night #1)

"Shall we?" He gripped her upper arm and guided her through a gate that creaked and then they traveled up a walkway. "There are two steps to the door." When she accomplished them without incident, he spoke again. "Griggs, this is my wife and duchess, Alice." Donovan gave her arm a gentle squeeze. "Lady Manchester, this is my—our—butler." Then he guided her hand into the gloved grip of an older gentleman who murmured a few words appropriate to the situation.

"Is she ill, my lord?" the man asked.

From behind her, Elizabeth gasped.

Alice frowned at the butler, and though she couldn't see his features, the doubt in his voice was unmistakable.

"She is blind, Griggs, and I trust you will not mention it again. I expect you to treat her no differently than you do me or Elizabeth. Is this understood?" A hint of a growl resonated in the duke's tone.

"Of course, my lord." The butler released her hand. "Your guests are waiting in the dining room, if you wish to join them?"

"Tell them we'll arrive directly." When Donovan once more took possession of her arm, he whispered, "I apologize."

She waved her free hand. "It is not his fault, and he didn't deserve a set down. There was no way he could have known."

Their heels rang on what were undoubtedly marble-tiled halls. Silence brewed between them, and finally her husband spoke.

"Forgive me. I am all too aware of how those around me might perceive you at first. I... simply wish to protect you." Emotion she couldn't identify graveled his voice. "Defend you."

"If the people you've placed on your staff cannot be trusted, then you have a larger problem than softening how they'll see me." She patted his hand where it rested on her arm. "Introduce me as your wife and leave it at that. I shall take care of the rest the way I've always done, and if your friends cannot support you—me—then you'll have your answer and can change accordingly."

He grunted. From behind, Elizabeth sucked in a breath. Then he chuckled. "Once again, you've put me in my place. I believe you'll find life as a duchess much to your liking if you continue with that spirit."

Pleasure flooded her and she smiled. "Only time will tell."

But it was as good a start as any.

The wedding breakfast was a boisterous affair. Excited chatter and congratulatory conversation filled a dining room that sounded as if it was an overly large area. In the space of an hour, Alice was introduced to so many of Donovan's friends, her head spun. She attempted to commit each of their names and titles to memory, for she couldn't see their faces to help in that effort. Elizabeth trailed after her, whispering pertinent details into her ear as person after person came up to her while Donovan entertained a few others from his end of the long table.

By the time she sat down to eat, her mind reeled from the abrupt shift in her life. Elizabeth went on to make the rounds herself, leaving Alice alone. She didn't mind, and contented herself with listening to the conversations around her. Donovan had a small circle of friends, which she found odd, for he was a duke, and didn't such men have a huge influence?

The sunshine streaming in from the nearby floor-to-ceiling windows caught the stones in her wedding ring, recalling Alice's attention to the bauble. She brought her hand close to her face in order to admire the piece of jewelry, and she gasped. A ruby solitaire winked at her from the middle of a daisy whose five petals were made of teardrop-shaped diamonds, all set in fine gold.

It's magnificent. And it kept with his theme of calling her his sweet country flower. How had he done it if he had it fashioned especially for her in such a short period of time? Or perhaps it was a piece of jewelry that went with his estate. Not that it mattered, for it was perfect. Tears misted her eyes.

"I'm glad for this opportunity to speak with you semi-privately." The speaker touched her fingers, and as he sat beside her, he lifted her hand to his lips, kissing her middle knuckle. "Do you know who I am?"

The faint scents of cedarwood and cinnamon drifted to her nostrils. "You are the man who sat next to Lady Elizabeth at the wedding ceremony."

"Yes." He released her hand. "I'm the Earl of Devon, but I'd prefer it if you'd call me Rogue. I'm your husband's closest friend."

"Ah, and you are here to make certain I am genuine, that I am not out to manipulate or use him." Her stomach muscles cramped. "Yes?" She stared at the flesh-colored blob that was his face, not seeing him but hoping her eyes told her story.

His laughter, separate from Donovan's, filled the space with a deep richness that would draw anyone closer to him. "I had to see for myself if you were as different as he said."

"Am I?" She arched an eyebrow, nearly breathless to find out.

"Refreshingly so." He patted her hand. "I'm glad Donovan chose you to take to wife. He needs a strong woman to lead him, help him. It's what's been lacking in his life."

She frowned. "What does he require assistance with?"

"It's not my place to say." He dropped his voice. "No doubt you'll discover that soon. And please, look past anything that may sound unpleasant, for understanding will be key."

Elizabeth joined them before Alice could question what he meant. "Leave the poor woman alone, Rafe. She's only just arrived and doesn't need your intrigue yet." Was that a tiny trace of fear in her voice? But why?

He snorted. "Always so managing." The man rose to his feet with murmured excuses to Alice. "I must take my leave. Being out in the daylight hours is… uncomfortable for me." Again, he took possession of her hand and kissed the back. "A pleasure to meet you, Your Grace."

Once the earl made his escape, the rest of the guests followed within the hour. Eventually, the room stopped echoing with laughter and conversation. Donovan came to her and assisted Alice to her feet.

"Now that the house is ours once more, shall we adjourn upstairs?" Into her ear, he whispered, "Where we can finally give into the desire that has been building between us since the day I pulled you off the public road?"

Heat fired in her cheeks. Out of habit, it was on the tip of her tongue to tell him such things weren't proper, but then she remembered they were married and bedding him was the next step. "I suppose."

"Dear Lord." Elizabeth huffed her annoyance. "Put a little romance in it, brother; otherwise, she will think you crude." She pulled Alice away from Donovan. "Perhaps you should partake in port or brandy while I assist your bride? No doubt she'll wish to relax and refresh before things... happen."

"Rogue was quite correct. You're extremely managing." But he laughed, and the sound sent awareness rippling over Alice's person. "Won't catch a husband that way."

Elizabeth huffed. "There is no man I want in such a fashion."

"Perhaps. We shall see." He came near and stroked his fingers along the side of Alice's face. "I give you into Elizabeth's tender care, but after that, you're mine."

"You're incorrigible." Her cheeks continued to flame. Perhaps she'd burn up before she ever made it to the marriage bed.

"No." Again he whispered into her ear. "I'm hungry."

"Come." Elizabeth took her hand and led her through the room. "You and I are about the same size. I'm going to lend you a few things until we can have seamstresses in and find you a lady's maid who you can work comfortably with."

An hour later, after Alice had been pampered with a bath of rose-scented water in a copper tub and had her hair washed with fine-milled French soap of the same flower, Elizabeth helped dry her hair, and once the tresses had been combed out and caught back with combs glittering with tiny pink jewels, she instructed Alice to don a nightdress of the palest pink silk, bedecked with frothy lace and ribbons. There was even a wrapper to match.

Embarrassment warmed her face as she offered yet another protest. "This is much too fine a garment for me. I'll make do with what I brought." The bodice pulled a bit tight across the bosom since Alice was rather more full than Elizabeth.

"Nonsense. This is your wedding night—er, afternoon as it were—and you should put on something that makes you feel beautiful." Elizabeth plucked at the folds of the nearly sheer fabric and nodded. "Honestly, it looks better on you than me."

"It feels crisp, as if new." Alice smoothed her hands down the front. Never had she worn such luxurious clothing.

"That's because I pulled it from the trunk that contains things I've put away for my own trousseau." She heaved a sigh. "For a wedding I'll probably never have."

"Why? I'd think you'd be snapped up," Alice assured her.

"Oh, there are specific reasons, and some I'm not at liberty to talk about until Donovan tells you…" Another sigh escaped. "Perhaps you and I can speak about this later in the week."

Alice frowned. There was too much intrigue that people around her new husband wouldn't reveal. Why was that? To alleviate Elizabeth's distress, she ignored the questions bubbling about her mind. "Do I look presentable?" Nerves fluttered in her belly. "I don't know what to expect… I always assumed the deed would be done in the dark and the man wouldn't need look at me…" Her cheeks burned. "Now I sound like a stupid country girl, and I'm truly not. My mother died when I was a young woman, and my knowledge is woefully inadequate, I fear, when compared to one so worldly as the duke."

"You poor thing." Elizabeth wrapped an arm about her shoulders and hugged her. "You're wearing a bridal flush, and it'll bewitch him. That is enough, but you must know that people indulge in intercourse at all times and in varying positions, and Donovan is…" She snorted. "Gah! I refuse to discuss my brother's intimate proclivities. It is much too weird."

They both shared a laugh, but Alice's nerves persisted.

"Is this your brother's bedchamber?" There was so much to still learn, when everything thus far had occurred with such alacrity she could scarcely make sense of it all.

"Yes. He has a sitting room attached to one side and a dressing room at the other side of the apartment." Elizabeth cleared her throat. "I would have no idea if he's planned for you to share the space, but if not, there is a matching apartment at the end of the hall. We never use it, for it's always been reserved for a duchess, and throughout the years, the women who've held the title haven't been happy in their marriages, and never wished to spend time with their dukes…"

Ah, more mystery attached to her husband's title. Cold foreboding slithered down her spine. "I'm already facing insurmountable odds."

Elizabeth blew out a breath. "Perhaps, but again, I cannot speak on the subject without Donovan's permission." Heavy silence brewed for several seconds before she spoke again. "Do you love my brother?"

Did she? Alice pleated the skirt of the silky wrapper. "I think I do."

"That is an excellent start."

She offered a smile in the event Elizabeth stared at her. "He's been nothing but noble toward me, and he's, quite frankly, wonderful."

"He's... different," the other woman finally conceded. "But, he's married you, so that is an encouraging sign." She touched Alice's shoulder. "Please be patient with him. He's not what you might fear. He's more than that."

"I'm afraid I don't understand." Why all the talk in riddles and unfinished sentences? What wasn't Elizabeth telling her? And more to the point, why did she suddenly feel as if she was a literal virgin offering ahead of a sacrifice?

"You will, and it's my fondest hope that spirit you've shown will carry you through." She dropped a kiss onto Alice's cheek. "I must go."

"Thank you. For everything."

"It's truly been my pleasure, and if you need anything, my room is the second door on the left from this one."

The soft snick of the panel closing alerted Alice to the fact she was very much alone in a foreign room.

Not wanting to snuggle into the bed, for that would feel odd, Alice wandered about the space. Thick Aubusson carpeting cushioned her bare feet. With her fingers, she explored the trinkets on the bureau top: a wooden handled brush and a comb, a pocket watch, a few coins, a bottle of cologne, a crystal decanter containing a burgundy liquid with a matching wineglass. She moved to a bank of windows where the drapes were still thrown open. What did his room overlook—a garden or the street? Everywhere throughout the room, the unique scent of the duke followed her, and kept the awareness she had of him heightened.

Another click of the door told her someone had entered—Donovan. The unmistakable turn of a lock rang loud in the silence.

"There is a certain amount of pleasure for a man coming into his bedchamber and spying a beautiful woman in such an enticing confection," he said, and his voice rumbled in the space to further ramp her anticipation.

"I told your sister this is the finest clothing I've ever worn." She could barely force the words from her throat tight with emotion.

"Ah, then you should know this is only the beginning of the luxuries afforded to you as my duchess." Then the dark blob that was his form came into her compromised vision. He tugged her into his arms. "I am glad you are here."

Before she could respond, Donovan claimed her lips in a tender kiss that sent heat sailing into her blood. The slightly smoky taste of brandy clung to him. She clutched his shoulders in an effort to remain upright. "You, my lord, are quite potent."

"And you, duchess, are beyond tempting." He stepped away. Clothing rustled into the silence, and tremors moved through her insides. "Finally, I've won you." Two decided thumps echoed, no doubt his shoes hitting the hardwood floor.

"Thanks to your overt charm." Never had she wished to watch a man undress more than she did now, but there was no use wanting something she'd never have. "Are you happy with your choice?" She stepped over the floor, following the sound of his voice.

"I am." Donovan said nothing else, so she couldn't gauge his feelings. Then he caught her about the waist, lifted her up and deposited her onto the high, wide, four-poster bed. She scuttled to the middle of it in a tangled cloud of lace-trimmed silk. "In fact, I couldn't be more pleased about life than I am right now."

Alice squeaked when the mattress depressed, and he dove into place beside her. She reached for him, traced his face with her fingertips and then dared to explore. He was once more bare-chested, and except for a sharp inhalation of breath when she swept her fingers down his torso to his abdomen, he remained still. "Since the first time we met, I've wondered about you, and once I dreamed of being with you in this way." Not even to Fanny did she admit such a thing, and she couldn't tell Elizabeth.

"Oh?" Donovan laid a palm on her belly, splaying his fingers, and the heat of each one burned through the thin silk of her night attire. "Did the dream satisfy your curiosity?" Slowly, oh so slowly, he slid his hand upward, where he manipulated the satin ribbons that kept the wrapper and night dress closed.

"No." Her throat suddenly dry, she forced a quick swallow. "I woke up wanting more, but I feared knowing you in such a way would never happen." Unable to let the moment happen to her, she plunged ahead, determined to act as a willing participant. He was strong and solidly muscled, and when she drew the fingers of one hand down his spine, he blew out a breath. Perhaps he needed her as much as she did him.

"Never fear any longer… about anything." He pulled the filmy fabric apart, baring her breasts. The cooled air in the room tightened her nipples. In a whisper, he added, "I won't hurt you."

"I trust you." Despite the intrigue and the words left unsaid, she had no reason not to. He'd been everything kind and considerate toward her thus far. Alice surged upward, catching his mouth with hers, wrapping her arms about his neck simply for the joy of having him to herself. After all the teasing kisses they'd exchanged over the past two weeks, now it would culminate in this one magical meeting.

The duke didn't answer in words. Instead, he plied her with kisses, each more gentle than the last, and her head swam with sensation. In a thrice he'd encouraged the silky clothing off her body, tossing it away in a rustle of fabric. As she lay naked and exposed for his perusal, he covered her body with his. All of his hard angles pressed into her softer curves, his weight atop her pleasing.

His attention seemed everywhere at the same time. He plied her lips, the side of her neck, her shoulders with fleeting kisses while he roved his hands along her body, leaving not one inch of her unexplored or untouched.

When he closed his lips on one pebbled nipple, her back arched involuntarily and she moaned with surprise. Donovan chuckled. He suckled the tip and then released it with a slight *pop* before he gave the other one the same attention. With each caress, each nip and nibble, her heartbeat accelerated and her blood turned to fire in her veins. She could barely breathe from the wonderful things he did to her body. Returning the favor was beyond her at the moment, for all she could do was writhe beneath him and revel in this new world of heady pleasure.

Just as she thought she'd become accustomed to the play he taught her, the duke slipped a hand between her thighs. He furrowed his fingers through her feminine curls, and when he glanced one of those digits over the hidden bud, the swelling center of her desire, she uttered a cry that had him laughing with masculine smugness.

"Donovan, what are you—"

"Enjoy. This, my sweet country flower, is what makes life worth living," he interrupted and began to tease that nub of flesh as he kissed her lips.

Alice feared she would dissolve into a puddle of hot, liquid need so great were the sensations he invoked within her. She clutched at his shoulders, digging her fingernails into his skin from the horrible pressure deep inside her lower belly increased and stacked. When would it end, and would she like it when it did? "I need..." She panted. Words wouldn't come. Passion fogged her brain. "I need something..."

"This." He circled that bud with his thumb and slid first one finger into her aching passage and then another.

"Oh, yes." It felt wonderful. She canted her hips in an effort to better receive him, and then she shattered, her body going stiff. When he didn't relent on the pressure, she went pliant as the most wondrous sensations swamped her being. Heat rushed through her veins from the roots of her hair to the tips of her toes and everywhere between. And between her thighs where he stroked his fingers in and out, her channel fluttered, contracting with the force of his attention. Alice collapsed against the pillows with a sigh. "I never knew it would be like that."

"We aren't finished yet." He removed himself from her, and when she uttered a weak protest, he chuckled. "Patience. I must undress all the way."

"Please hurry." Was it wanton of her to wish for a repeat of what just happened? While she stretched with a languid grace she'd not known before, the whisper of a garment hitting the floor broke the silence. "Is this the part where you applied the blindfold to your mistresses?" She gasped. What was wrong with her that she'd utter such a thing now?

His chuckle smoothed her worries; he wasn't offended. "Actually, I would blindfold those women the second I invited them into my rooms." The mattress depressed, signaling his arrival upon the bed, and then he joined her once more, his body warm and strong over hers, his hips nestled in the cradle of hers.

"Why?" It was the only word she could utter, for the simple joy of having his strong form in her arms and between her legs.

He lightly nipped the side of her neck. "I didn't want those women to see me during such an intimate moment as finding release." Slowly, gently he spread her legs, and as he did so, the tip of his hardened member brushed her opening.

"Isn't that one of the most important aspects of intercourse?" She wriggled her hips, but he didn't move. "I want to see you, Donovan, watch the emotions shift through your eyes, see your face and know this is where you wish to be." Her voice faltered. "With me."

"Of that there is no doubt." He captured her lips with his, and when a powerful flex of his hips, he slipped inside her, breaking past her virgin barrier, and didn't stop until he was fully seated and they were pressed together as intimately as any two people could be.

Alice gasped from the sharp prick of pain. She dug her fingers into his shoulders, but as he began to move within her, the discomfort faded and in its place came showers of sensations so pleasurable she moaned from the sheer delight of what he did to her.

He gathered her closer, gripped her hip with one hand and with the other encouraged her to wrap a leg about his waist while he increased the intensity of his thrusts. "Quickly, Alice. I won't last, for I have been teased by wanting you for too many days." His breath caressed her cheek, ruffled the baby-fine curls on her forehead.

What did he want her to do? She had no idea, but she moved her hips in time to his and soon they fell into a pleasing rhythm. With each stroke and undulation, the pressure inside her built and grew once more. Harder and harder he pushed, scooting her back deeper into the pillows. Faster his hips worked until all she felt was him, his turgid length inside her, his strong, solid body rubbing along hers, the crisp hair on his chest scraping over her sensitive nipples and adding another layer of awareness.

And then, quite simply, she broke, crying out, into a million pieces of light, fell into a world where there was no sound. Higher and higher she shot, her body drifting in clouds of sparkling white light, and as she floated back down, her body tingled and shuddered as spent desire pulsed through every nerve ending.

Donovan bit back his own shout of completion. He ground his hips into his while his member jerked, but he pulled out of her body seconds before the warmth of his seed jetted out and spattered over her thighs and belly. He collapsed against her and then pulled them both onto their sides.

As she returned to herself and her heart didn't pound quite so fast, Alice frowned. Why did he feel the need to not complete the act? If he didn't wish for her to get with child, why didn't he first speak with her about that? As pleasant lethargy seeped through her limbs and she snuggled against his sweaty chest, she pushed the thoughts to the back of her mind. There was much to talk with him about, but the questions would keep.

This was her wedding night—afternoon—and she vowed to enjoy every second of it, for her first experience in love making had been everything wonderful.

CHAPTER TWELVE

Donovan woke from his doze as the three-quarter full moon began its rise in the sky. Its illumination filtered through the trees and made its way through the windows that had yet to have the curtains drawn. Alice, as sweet in slumber as she'd been when he'd finally claimed her body, lay with one hand tucked beneath her cheek on the pillow. The other lay haphazardly on his chest, the ring on her finger winking in the lunar glow.

Bloody hell, I'm truly married.

He'd said vows, gave her a ring—a piece that had belonged to his mother's trousseau as part of her bridal jewelry—all because he wanted to lay with Alice… and have a chance at breaking the curse. Memories surfaced through his mind of exiting the church behind her and Elizabeth as he'd walked with Rogue. He'd caught the viscous whispers from the handful of people who'd come to witness the ceremony, or to gawk. If nothing else, he wished to prove every one of them wrong; Alice was indeed good enough for him.

I'm the one who doesn't deserve her love.

The truth caused his chest to squeeze. Again he looked at his wife. Her hair, loose with jeweled combs holding the tresses back from her face, pooled around her head on the pillow like melted chocolate. It was glorious and he wanted to tangle his hands in it. They'd come together before the bedclothes had been turned down, and she reposed naked on her side, her mons hidden from view, strands of her hair obscuring her pale breasts.

Damnation, he wanted her again, if only to claim her in the moon's light, the time of night he felt most comfortable.

Perhaps soon, for there was nothing to hold him back; they were legally man and wife. The muscles of his stomach cramped from his deception. He stirred, carefully slipped from the bed so he wouldn't disturb her, for the longer she slept, the more time he'd have to figure out how the deuce he was to reveal his damning secret to her. Already, the words danced on the tip of his tongue, for after every joining, no matter the woman or the reason for the bedding, the curse compelled him to confess all.

At least this time you had the sense to marry the female before bedding her. Now she's legally bound to you with nowhere to go, his wolf was quick to remind him.

A bird in a gilt prison. Until she broke the curse. Not caring that the water from her earlier bath was cold, he sank into it and hurriedly scrubbed himself with the rose-scented soap still resting on a small round table.

Finding release with Alice had been everything he'd hoped, and where she'd lacked experience or nuance, she made up for with enthusiasm and feeling. The woman loved him, of that he had no doubt, and he looked forward to teaching her the finer points of love making before the full moon arrived. He had just under a week to enjoy a honeymoon period, of sorts, before fate came into play. After that, he'd embrace his life as a full human and enjoy it to the hilt.

Without her? In his mind, his wolf glared at him.

I don't know. The future had become murky, and he didn't appreciate that.

His wolf snapped his jaws. *But she's soft and sweet and her eyes sparkle when she comes undone.*

That they do. Donovan shoved those thoughts as well as his wolf's commentary to the back of his mind as he dunked his head beneath the water and gave it a vigorous scrubbing. Then he did the same to his body. By the time he'd dried himself with the leftover towel draped across the back of the tub, his wolf waited.

You do not wish to impregnate her? Do your duty to the title?

Did he? Not at this time, for if the curse wasn't lifted and Alice bore him a male child... He shook his head. *I'd rather wait to see what happens.* Damnation, but he was a coward of the first order, yet he refused to put a child through the hell he'd grown up with—the not knowing, the fear, the pain that came with shifting, the sense of being out of control and fighting with the beast. He snorted. *All of which I still am subjected to.*

There are worse things, his wolf countered.

Donovan glanced at the bed—his bed—where his new bride still slept. *What have I done?*

Inside his head, his wolf whined. *Will we run tonight?*

No. He rubbed a hand along his jaw where rough stubble had formed. If all went well when he told Alice everything, he intended to indulge in a different form of exercise, for her body truly was made for sin, and since they *were* married...

Perhaps he was beyond redemption after all.

He strode across the room to the basin in the corner, and after dipping a clean rag into the water, he returned to the bed. With gentle movements, he cleaned away the evidence of his lust from her belly and thighs. With each pass of the damp cloth over her skin, soft sounds loosed from her throat. She stretched and shifted, briefly splaying her legs and rolling onto her back, putting her breasts on full display. *Dear God, she is perfect... just not for a lifetime with me.* Still, his length twitched to life, bringing his own naked state into stark relief, and he tossed the soiled rag in the direction of the basin.

"Alice." Donovan joined her on the bed, layered himself to her side and pulled her close. "Are you sufficiently awake?"

"That largely depends on why you wish it," she said with a smile that spoke of deliciously wicked things in his immediate future. His wife stroked her fingers over his face, and he grinned for her benefit even though anxiety clawed at his insides. When she explored and ran her digits through his wet hair, she frowned. "You bathed?"

"Yes." He pressed his lips to hers in a series of gentle, teasing kisses designed to lull her into a warm cocoon before he shook the foundations of her life. "How did you sleep?" he whispered against her mouth as he reminded himself another bout of bed sport could come later once he'd told her his secret.

If she'll still have me.

"Extremely well, and it's so decadent to do so during the day." Alice looped her arms about his neck while she snuggled closer. Each innocent movement created friction against various parts of his body that were already primed. With her nose to his, she stared into his eyes. Hers reflected wonder and a new feminine knowledge that sent heat curling through his blood. "Will there be a second session soon? I find I'm ready for another go."

The fact she'd taken to coitus intrigued him. In other circumstances, if things had been different, perhaps they could have gotten on well together. Donovan forced a swallow into his suddenly tight throat. "If you so wish it, but first, there is something I must say."

She went still in his arms. Concern clouded her gray eyes, the silver flecks fading. "This is what you and your sister have hidden from me." It wasn't a question.

"Yes." The word came out in a strangled whisper. He relaxed his arms in anticipation for her flight. Urgency compelled him to not only tell her of his alter-ego but to also confess all, that perhaps if he conveyed the truth now, it would go better for him in the future. His wolf, pacing about the confines of his mind with a certain restlessness and need to claim her once more, didn't help to promote calm. Donovan shoved everything he could from his consciousness in order to concentrate on the more immediate problem. "Long ago, my family line—as well as a handful of other titles within the *ton*—were cursed by a gypsy witch."

Alice frowned as she pushed up from him, a hand lingering on his chest. "What does that mean?"

"For the insensitive and uncaring actions of a distant relative, each male relative in the line must pay penance until such time as the curse is lifted." He cleared his throat. Never had this conversation been so difficult, for Alice looked at him with trust in her eyes and empathy in her expression. It was almost as if she understood. "My portion of the witch's curse is shifting into wolf form at night—every night—running as the beast, going where he goes. I… I have no choice."

A smile curved her lips. "You are having me on, you naughty duke. Why would you tell me a tale like this?"

"Alice, I'm dead serious." He removed her hand from his chest and pressed it to his face. "Look into my eyes." His body tensed as she explored his face with lighter-than-air touches. "In fact, you have met me while I occupied my beastly form." How much would saying the words cost him? For if she didn't believe and her tremulous feelings for him hardened…

She held his gaze with hers, and while she did so, he loosed a bit of his control in order for his eyes to turn amber like his wolf's. "It *is* you." Alice reared backward so quickly she toppled into the bedding. Then she scrambled away from him, pulling at the counterpane, using it to shield her nakedness from him. "*You* are the wolf from our first meeting. I knew there was a canine of some kind there that day."

Donovan remained where he was for fear any movement on his part would startle her from the room. "Yes. I'd been hunting as the animal that morning when I saw you in peril. I had no time to act; I just ran toward you and shoved you out of harm's way."

"There was another time." She shook her head as the truth finally sank in. Horror clouded her eyes. The hand holding the bedclothes to her breasts shook. "You attacked Joe, nearly killed him the day of our engagement."

He moved into a seated position as anger swirled through his chest at the remembrance. "Because you were mine." The explanation came out louder and more forceful than he would have liked. Damn wolf.

You might as well tell her that too, human.

Alice's eyes went round as saucers, whether from his tone of voice or the sentiment, he couldn't say. "You assume I belong to you, that I'm your… property… and that I'll do everything you command because you're a duke." She slipped from the bed trailing the sheet and counterpane behind her.

"No. Perhaps a bit, but..." He was mucking this up beyond repair. "Please listen to the rest of it before you decide you hate me. It is an affliction, and I hinted about it to you before. Just like your sight challenges, I have no choice except to live with this."

A bark of bitter laughter escaped her, which was so foreign that he gawked at her. "No, my lord. Your affliction and mine are not the same for one reason alone: I never hid mine."

"I did so to protect you." *Protect me.*

"In the event that you haven't been paying attention, I am capable of taking care of myself. I'd done well until you came along, and you made me feel..." She stifled a sob. "You made me believe that I..."

"Alice, please." *What should I say to calm her?*

Ironically, his wolf declined to comment.

"This marriage, it was a mistake." She turned her horrified gaze to him once more. "You went along with it to bed me, and then what? Kill me in my sleep when you become the beast? To what purpose?" Her voice rose with every question she put to him.

Donovan cringed. With a tight chest, he left the bed but kept that piece of furniture between them. "I will not kill you."

"How can I know that? You nearly killed Joe, and if I hadn't intervened..." Her mouth worked but no words poured forth. "You lied to me, married me for reasons that are still only known to you."

"No, I withheld a truth. There's a difference." But was there, really? Wasn't the sin the same no matter how one looked at it? He stared at her, wondering, hoping. In a quiet voice, he asked, "Do you regret saying vows to me?"

"Yes." She shook her head. "No." The delicate tendons in her neck worked with a hard swallow. "I am not certain." Alice looked across the bed at him, her unseeing gaze holding his. "I believe you are a good man, Donovan. Or so I hope, but you lied about your wolf. What else are you not telling me?" She dropped her voice. "What is the real reason you married me?"

At least she hadn't run screaming from the room, and she hadn't thrown anything at his head. Yet that didn't alleviate the self-loathing that filled every pore of his being. His jaw worked. Finally, he uttered the words dancing on his tongue. "Every five years, there is a chance the curse might be broken. This only occurs during one full moon a quarter in that five-year span—we don't know which moon."

She blew out a breath that ruffled the baby-fine curls on her forehead. "And somehow you believe I can help break this curse." Her eyes narrowed. "How?"

"Only when pure, unselfish love crosses my lips beneath the full moon can the curse break." Every word felt pulled from him, for with each one she wilted a little more.

"Oh." Alice bowed her head, and he gasped at the severed connection. "You knew this all along, so you manipulated me, courted me with every intention of making me fall in love with you." Disappointment wove through her voice to further chill him.

"Yes, but we get on well together, and I truly believe you'll do the title of duchess proud." That wasn't a lie. Every day that went by she impressed him even more.

"Poor consolation for a woman who is now trapped." When she raised her head, her eyes flashed silver lightning. "You wanted my body."

How could he deny it when the bald facts were already there? "Yes, but I—" But what? Have no plans to set up housekeeping with her or even welcome her into his life once the curse released its shackles?

"You knew all along you wanted specific things from me." Each word cut through his chest with the accuracy of a sharp dagger. "You charmed me like you've done countless others." She threw a glance about the room and gasped, clutched the bedclothes higher up her person. "Oh, God, how many mistresses have been in this same room, that same bed, the place where you... where we...?" Tears pooled in her eyes, magnifying the gray depths. "This somehow cheapens what we've shared." She struggled for control. "You used me then and now you'll do so again." Her gaze bore into his. "As if I wasn't worth the truth."

"You were, and I should have done things differently." Yet he could hardly have asked her if she might consider falling for him to break a curse after he met her on that public road, naked.

Anything he'd say now would sound trite. "I am truly sorry."

Tears fell to her cheeks. "I am, too."

Those crystalline drops of moisture tore through him. Yes, women had cried in his presence before, but those had been crocodile tears designed to make him offer gifts or trinkets and baubles. Alice was truly in distress, her sadness and suffering caused by him alone. "It sounds horrible when spoken aloud, and I'm not saying my part in this debacle wasn't heinous. However, time is of the essence, and I am desperate to banish the curse." Perhaps it would mean more if he tried the honest approach. He took a few steps toward her. "I've been a slave to the beast year after year since I was old enough to become aware of my differences. It has grown weary. I wish to live as a free man—a fully human man. Is that such a bad thing?" He snatched up an Oriental-style dressing gown that lay on the foot of the bed and thrust his arms through the sleeves, tying the sash as the silence grew between them.

"No." Alice wiped at the moisture on her cheeks. She took the first tentative steps toward his location. He couldn't breathe the closer she drew. "No, it is not too much to ask, for if given the chance, I too would choose to be free of my affliction." When she closed the distance and lifted a hand to his face, he concentrated on his rapid pulse and the coolness of her fingertips on his skin. "This doesn't mean I'm not still angry with you."

"I understand." It was a start, but there was much ahead of them to overcome if she could indeed lift the curse. "Above everything, I regret breaking your trust."

"Words are meaningless. Show me you've changed by your actions." She brought her nose close to his, her breath fanning over his cheek. "Is it horrible living with a beast inside you? I cannot imagine what that must feel like."

Donovan dared to cup her face between his hands. "Think of it as a never-ending conscience that doesn't mind his own business." When she smiled, he dared even more and brushed his lips over hers, but she pulled out of his arms.

"I'm not ready for a return of intimacy between us so soon." One of her eyebrows rose. "And most assuredly not in that bed." Her tone brooked no argument.

"I deserve that." He sighed. Most times, when a woman went out of temper with him, he bought them a gift and their mood cleared. However, negotiations with Alice were more delicate. She demanded better of him and the situation. "Perhaps you'll adjoin to my sitting room with me?"

She nodded and held out a hand while still clutching the bedclothes to her chest with the other.

"Good." Donovan caressed his gaze along the slender slope of her back. She had the dearest dimple at the base of her spine that he couldn't wait to press his lips to. Tamping down his growing reaction, he took her hand and led her out of the sleeping chamber into the room beyond, a private area where he often read or shut himself away from his responsibilities. "Do you wish to know more?"

"I do."

"Even better." He took a seat on a low sofa of navy crushed velvet and pulled her down with him. "However, it is complicated."

"As are you." She didn't protest when he kept hold of her hand and threaded their fingers together. "But I do understand why you did what you did."

Donovan sighed as he leaned against the furniture's high back. "I have made mistakes in my past before I realized how dangerous I could be without control of the beast. During the war, I killed many men, but war isn't an excuse to give the animal its head." He remained silent and she didn't interrupt. "I refuse to be that man again, so I constantly fight with my wolf. He is more violent than I am, he has a completely different way of thinking."

"Which one of you wins?"

"Whichever of us is stronger that day." He sighed. "I try not to let the wolf have control over me, for that would not end well. But the most I want you to know is that I'm not a savage, nor do I kill people... unless threatened."

She turned her head toward him. "Would you have murdered Joe that day?"

"Honestly?" When she nodded, he said, "I perceived your life was threatened. He very nearly raped you. That is an unforgivable crime, and the beast doesn't take kindly to that. I didn't think; I just shifted and let the animal have his way. I knew in that moment I wanted to protect you from every bad or foul thing that might come against you in life."

"It is dangerous, what you do." Alice put her face close to his and studied his eyes. "While you are struggling, please be careful. Though I'm annoyed with you at present, you are my husband, and this is my life now. What affects you affects me also, and I will support you in any way that I can." She searched his eyes, and he hoped she'd find something redeeming in him. "Don't act the arse merely because you aren't fully human."

Relief poured into him. He kissed her cheek. "Thank you. I'll endeavor to make your days pleasant until the full moon."

"And after that?" Trepidation hung on the question.

"Only time will tell." The lie came easy, but his gut felt as if he'd been punched.

When will your penchant for using people end? his wolf wished to know.

This time it was he who remained silent.

CHAPTER THIRTEEN

September 27, 1815
London

Alice had spent much of the morning familiarizing herself with her new home as well as the staff who worked there, and with Elizabeth as a companion and guide, it hadn't been as overwhelming or daunting as she'd assumed.

As she moved through the rooms starting with a drawing room where she touched sculptures, bowls, figurines, curtains, and furnishings, Elizabeth described the pieces or gave brief histories, if any. The anecdotes made Alice feel as if she were more connected instead of a recent transplant.

She gave the same treatment to any member of the duke's staff she encountered, from the grouchy butler to the eager footmen to timid maids. Every face she felt, every smile or frown she traced, and if they thought her odd, they were too well-trained to say so. With each meeting, Elizabeth said their name and their place within the household, described their hair and eye color, gave her an insight as to what they enjoyed and what they excelled at.

Throughout the tour, she remained distracted regarding the duke's revelations of the night before. Long after he'd stopped talking, she'd sat next to him in the quiet, listening to the sound of his breathing, reveling in the heat of his body as it had seeped into hers, traced her fingertips up and down his arm until he'd attempted another bout of love making, but she declined and had retreated to the duchess suite at the end of the hall.

Even now her heart twinged, for she'd meant what she'd said—she wouldn't have relations with him in the same apartments where he'd entertained countless other women. The fragile state of her budding emotions weren't strong enough to survive her mental comparisons.

Donovan had greeted her in the morning room for breakfast, and then he closeted himself away in his study with his man-of-affairs as well as his solicitor. The legalities of their new union bewildered her, but he didn't share his thoughts, nor did he tell her what he'd intended with the newly drawn up documents.

"You are wool-gathering," Elizabeth said softly as they wandered through a parlor.

"I apologize." She stopped when the other woman did, and she slid her arm from hers. "I'm afraid my mind is on Donovan."

"That's understandable. You married him yesterday. No doubt there will be an adjustment period... to everything." Elizabeth took her arm once more and led her through the room and into the corridor beyond. "This morning, my maid informed me that you'd slept the night in the duchess suite." Curiosity lingered in the statement, but she didn't outright question why. "Is this where you'll remain going forward?"

Alice heaved a sigh. "I'm not certain."

"My brother told you, didn't he?" Resignation clung to the words.

Does she fear I'll leave?

"He did." Content to let the other woman guide her through the corridors, she continued. "You knew what your brother was about, yet you didn't say so to me, or at the very least warn me." It wasn't an accusation but a mere statement of fact. Everyone around her concerning Donovan had secrets to keep. Was it for her protection or his?

"What could I do?" Elizabeth slowed her pace as she lowered her voice. "I'd already lectured him against hurting you, breaking your trust, but he has always wished to lift the curse and live free. How could I begrudge him that, for I cannot imagine what his life is." She squeezed Alice's arm. "I'm afraid it's a conundrum at best."

"Definitely a puzzle." But did Donovan wish for someone to solve it? She had no interest in the few rooms Elizabeth pulled her through, for her mind was consumed with her new husband. "Has he ever been in love with a woman?"

Elizabeth paused in what she called a sunroom that was at Alice's disposal if she wanted to work on correspondence, household menus, and event planning or the like. It certainly lived up to its name, for a wealth of windows on one side allowed sunshine to pour in and warm Alice's face. "Once. The lady broke his heart upon finding out about his truth. She was quite cruel about it." A stretch of silence grew between them. "Donovan was devastated. That was five years ago—the last time the curse could be broken. He's stopped trying for love in recent years. I think he fears it's impossible."

"Considering the history of previous title holders, it's no wonder he's concerned."

"He told you of the previous dukes?"

"He briefly touched on it, so I put together the rest myself." Alice smiled. "Also, your servants talk. I might be blind but I am not deaf." Everyone assumed if one had a handicap then they must be deficient in other ways as well. "I shall make it a mission to educate them."

"I'm so sorry." Elizabeth hugged her and then released her as abruptly. "It seems an adjustment period on the part of everyone is mandatory, but please know that I, as well as the staff, are pleased you've come to us and have married the duke."

Shock moved through her. "Why? What difference can one woman make?"

"Donovan, for all that he's a good man, is often troubled and moody. When he's wrestling with the beast, he's quiet, sullen and at times snarly. And the women he's kept company with are nothing but grasping, vain creatures who add no value to life." Elizabeth's laugh swept away some of Alice's concerns. "With your arrival we are all hoping for a breath of fresh air, so to speak. A chance at new life."

"Such a lofty goal and large weight upon my back," Alice murmured. Since her companion mentioned it and Alice's curiosity ran rampant, she asked, "He's had many mistresses?"

"Yes. I think some of those women have been curiosity seekers, for the curse on his name has long been bandied through the *ton* as rumors. But since meeting you, Donovan has stopped all such behaviors. He hasn't entertained a woman for weeks even before you met." The smile in her voice was more than evident. "I noticed the change in him even if he denies it, so I look forward to what's in his future."

Hope warmed her and shimmered in her mind's eye as a cloud of sparkling opal. "I hope you're right."

Elizabeth set them into motion once more. "It sounds trite, I know, but only time will tell."

Time, the great equalizer and healer. Alice smiled. "Will he ever let himself love again?" It was one thing for her to love him, but if there was no chance of the man returning those feelings? Life would stretch long and empty indeed. Could she survive?

"I am not certain." Elizabeth sighed. "It largely depends on the woman, for our parents' union was fraught with animosity and resentment. There was no real love there, and I think Donovan fears he will suffer the same fate."

"Ah, and he keeps his relationships shallow to thwart bearing his heart." Perhaps she understood him more now, but that didn't lessen her worry.

"Yes, because of the curse. It's a horrible task master and leaves him isolated. There is only so much I can do for him."

"I understand."

Elizabeth squeezed her arm. "Please say that you'll try with him. I..." Her voice wavered. "I want my brother to find happiness. For too long he's struggled with a life not of his own design. No one deserves that."

Tears prickled the backs of Alice's eyes. "I will stay true to the vows I said to him, but eventually, he will need to help himself. A man makes his own decisions regardless of his situation."

Please, God, give me the strength to endure what will, I fear, be a long road.

The tour of the duke's townhouse resumed. They inspected a lavish ballroom, another drawing room, an additional parlor and then went down into the kitchens where Alice was given copious snacks, which she exclaimed over, much to the cook's delight. With promises to meet and go over menus soon, she and Elizabeth moved on. She met Mrs. Bailey, the stalwart housekeeper, who fussed about her as if Alice were her long-lost child.

Alice enjoyed the attention and the warm welcome. After the coldness of Shalford, the difference was startling. Scullery and kitchen maids rushed to meet her, having already heard of her arrival from others. A few groomsmen and footmen lingered through the servants' halls to greet her. The butler, Griggs, apologized profusely for his hard words from yesterday, which amused her, and then went out of his way to show her around his domain.

Devil Take the Duke (Lords of the Night #1)

With a laugh, Elizabeth guided her back up the stairs. Once more on the second level, they went through the morning room where breakfast had been served, walked through a library that smelled of leather and old books, and her companion pointed out Donovan's study, but neither of them had the courage to interrupt the duke from his business, though Alice suffered an attack of butterflies in her belly when she heard the deep tenor of his voice through the closed door.

"And this," Elizabeth said once they'd continued the tour, "is the last room on this level. It's a little-used music room, and I cannot remember the last time it was opened."

"A music room?" Alice's heart beat a little faster. "How amazing." She released Elizabeth's arm in order to explore about the space. "Everything is covered in sheets." Her hand encountered such draperies, and then deciding to utilize her authority as duchess, she tugged the sheets from every piece of furniture or musical instrument she found, especially those she discovered on a small stage three steps up from the floor.

"As I said, this room has been rather neglected." Humor wove through Elizabeth's voice. "Obviously, this makes you happy."

"Oh yes." Then Alice sucked in a surprised breath. "A pianoforte." She moved to the next instrument. "Oh, dear heavens." She couldn't believe the evidence of her fingers as she plucked at familiar strings and light, lilting notes released into the air.

"What is wrong?" Ever on the alert, Elizabeth swept across the room to her side.

"You own a harp." She couldn't prevent the awe that fell over her as she continued to stroke her fingers along the graceful lines of the instrument and work its strings. "I know this instrument. I played one and was quite proficient before I was tossed from the baron's home." She swallowed around a lump of tears in her throat. "It was the one lady's skill I conquered."

"Did you enjoy it?"

"Oh, yes." Alice smiled as she played a quick scale on the strings. Heavenly music, somewhat out of tune, floated around her. "It allowed me to express myself in a way that made my blindness fade." She continued to pluck at the strings, anxious to sit with the instrument and rediscover that long-ago joy. "While I played, I imagined myself whole, and as I lost myself in the songs, for a while I was free of judgment, of the slights, of the resentment at being a poor relation, of the sadness of being alone."

"That's a beautiful way of looking at life, Alice." Elizabeth laid a hand on her shoulder. "I'm so glad you're here."

Her smile widened. "Why is this room never used? Do you not play an instrument?"

Elizabeth snorted with laughter. "I am not skilled, nor do I have the patience. Please, make use of the room and all that's in here. I'll have someone in to tune the pieces."

"How splendid! I look forward to countless hours finding my music again." As tears swam in

Devil Take the Duke (Lords of the Night #1)

her eyes, she impulsively grabbed the other woman in a hug. "That means so much to me." She peered into Elizabeth's face, caught the surprise in her brown eyes so much like Donovan's. Then she pulled away. "You and your brother have been so kind. I keep wondering when the dream will end." A shiver ripped up her spine and she gave into it. "Or when I'll have to return to Shalford and my tiny room where I was an obligation to everyone."

And mayhap it would end, and soon, for Donovan didn't want her for anything beyond breaking his curse, but being here in London, in this townhouse with the duke and his sister was so different than the life she'd known previously, she didn't know quite how to act. And having the title of duchess behind her, which could effect change to anyone she so wished both staggered and humbled her.

"It's best to remember this isn't a dream." Elizabeth patted her arm. "You are truly here. This is where you belong now—with people who love and appreciate you."

"Except for your brother," she added in a harsh whisper.

"Alice, please know you have brought a change to my world simply by marrying Donovan." Elizabeth grasped her hand and squeezed her fingers. "Do not give up on him, even if things seem hopeless. Sometimes men take longer to convince their hearts of what's there in front of them."

A tear fell to her cheek, and she dashed it away. "I shall try my best, for I do care for him, despite my misgivings." Her voice wavered. "If only he knew how valuable he is even with the curse."

"Oh, you dear girl." Elizabeth laughed, and the lightness of the sound wrapped about Alice, further bolstering the hope that bloomed in her chest. "He's never seen it, though. Perhaps you can help show him the way. Lord knows I've tried for years, but all he can see is the curse, how he is unsavory because of it."

Companionable silence fell around them, and once more Alice drifted to the harp. She rapidly played a scale and then plucked out a few lines of a favorite song.

Eventually, Elizabeth sighed and roused herself. "Come. You have fittings this afternoon and menus to approve and invitations to look through. Your new status of duchess might attract curiosity seekers, but I'm hopeful that some of the invites are genuine and that you'll forge an unforgettable path through society that Donovan hasn't been able to make."

A near hysterical laugh escaped Alice, and she sighed. "My biggest fear is failing at being his duchess. It is quite an overwhelming responsibility, even for a woman at full sight." She worried her bottom lip with her teeth as she stepped away from the harp. "Perhaps I made a mistake in marrying him."

"No." Elizabeth squeezed her hand. She assisted her down the steps and then led her from the room. "You are here, and that in itself is an enormous step for my brother. Forget the reasons why he did it; it is done, and he cannot erase that. Spend time with him. Show him you won't reject him or let him down. Mayhap fate will give him a nudge."

How much did she already appreciate having a sister? Alice nodded. She blinked away the remaining tears. "Let us hope for the best, and you're right. I'm here now. I won't waste the opportunity, for many things." With excitement trickling through her voice, she told Elizabeth about her dream of opening a school for children with impaired vision and to help them integrate into society with confidence.

"How wonderful that sounds!" Her genuine enthusiasm echoed in the corridor. "I, myself, work with the poor by bringing them bread a few times a week. Just now that takes me into the Dials, much to Donovan's chagrin."

"Does he accompany you?"

"He does not." She lowered her voice. "At least he doesn't in human form, though I suspect he might follow me as the wolf. For protection." She giggled. "It makes me feel safe, but he never interferes and thus allows me to have my work as mine alone."

A twinge moved through Alice's heart. "I'm glad for you." He must have some honor about him if he played at being his sister's watchdog.

Elizabeth leaned closer. "For what it's worth, Donovan has ordered his apartment renovated."

"Truly?" He'd taken what she'd said to heart?

"Oh, yes." Elizabeth chuckled as if she found everything concerning her sibling a great joke. "As of this morning, in fact. It has thrown poor Griggs into a tizzy, but my brother is quite adamant. Says he cannot live with the old décor." She snorted and another peal of laughter escaped her. "He has even ordered every piece of furniture replaced. Can you image the upheaval he's causing?"

"I can, indeed." Alice smiled, and a host of tingles erupted inside her. "How… encouraging though." That the powerful Duke of Manchester had abruptly ordered a change of his whole suite of rooms after she'd vowed not to lie with him there amused her. Perhaps there was hope for their union after all.

"Yes. You know the whims of dukes," Elizabeth replied with a grin in her voice. "Or perhaps the quiet direction of their wives." Another laugh tinkled from her. "Oh, you and I are going to have such fun bossing him. He'll be quite the changed man once we're through."

Alice kept her own counsel, but the smile wouldn't leave her lips.

CHAPTER FOURTEEN

September 28, 1815

Donovan sat at the head of the table while dinner stretched on. He wasn't particularly hungry, at least not for the fare on his plate.

He'd been married to Alice for just over two days, and for the most part, he hadn't seen her since she'd left his bedchamber after they'd talked on their wedding night. Yesterday, as his sister familiarized his wife with the townhouse and the staff, he'd spent his time with his solicitor, drawing up legal documents that would see Alice cared for if something untoward happened prematurely to him. He may be a scoundrel and a rake, but he took his duty to the title seriously. His man-of-affairs had also been summoned, for there were properties to catalogue and put into her name.

If nothing else, she'd married him, and he had a responsibility toward her.

The lilting notes of her laughter recalled him to the moment, and he rested his gaze on his wife. She talked animatedly with Elizabeth on a variety of topics. As the dulcet tones of her voice washed over him, his wolf paced restlessly inside.

Want to run. Need exercise.

Not tonight. He picked at the roasted pheasant on his plate but kept his focus on Alice.

Want her.

So did he.

She is ours and we should be with her.

He ignored his wolf.

Last night she'd retired to her suite of rooms while he'd had no choice except to either bunk down in his study or sleep in the room next to Elizabeth's. His wife hadn't requested his company and he'd not pushed the issue for fear she'd reject him. It was one of the reasons he'd stayed away from her yesterday as well as today; he didn't wish for her to leave, especially not before the full moon. But he'd trailed after her a few times throughout both days, watching her as she embraced her new role with enthusiasm.

The warmth of hope stirred in his chest. It was all to the good she hadn't slipped out of the house in the night. Neither had she spoken to him about the curse. The hope faded as anxiety clutched at him. Were they already estranged so early in their union? Even his parents had lasted longer than that, or so he'd assumed.

"You are quiet tonight, brother," Elizabeth said, and once more he was yanked out of his thoughts.

Desultory rain tapped against the windows at his back and further added to his maudlin mood. "I apologize for not attending the conversation. My mind is on other matters."

"So I can see." She bounced her gaze between him and Alice then back again. A grin tugged at her

Devil Take the Duke (Lords of the Night #1)

lips. "Perhaps, since it's raining, you should take your nightly constitutional by walking the house." His sister gestured with her head toward Alice. "It might be nice, and I don't wish for you to catch your death in the wet."

Again, he flicked his gaze to Alice, who looked fetching in a green satin gown. The pale blue wrap she wore to ward off the autumn chill reflected in her eyes. "Perhaps you're right. Thank you for the concern." When his wife turned her head and glanced at him, a faint smile curving her kissable lips, her upswept hair curled and cascading from new glittering combs, every muscle in his body tightened.

"I know you're both talking about me," his wife said in a soft voice. "I'm not deaf."

Donovan exchanged a laugh with Elizabeth. "We meant no disrespect." He shoved his half-eaten dinner plate away. "Alice, will you do me the honor of walking the house once we're done here?" Regardless of what the future held between them, it would behoove him to continue courting her with charm and romance to ensure the feelings she held for him didn't fade.

"That sounds lovely." When a footman came forward and whisked away her empty plate, she smiled up at him. "Would you please tell Cook that I will pop down later tonight for her dessert. I'm not in the mood for it at present." Then she slid a glance to Donovan, and the twinkle in her gorgeous eyes had tiny fires erupting in his blood. "My time has been otherwise engaged."

"I will, Your Grace, but you don't need to come down. Just ring and someone will bring it up with tea," the footman responded with a besotted expression.

Donovan tamped the urge to roll his eyes. How had she enchanted the bulk of his staff in forty-eight hours? It had taken them years to warm to him. He grunted. Of course, he wasn't the most congenial of men due to the curse.

"I know that; I enjoy chatting with Cook and the maids."

The young footman gawked. He frowned. "But you are a duchess, my lady, and they—we—are servants…"

Alice's eyebrows rose. "People are people, Thomas. Should I not treat everyone around me with kindness despite my elevated station?" She shook her head. "I rather think that's unfair, for I know what it's like to be ignored or taken for granted."

When the footman opened his mouth to argue, Donovan cleared his throat. "That will be all, Thomas. Thank you." Once more he contemplated his wife. His respect for her rose. Yes, she'd been a perfect choice for his duchess, and she managed to convey a regal elegance while maintaining a humbleness of spirit. How? How did she find balance in everything?

Inside his mind, his wolf whined at the delay. *Go to her, kiss her, claim her. Spend more time with her.*

Do shut up, beast. Subtlety is needed lest she tip the delicate truce we have. But Donovan pushed back his chair and stood. "Apologies, Elizabeth, but I intend to steal Alice away for a while." Slowly, he made his way around the table to his wife's location, almost stalking her, tracking her. Did she realize she was already caught?

She is not an imbecile, his wolf was quick to remind him.

Elizabeth squeezed Alice's hand that rested on the tabletop. "I shall see you tomorrow when we interview women for your lady's maid. Call for me in the night if you need me."

"Thank you." Then she turned her full attention to him as his sister departed the room. "Impatient, are you?"

"Perhaps." He assisted her into a standing position. "I simply wish to spend time in your company, for I haven't seen you since our wedding night."

"Are you blaming me?" One of her eyebrows rose in challenge.

He grinned. "I believe we are both at fault." As soon as he drew her hand through his crooked elbow, he led her from the dining room. "However, I promised to make this week unforgettable, and now that my business has concluded, I will do just that."

The soft intake of her breath was barely noticeable. "Before you are free of your responsibility. You'll either send me to another property or you and I will reside here, growing more cold toward each other until resentment is the only thing we share."

Silence was his answer. After all, what was there to say, when exactly that would happen?

You are a coward, said his wolf.

Silently, Donovan agreed. The aroma of apricot and vanilla fanned the flames of his hunger. "You smell nice. I like it much better than roses, which is my sister's scent."

She turned her head and focused on his face. "The perfume was delivered to me yesterday, from a shop in St. James Square." Then a tiny smile curved her lips and he couldn't tear his gaze away. "How did you know?"

Perhaps he wasn't as big a coward as he thought, for he grinned. "When I was out yesterday, I dropped by a perfumery and described to the chemist the scent I was after." He shrugged. "The man immediately knew, so I bought a bottle. I thought you might have missed it from home."

Her hand trembled in his hold. "I appreciate your kindness. The one bottle I owned, I'd used the last drop the morning of our engagement. I'd had it for years, barely using it to make the scent last."

"It's special to you?"

"Yes. It was a perfume my mother favored. She'd given me a bottle for my birthday before she died." Her voice wavered. "I kept it for years, only wearing it on days I wanted to feel particularly feminine, to remind myself I was more valuable than people assumed."

"Never let the opinions of others tear away at your own self-worth." Donovan escorted her into the music room. Elizabeth had informed him of Alice's pleasure regarding the harp, and she'd had a man in that morning to tune the instruments. "Do you know where we are?" he asked quietly as he left her side long enough to close the door. A quick turn of the lock guaranteed their privacy. "Would you like for me to light a candle?" As it was, the room resided in shadows. The moon's glow didn't penetrate the cloud cover.

Remarkably, Alice laughed. "I am blind. Illumination has little effect, but if you are uncomfortable in the dark…"

"I am not, for darkness is very much a part of my soul." The words held a bitter edge he wasn't proud of.

"Poor Donovan. Can you not let yourself see the light that is always there?" She moved about until the toe of her slipper hit the first step of the raised stage. "You brought me to the music room. Why?"

"I would enjoy it very much if you would play the harp for me." It intrigued him that Alice had such a talent. It would seem she was indeed every inch the duchess, even if she hadn't been bred for such a station.

"You are interested in this, when you've previously shunned music?"

"I never shunned it; I merely didn't wish to cool my heels in such an activity." He chuckled. Clever girl who thought it was he who had ordered the room closed. "Since Elizabeth doesn't play and none of the other females in my circle did either…"

"Are you quite certain that's the only reason?" she asked, and her quiet inquiry reached through his chest to tug at his secrets. Perhaps wisely she ignored his reference to previous females in his life.

The heat of embarrassment crept up the back of his neck. "For a woman who has abbreviated sight, you certainly see much." He clasped his hands behind his back. "My mother used to play the pianoforte when Elizabeth and I were small. I have enough sadness and angst in my life that I don't wish to come here and gather even more." Never had he admitted such a thing, not even to Elizabeth.

Alice moved onto the stage. Navy velvet curtains shot with gold thread draped the walls in an effort to provide better acoustics. She slipped onto the brocade stool that sat beside the white-painted harp with gilded swirls and feathers. "Then remember your mother in the happy times. They are the only recollections worth bringing forth."

"I'll endeavor to keep that in mind." Donovan sat in a chair with a blue brocade seat and back. Its dainty frame was painted gold—another relic from his mother's time as duchess, before she died of a broken, lonely heart.

A product of the curse when his father toiled under it.

"Please, play for me." Emotions strained his voice, whether from old memories or the fear Alice would follow the same path, he didn't know. In his mind, his wolf restlessly paced, hated the inactivity, deprived of his nightly run, while Donovan drummed the fingers of one hand upon his leg.

"I might need a few attempts to remember the notes, but I'll do my best. I tinkered about yesterday while your sister was with me." She uttered a self-deprecating laugh. "I haven't played for years, but this is an unexpected treat."

"Take all the time you require." He rested an ankle on a knee and attempted to quiet the beast within, but the wolf grew ever more anxious. Nerves crawled within Donovan.

Why are we waiting? She is ours by law now, his wolf complained with the snap of his jaws. *Claim her, lay with her, impregnate her.*

Not until after the full moon. He didn't wish to risk anything, for Alice was too valuable to his plans to spook her.

No! Now. We need her.

Donovan ignored the wolf in favor of attending to the actions of his wife. She'd begun to play more than practice scales. Now, it was as if her fingers were the instruments of magic, for the music she wove was transcendent, almost magical, ethereal.

Internally, his wolf immediately quieted, and all the while, Donovan stared. The sound of her playing built into billowing crescendos only to fall in low swoops as if the notes rushed down a hill. Never did she falter, so sure and swift were her fingers on the strings. The notes wrapped around him, knitting a soothing cocoon of invisible comfort until he could only gawk at the woman he'd wedded.

She was beautiful—there was no other way to explain it. With her eyes closed, she swayed slightly to the music she created—that she felt and wore like a gilded, shimmering garment. Essentially, Alice spoke with the notes, the melody, the moving passages, and the stories those notes told went straight to his heart.

His mother had loved music, but Alice *embodied* it. In her, the passages, the melodies became a living, breathing entity, and if he wasn't careful she'd float right out of his life to return home to Olympus where the other Muses dwelled, for she was no longer part of this world.

Donovan watched her, entranced, as the music throbbed through his body, pushing through every nerve ending until he breathed in the magical notes and it gave him new life. While playing, she imparted a piece of herself, gave that white, shining bit into his keeping whether she was aware of it or not. And it stunned him, not knowing what to do with it, for no one had ever offered such a gift before.

He sat captivated through two additional songs, and then he launched to his feet, had to be with her, needed to touch her. "Alice." His feet didn't move fast enough, and he stumbled to the stage, lurched up the few steps of the rise. "Dear God, you are amazing." A certain reverence filled his voice as he gently maneuvered the harp from her. Then he took her hands and pulled his wife to her feet, tugged her into his arms and brought his mouth crashing down on hers.

They communed without words. There was no need. While she twined her hands around his neck, her magical fingers furrowing through his hair, he drank from her as if she held the last drop of water on Earth and he wanted it. So thoroughly did he kiss her that they remained locked together, pressed into each other, fitting completely until they were seamless in perfection. She filled the spaces in him that were empty and he borrowed from her strength, gave her the same until he hoped she felt as whole as he did in that moment.

He might not love her, but in this kiss, after hearing the exquisite music she'd created, he shared *something* with her he couldn't ignore. No longer was he the same man who'd entered the room earlier. A tiny shift had occurred, and he refused to contemplate what that might mean for his future. For now, he couldn't have enough of the woman in his arms.

He broke the kiss to trail his lips along the underside of her jaw. When she moaned, he held her close, framed her face with his hands while she clutched at his arms, his shoulders, anywhere she could find purchase. "Ah, Alice, you never cease to surprise me." Donovan rested his forehead against hers. When she closed her eyes, he did the same, content to inhale when she exhaled, exchanging the give and take of air, quite literally breathing her in, then when she stirred, he kissed her again, more intensely, chasing her tongue with his, seeking, asking, claiming her until they both panted with need.

"That is an encouraging sign," she responded, her words breathless and she inclined her chin as he dragged his lips down the side of her throat.

"Quite so." Donovan traced the bodice of her gown with his lips, licked the satiny skin. Then he pulled away from her, and when she uttered a protest, he grinned, vaulted off the stage, only to turn, grip her hips and bring her down to him. At her slight squeak, he chuckled. Damn, but he adored the sounds she made. "So very encouraging," he murmured against her lips as he claimed them again in a searing kiss that broke the shackles on his control.

He urged her backward, bent her over his arm in an effort to kiss her so deep that he might reach her soul, and he laid her down upon the polished wood of the stage, her legs dangling, his gaze connecting with hers. In the silver-gray depths of her eyes, the same desire glimmered that rode him, and he kissed her again. Alice fisted one hand in his shirt. The other she slipped to his nape and encouraged him closer.

"I need you, Donovan," she whispered, and the words swept away his hesitation.

Again, he didn't answer with words; he didn't have to. In this moment, there was complete understanding between them. As if he couldn't bear a parting from her lips, he kissed her, made love to her mouth, hinted at what was to come, and slowly, he drew her skirts upward until the fabric bunched at her waist.

His member pulsed with urgency. This joining would go swiftly, but he didn't care. He fumbled with the buttons at the front of his trousers, shoved the panel out of the way and then he gripped her hips, fitting his tip to her ready opening.

"Wrap your legs about my waist, love." He could scarcely force out the words from the tightness of his throat.

A groan escaped him when she followed his command, and he couldn't hold back any longer. Donovan thrust into her snug passage, plunged into her honeyed heat, and for the first time in his adult life, tears pricked the backs of his eyes, for she felt so bloody wonderful around him, as if he was where he was supposed to be all along.

Alice gasped. She squirmed beneath him as he angled along her body, leaning over her for maximum friction. With every movement, hot sensation raced up his member and settled into his stones. She smiled, looking directly at him, and he fell all the harder into the glory that was his wife.

He closed his eyes to block out the adoration in her expression; it was too damning, too guilt inducing, but he wouldn't give up this moment with her. Over and over, he stroked into her body, rocking them both in a rhythm as old as time. Deeper and deeper he drove, wanting to touch all of her. Soon, the urgency riding him changed into blinding need. Donovan dug his fingers into her hips, grunting, hoping that he left marks in her skin—his marks—and he drove into her, wishing to forget what he was, what he'd done, what he still had to do...

Her moans blended with his, and all too soon she shattered in his hold. His name, sweetly uttered upon her lips and keening through the room on the wings of the same notes she'd played earlier, burrowed straight to his soul. As bliss claimed her and she contracted around him, he pushed through the waves that beckoned, grabbed at him, called his name until he, too, surrendered to release and let the heated tide consume him.

As his pulse roared in his ears and sweat plastered his shirt to his back, Donovan thrust once more in an effort to prolong the pure sensations, but he was spent and he collapsed upon her chest, wrapping his arms around her. Alice's heartbeat raced wildly beneath his ear, her breath skated along his cheek and brought him back to Earth. Oh, to have it always like this between them... but how could it when the whole of their life together was based on his lies?

Cold loathing crept in to steal the temporary post-coital euphoria. Biting back a string of vulgarity, Donovan pulled out and away from her body. Only then did he realize he'd been so lost in the moment, in her, that he hadn't attended to the act as closely as he should—he'd spilled his seed inside her. *Bloody hell.* He did up the buttons on his trousers and then sank to the floor, his back against the wall of the stage. Damnation, he was a prick, and she didn't deserve him. Not at all. Yet here they were, both careening down a path from where there was no return. And what if the coupling left her with child?

"Are you well?" Alice righted herself. Seconds later, with the faint scent of apricots stirring in the air, she settled onto the floor beside him. "Tell me what troubles you."

How could she know? But then, she'd always possessed a sixth sense when it came to him. "I apologize for the distraction. Much weighs upon my mind."

"The curse."

"Yes." The word sounded strangled even to his own ears.

"Perhaps we should talk." Alice slipped her arms around him and laid her head on his chest as she snuggled into his side. "What are you dearest hopes for your life? A man must have dreams, after all, for what is the purpose of living without them?"

"Ah, dreams." Her touch, her warmth, her trusting presence with him in the darkened room brought a modicum of comfort. Donovan pulled her into his lap, cradling her in his arms, his cheek against her silky hair, her skirts flowing around them. It was odd, this intimate sharing, cuddling after release had been achieved. With the women before Alice, he either left their residences shortly after, or they left his, for before, there'd been no intimacy in those connections. Bizarre, but this was somehow... addicting. "For the whole of my life, I have focused on being free from the curse."

"But?" She played with a button on his evening jacket. "There is a question?"

"I am struggling morally with the decision." He drew in a deep breath and let it ease out. "Once the curse is gone, so will be my wolf, and how can I live with myself for the rest of my life knowing that I essentially killed a living being for the sake of having a life of my own?"

"While I cannot pretend to understand what such a thing must be like for you, ask yourself this. Does the beast enhance your life? Does he help you better the world around you?"

"I'm not certain." Surely he hadn't used the power of his wolf to do anything for anyone. It was all a selfish intent.

"Ask yourself why you wish to be free of him then."

Finally, his beast roused from the stupor that had calmed him. *Don't you like being with me, human?*

Botheration. Donovan ignored the wolf. "It is a weighty problem to contemplate." No matter what decision he made, someone would hate him, and he would despise himself more.

Alice pulled slightly away in order to peer into his eyes. The concern clouding hers nearly had him undone. "Are *you* making a difference?" When he remained silent, already knowing the answer, she continued. "Wanting to help others in this world but having no power or voice to do that is dismal at best. That is what I struggled with before I married you. However, I plan to do all that I can with my new title."

"You are more noble than I." He attempted to keep bitterness from his voice.

"No, but perhaps I am more resourceful, for I know what it's like to struggle. Wielding massive amounts of influence throughout society, having the reach you do, you are able to affect change, and that is staggering. Discover what you can do instead of despairing on what you cannot because of what you feel holds you back or makes you different."

"But with the wolf, I am unable to—"

Devil Take the Duke (Lords of the Night #1)

"Hush." She laid her fingertips over his lips. "Discover your place in the world, my lord, and find what makes you happy, for life is hard enough if you are your own worst enemy." With a tiny sigh, she settled against his chest. "Despite your affliction, you have great power. You are a duke. Countless peers look up to you. Don't squander your potential on empty pursuits of pleasure."

Silence fell over them as Donovan contemplated her words. There was much soul-searching to do before the full moon arrived. In a rare moment of honesty, he said, "I feel I've started to make a difference by marrying you." Shock moved through his chest. Yes, it was true. "You have helped me change my mindset on a few subjects. And I... I rather like it." What was happening to him?

"How wonderful." Alice moved slightly to look into his eyes. Her smile could have brightened the whole of London-town, and that gesture echoed deep in his heart, where he captured that light to use later when he was without hope—without her. As before when he'd made love to her, *something* passed between them, and their relationship shifted again.

"It is, quite," he whispered with a grin of his own. He encouraged her head down upon his shoulder once more and he held her tighter.

Perhaps there was a chance for him after the full moon. Mayhap she would stay. Did he want her to? His whole life would transform, and he wasn't certain he wished it to, for it would mean a pain more exacting than going through the shift into the wolf.

Yet without change, there was no growth. A conundrum of a different kind indeed.

CHAPTER FIFTEEN

September 29, 1815

Life kept Alice busy as the ball—and the full moon—approached.

Yesterday, the duke spent his day away from the house as business occupied his attention. That night before dinner, he disappeared to parts unknown, and she suspected he ran as the wolf, though he didn't confirm it when she'd asked at breakfast this morning.

Was that a part of life she'd need to come to terms with if the curse didn't break? It definitely needed consideration. Married to a man who became a beast, regularly missed meals for the wide-open spaces and chasing down livestock, delighted in the times they came together carnally yet didn't know exactly what occurred when he was the wolf. Wife to a man whose devotion was split. If he'd ever come to care for her, would that make a difference?

That afternoon, Alice drooped with fatigue and rested in the family's private parlor, recovering from the rigors of a seventh fitting for her ball gown in two days. Elizabeth occupied a settee across from hers with a sheaf of papers in her hand.

"Your lady's maid is meeting with the housekeeper as we speak. If she passes muster, she will be installed and available for your use this evening."

Alice nodded. "I look forward to it." The young woman, not much older than twenty, had come recommended from the Mayfair household of a friend of Elizabeth's. Her name was Mary, and she was a bright, energetic person who had infinite patience and didn't treat Alice differently due to her vision impairment. What was more, Mary's younger brother suffered from blindness of his own, a different sort than Alice's. "She and I will get on well together."

"I feel that, too." Elizabeth referred to another paper. "Regarding the ball, here is a list of things outstanding that you'll need to look over and either approve or reject." She began reading out various subjects, and Alice's mind wandered.

Certain aspects of being a duchess overwhelmed her. How did other women manage it? A niggle of cold fear threaded through her insides. What would become of her life once Elizabeth relinquished the organization of tasks to her? Eventually, her sister-in-law would want to follow her own dreams. Alice forced a swallow into her tight throat. Of course, there was every possibility that once her husband was free of the curse after the full moon, he'd have no more use for her anyway…

A prickle of tears stung her eyes. She'd thought that after what they shared in the music room, things would have been different, that he might have come to care for her above and beyond his affliction.

Why do I continue to hope for things that never come to pass?

"Leave off with badgering my wife, if you please, Elizabeth."

Alice blinked away the want to cry as Donovan came into the room. Though he was but a blob in her white-fuzzed vision, she straightened her spine while silly little trembles of excitement bounced through her. "What are you doing here?"

"I live here." He came closer, now a blob of bottle green from his jacket. A tan blob made its presence known in the form of his breeches.

"No, I mean… I presumed you'd have business today that demanded your time."

He took her hand and gently tugged her into a standing position. "I have managed to clear my schedule." The duke brought her hand to his lips and kissed the back of it. "I wish to take you driving. In my open carriage since the afternoon is lovely, and it *is* the fashionable hour."

"That is a splendid idea, Donovan," Elizabeth enthused. "I've hoped you'd circulate through society on a more regular basis now that you're married. It will go a long way into removing the stigma attached to your title."

He grunted. "I'm not sure anything can help in that quarter. However, I'm willing to enter the nest of vipers for Alice's behalf. It's not her fault she married a cursed lord."

"Why would you do this now?" She couldn't help narrowing her eyes. "This is suspect—you have nothing to gain except perhaps a more positive reputation." So again, he would use her to further his own agenda. The offer of a drive had nothing to do with romance.

Both he and Elizabeth laughed. His sister said, "It seems she's not one to let you use flattery or charm any longer to coerce her."

"Why would I do this?" He tightened his hold on her hand. "Honestly, I wish to show you off to the city. I cannot wait until the ball for London to see my beautiful bride." No trace of dissembling rang in his voice.

Despite knowing he only did or said such things to further solidify her affections for the purposes of the curse, her heart trembled. His spicy, citrus scent worked to draw her into his web. "I should at least change clothes." She simply wasn't ready for London society, however informal the meeting.

"Pish posh, my dear." Donovan lifted her arm and gave her a twirl that set the skirts of her pink day dress flaring. The tails of the white satin ribbon fluttered. "You will steal all the men's hearts and make the women green with jealousy just as you are."

Elizabeth tittered. She laid her folio aside. "It's rare my brother is so eloquent or even teasing when he has nothing to gain. Best take advantage of this, Alice."

For the moment, her worries fled. "I think he's adorable." His words and attention might be more of the same to keep her happy and content so she'd break the curse for him, and she would allow herself the dream that he might change. She hated having to second-guess every aspect of their life together, but he seemed so earnest and genuine…

"See, Elizabeth, I'm adorable," he joked. "You should take notes. I'm not as frustrating or hopeless as you thought."

His sister uttered an unladylike snort. "Oh, but you are, brother. Make no mistake." There was a smile in her voice.

Alice loved the interaction between them. "Will you accompany us, Elizabeth?"

"Oh, no. I want no part of Donovan's spectacle, for he'll no doubt do up the romance while he has you on display. It'll be quite sickening, mark my words." She laughed. "I'll see to a few of these last-minute tasks, so you won't need to."

"Thank you." Her voice wavered. "All of these things threaten to pull me under and drown me. I don't know where I'd be without your help."

Donovan slipped an arm about her waist. "One might become a duchess overnight, but one doesn't learn how to actually *be* one until time has passed." He fit his lips to her ear. "You are doing splendidly."

A blush burned in her cheeks. "I am trying my best."

"That is all I have ever asked." Then he escorted her from the room, but the words didn't alleviate her worries.

Driving through Hyde Park in an open carriage was much different than when he'd taken her out in his curricle that seemingly long-ago day. It was more exciting. The crush of carriages on the street slowed their progress, and the shouts of greetings blended with the low buzz of excited conversations all around them.

"Is all of London here?" Though she had a light wrap about her shoulders, the slight chill of autumn sent a shiver through her.

"Could be. I usually avoid the park at this time of day," Donovan responded with humor clinging to his voice. "And, in the event you are wondering, yes. There are plenty of eyes on you, so smile and pretend you are happy with your life."

She turned her face toward him, leaned close enough to catch the wink of the emerald stick pin in the pristine, snowy folds of his cravat. "I *am* happy, Donovan."

"Because you married me?"

"That's part of it, of course. I feel pulled out of the shadows now that I'm with you, but I was happy in my life before you came along." She placed her hand over his free one that rested on his thigh. "If a person isn't happy with current circumstances and themselves, they will never find that or contentment with what comes after."

"You are all too wise, my sweet country flower. And that is dangerous to a man of my position, for it sets me to thinking." His shoulder brushed hers as he manipulated the reins.

"Introspection is oftentimes cleansing." Alice smiled. In the short time she'd known him, he'd grown, even if he didn't see it. She didn't wish to change him into something different entirely, merely to enhance what he already was.

Even if he's a wolf part of the time?

She didn't have answer for that. How could she accept his other life when that persona labored beneath a curse, but how could she not, when both halves of him made up the duke that he was, the man she loved?

And if she couldn't, did that mean she didn't love him enough?

"The fact you find peace in your life despite everything intrigues me. I almost envy you." He kept his voice low, for there wasn't any privacy in the crush of vehicular traffic. At times carriages stopped alongside theirs on both sides and greetings were exchanged, interrupting conversation. During a lull, he said, "My father never came to terms with the curse." When she drifted as close as she dared in such a public setting, she caught the tick of a muscle in his clean-shaven jaw. "He never understood how to balance the two halves of himself. This alienated my mother. She loved him, but he couldn't keep out of his own head enough to return her regard. Perhaps their union became a casualty of the curse, for it does state all males are destined to live their lives unloved."

She thrilled that her husband deemed it wise to open up to her. "I'm sorry to hear that. My parents, on the other hand, showed their love often. Anytime they could, they held hands or shared kisses, regardless of who was around." A smile tugged at her lips. "I liked seeing their obvious affection for each other. It was... encouraging, gave me hope for my own life. Of course, my father, though connected loosely to the *ton*, wasn't nearly as high on the instep as yours, but titles shouldn't matter where love is concerned."

Donovan remained silent for some time as he navigated traffic. "You were loved, felt that love, as a child?"

"I did. Until my parents died. After I went to live with the baron, I didn't experience any such thing again. It was a lonely time, and I had difficulties adjusting."

"Understandable." He squeezed her fingers. "My childhood was much different than yours. Father gave his wolf control more days than not. He wasn't home much, chose to spend his days at the country estate, for he'd been black balled in the House of Lords, so he had no obligations to spend time in London. The title is still not accepted."

"Except his wife was there." His must have been a sad and dismal life with his parents so broken.

"Yes. Mother tried, but Father couldn't—wouldn't—let her in. He kept to himself, tortured by the beast and knowing there was no escape. It made for a dreadful childhood, especially when I suffered the same fate."

"He didn't help you, guide you through the awfulness of shifting?" Was that how all *ton* families worked? Fingers of anxiety clawed at her insides. Would Donovan act the same if they had children?

"No. He was riddled with self-loathing and anger. He allowed no one close. Mother, Elizabeth, and I were left to our own devices until the day Mother died attempting to birth my brother. Perhaps losing them both helped to drive my father further over the edge." Donovan released her hand, and then was distracted by a greeting from someone he apparently knew.

"Is that the fate you are heading for?" she asked in a small voice and leaned away from him. "Losing control and shunning life?"

"I don't know." He offered nothing else.

Wisely, Alice kept her own counsel. She tipped her face to the sun and reveled in the warmth.

After a while, he resumed his story. "Living as the wolf wreaked havoc on my life, especially as I grew into a man. By then, Mother had disengaged from life and Elizabeth was away at finishing schools. I was angry, unsure... randy as hell once I'd returned from the war." He laughed, but there was no bitterness in the sound, only memories. "As a duke's son and heir, women showed interest in me. I explored." He shrugged. "I sowed wild oats, many of them. Such... activities appeased the beast for a time, since I'd had my fill of fighting, killing men in battle."

She didn't wish to hear this, didn't want to know the sordid details of his life before her, but it had helped make him into the man he was today.

"Did you fall in love?" Mindful of Elizabeth's story, she didn't say more.

"Yes." The word sounded pulled from him. "Shortly after I came into the title, I met a woman, bedded her, fell hard for her." His voice took on an edge she'd not heard before, and it frightened her. "Compelled by the curse to tell her of my affliction, I proposed to her and after my declaration, I revealed everything."

"And she left you." Alice's heart throbbed in sympathy for him. "That is why you only wish for shallow relationships and have had a string of mistresses." Then she gasped. "You refuse to engage your heart for fear of being hurt again." *He will never love me.*

"I'm sorry." The whispered response stabbed through her chest.

"So am I." She scuttled further away on the bench until she butted against the side of the carriage. Tears threatened, and she fought them, unwilling to embarrass herself or him by becoming a watering pot in public.

The carriage stopped once more in the crush. "Alice, please come back." Emotion graveled his voice. "This life is difficult enough without feeling censure from you—my wife." He cleared his throat, lowered his voice. "This isn't about making a public appearance or a united front. This is about me telling you my history and hoping you'd understand me better." A note of desolation crept into his tone. "I have few friends within the *ton*. I'd hoped… you could be one of them."

If she wasn't already in love with him, she tumbled headlong into that state now. He was so broken but yearned for acceptance, the same as she. "Oh, Donovan." Alice slid back to his side and took possession of his hand. "Of course I'm your friend." Despite being surrounded by prying eyes, she raised his hand and kissed a gloved knuckle. "Tell me of the people who are closest to you, of the Earl of Devon. He is a friend, yes?"

"Yes." There was no mistaking the grin in his voice. "He's my oldest friend, around my age. We grew up together, for there are a handful of accursed titles in the *ton*. Naturally, those families associated with each other since we are all outcasts from proper society."

"What," she dropped her voice as the sound of close-driving carriages increased. "What is his affliction? Is it the same as yours?"

"No. We all suffer differently. He is a vampire."

"How utterly fascinating. I had no idea when we met at the wedding breakfast." This world she'd married into was shocking, of course, but intriguing as well. It went beyond fairy stories into something real and raw and painful. "I'm glad there are people you rely and depend on. You are lucky in that regard."

He grunted. "Fortunate is never something I associate with myself."

"You should start. It could be much worse." She squeezed his fingers. "Tell me about your wolf."

Donovan blew out a breath. "No one has ever cared about the beast before."

"I do."

"I believe you." He threaded their fingers together. "He leans toward being sarcastic. He's extremely loyal. He loves to run, hates the city. He likes you."

"What?" She started. "He knows about me?"

"Of course. He's always in my head, always talking to me, arguing with me, like a damned furry conscience, but when I shift, he is fully in control, and once blood comes into play…"

"You lose yourself to the unique madness of being the beast," she finished for him. Alice moistened her lips, and even as her heart pounded, she leaned closer to him and asked, "Will you let me see you in that form?" Now that she was beginning to understand him, she wished to know how to make his life better or more endurable.

His Adam's apple bobbed with a hard swallow. "Do you wish to experience it?"

Did she? "Yes." She nodded. "If I am to accept you—all of you—I want to know everything, see you as you are."

"Ah, Alice." Donovan squeezed her fingers. "You may, but after the ball. I don't wish for you to hate me for it."

Before she could reply, someone hailed him from the street.

"Ho there, Manchester!"

Since the carriage was already halted, Donovan half-turned toward the voice. "Rogue. How serendipitous to find you here." To her he said, "It is the Earl of Devon." Then to the other man, he asked, "How is it that I find you out and about in the daylight, beneath the sun?"

"I am well enough cloaked, and I've had fashioned spectacles with tinted glass that shield my eyes. Makes for better tolerance." He chuckled. "Meet me at Gunter's, old chap," the other man said. "I'll secure us a table and we'll have a chat. A pleasure to see you again, Lady Manchester."

Alice waved in his direction while Donovan attempted to guide his carriage through the crush in order to park along the curb.

Her first time at the renowned bakery and sweet shop in Berkeley Square, Alice sat captivated at a darling little round table with her husband and the earl. Eating sorbet of all things. The frozen lime concoction danced upon her tongue in a burst of tartness, and she exclaimed upon it so enthusiastically that the men laughed at her.

"I've never had such a confection before," she said by way of explanation.

"Enjoy it," Donovan encouraged as he sipped at a glass of lemonade.

"It's refreshing to see such genuine delight in the *ton*. Too often the ladies of our acquaintance are bored with life, have no interest," the earl said. He leaned closer so that he might enter her line of sight—had Donovan told him the extent of her vision loss? "How are you adjusting to married life, Lady Manchester?"

It was odd, hearing her title, but she replied as honestly as she could. "It's an emotional quagmire that has glimmering moments of wonderful embedded within it."

The other man chuckled with indulgence. "Ah, then the duke has told you of his secret?"

She drummed her spoon against the remainder of her treat. "Yes, as well as his need of me at the full moon."

"I thought we had an understanding, dearest, that we would keep facts of our married life to ourselves," Donovan interrupted. He tapped a piece of sponge cake against her lips. "Sample this. It's marvelous."

She rolled her eyes as she accepted his offering, no doubt to stem her words.

The earl laughed in earnest. "The best of women will always keep their men on their toes." He continued to chuckle while Alice chewed and swallowed the cake. "In the event the curse isn't broken, you'll still have the wife, Donovan. I hope you'll appreciate her."

Her husband grunted. "I'm well aware of what the future entails if I cannot lift the curse."

Trepidation climbed her spine, and suddenly her appetite for the remainder of her sorbet fled. Obstacles had already peppered their union. What were his plans for her after the full moon? It was a subject they'd danced around but never discussed.

The earl leaned toward her husband. "There are worse things than having a woman who loves you by your side, despite the affliction. I envy you, Manchester." Longing roiled through his warm tone.

Devil Take the Duke (Lords of the Night #1)

On impulse, Alice touched the man's hand, and Donovan growled, much to her amusement. Was he... jealous? "Promise me when you court your lady for the same purpose you don't begin your relationship with lies. Trust, once broken, is difficult to regain."

"Note taken." When she nodded, he continued. "I fear the year draws short for me."

A slow smiled curved Alice's lips. "There is always Elizabeth to consider. She's wonderful."

Donovan straightened beside her. "My sister does not need such a life." His tone brooked no argument. "I wish a match for her with a *human* man."

"She is stronger than you assume, Donovan," Alice protested. "And if you can marry but are only partially human, why cannot your sister fall in love with a cursed man?"

"That is not up for debate." A warning growl went through his voice.

The earl cleared his throat. "Perhaps at one time there might have been something between us, but now it's impossible. Elizabeth and I share history that isn't exactly pleasant."

"Oh?" A strong note of annoyance had entered Donovan's voice. "Such as? She's never said so to me."

"It is a private matter and a story for another time. I should go." The earl stood. He brought Alice's hand to his lips and kissed her gloved fingers. "However, I shall see you at the ball."

"Perhaps we will have more time to visit then," Alice said. Now that she knew how close this man was to her husband, she wished to cultivate a friendship of her own with him, to better understand Donovan.

"I look forward to it." He released her hand and addressed her husband once more. "By the by, Lady Cecily sends her regards. I saw her briefly in passing last night at the opera."

Alice frowned. Who was Lady Cecily?

Donovan's growl was more pronounced and riddled with annoyance. "Lady Cecily can buggar off for all I care. She and I are done. Elizabeth threw out the belongings she left behind."

Ah, she'd been his last mistress, but his assurance that she was no longer in his life prevented a blue mood.

The earl chuckled. "Good to hear, old chap. I much prefer the woman in your life now."

"As do I, and in the event you wondered, she is taken, Rogue."

"Don't I know it."

When he departed, Alice took Donovan's hand. "How can I help soothe your ruffled feathers?"

He snorted. "I'm a wolf, my dear, not a goose. I have fur not feathers." But he grinned, which prompted one of her own. "Perhaps we shall enjoy the afternoon before returning home for tea. I find I'd like to further stake my claim to you since Rogue had the audacity to touch you without my permission."

A delighted laugh escaped her before she could recall it. Yes, her husband was jealous, and she rather liked it. A man didn't fall into the grip of such emotion without being somewhat attached to a lady. "I wouldn't say no to another bite of sponge cake."

"I live to serve," he murmured, but there was a certain note of satisfaction in his voice.

CHAPTER SIXTEEN

September 30, 1815

It was well after midnight when Donovan returned from a run as the wolf. Despite the late hour, he ordered a bath, needed to wash the blood and grime from his person, for his beast had been particularly intent on hunting this night.

As he stood from the dirty water and stepped from the copper hip bath, the door to his temporary room opened and Alice came into the room. The soft *snick* of the panel closing echoed in the silence.

Clad in frothy, lace-trimmed night garments of silver satin, she resembled a creature made of fairy tales in the light of the single, flickering candle that rested on a rose-inlaid table near his tub. "Good evening, Donovan."

Tendrils of surprise threaded through him. "I thought you were sleeping." He grabbed a towel from the back of the bathtub and hurriedly wrapped the cloth about his waist.

She moved toward him, her skirts whispering over the floor. "I was, but the rain woke me and I wondered what had become of you." Even in the shadows, the blush on her cheeks was evident. "I thought you might visit…"

Was there any more adorable woman than her? Alice's appetite and enthusiasm for marital relations kicked his own hunger up a notch. His member twitched to life. "I apologize. The day was eaten by business endeavors I couldn't beg off from, and then the beast demanded my attention."

"You missed dinner."

"I know. When the wolf calls, there are times when I cannot ignore him." He didn't mention the metal claw traps laid in the woods around Shalford. Someone hunted him, which wasn't an issue if he stayed away from the area. Still, it was troubling. But there were other rural counties rich with livestock.

His wife took another few steps toward him. "Are you tired?" Her eyes, wide and sparkling, were shadowed in the candlelight. What did she think of such a frank discussion?

"Not more than usual." Shifting took a toll on his body and left him exhausted most of the time. He eyed her as she crept closer. Her brown hair, glimmering with highlights in the dim illumination, flowed down her back in mussed waves, tied back with a simple with ribbon. So innocent yet so seductive. A shudder of need ripped up his spine. "Ah, allow me a few minutes to dress, and then perhaps you might accompany me to the kitchens? I'm famished after the run."

She'd drifted close to him, reached out a hand and cupped his cheek. "Please don't cover your body just yet," she whispered. Her pupils had dilated, a clear hint of how she felt. She rubbed her palm along the stubble covering his jaw, went so far as to draw the inside of her wrist against those short hairs. Hunger reflected in her face.

"What... what are you doing?" The words were tugged from a tight throat as her feather-light touch heightened the awareness he always had every time she came near. Every hair on his body stood to attention.

"Exploring you since I've not had the opportunity to really see my husband." She stood in front of him, smoothing her palms along the sides of his neck and sweeping her hands along the breadth of his shoulders. With each glance of her fingers, need shuddered through him. Hints of something deeper, stronger pulled at his heart.

"Do you like what you see?" he couldn't help asking, for vanity demanded she acknowledge his face and form.

"Very much so." She ran those digits through the mat of hair on his chest, and she sighed. "I adore how hairy you are. It's so crisp, coarse. I cannot stop petting you."

He alternately wished she would and would not, for he craved her touch.

Alice took his hand and guided him away from the bathtub into a clear space. Then she returned to her exploration by slipping behind him and smoothing her hands over the planes of his back. She gasped as she squeezed his biceps. "You are quite lean, muscled, powerful." His wife ran her palms over his skin, and with every pass his need for her grew. When she pressed her mouth to his left shoulder and lightly nipped him, an involuntary moan escaped him.

"Do you know what you do to me?" he asked in a barely-there whisper. He stood still, not daring to move and break the spell she wove over him.

She smiled against his skin, and he felt every bit of that gesture. "Perhaps you are not the only one who can master a seduction." Alice remained behind him, tracing her fingertips down his spine, and when she plucked at the towel, it fell away from his waist to land on the floor at his feet. Then her hands slid over his hips, holding him, measuring him, and when she gripped his arse cheeks, he sucked in a sharp breath. "Such beauty of form." A trace of awe lingered in her voice. "You resemble a statue of a Roman god I once saw in the baron's home."

"Alice..." His length hardened. "Please." Was it a plea for her to cease her ministrations or for her to let him take her into his arms?

Finally, she came back around until she faced him, and she smiled as she cupped his equipage in her soft palm.

Damnation, he would spend if he wasn't careful.

But his wife wasn't done with her torment. She fondled his bits before leaving off and kneeling. She swept her hands up and down his legs, glanced her fingertips along the inside of his thighs, exploring every inch of him. When she reached his ankles, she came back up until she finally paused with her hands primly folded in her lap.

"Well?" The question was breathless, dancing over the last of his control. Donovan furrowed his fingers into her hair in an effort to do something that wasn't throwing her to the floor and having his way with her.

"Most satisfying." She tilted her face upward, her gaze connecting with his even though he knew she couldn't see him. "Please shift into the beast for me."

"No." He shook his head. "Not now." They were newly married, and he'd rather lie with her than show her the unsavory side of himself. Doing so might tip his hand... or force hers.

The pout upon her kissable lips nearly undid him. "Please, Donovan. I need to see you in wolf form." She placed a hand on his knee, the heat of her seeping into him. "In order for me to understand all of what you are burdened with, I must see the other side of you."

"It will change your mind about me, about the curse." He curled his free hand into a fist. Everything would turn to muck once she saw...

"Or it will firm my decision to help you." Alice gained her feet. She framed his face with her palms, put her forehead to his and peered into his eyes. "I love you, Donovan. Through everything, that hasn't changed. I want to see you in your entirety." After brushing his lips with hers, she said, "Please. I'm made of stronger stuff than you think. I won't cower or run away." She traced his bottom lip with her thumb. "I promised you my fidelity, and you will have that for as long as you need, but don't shut me out."

The sincerity in her voice, her manner, pulled him under. He longed for the sanctuary she represented but life had taught him not to hope, for women were fickle. Yet the longer he stood before her, his gaze locked on hers, the more he wanted to believe. His pulse throbbed through his being in both fear and anticipation.

She wishes to see you, human, to see me, his wolf urged, adding fuel to his confusion.

Can I survive if she reacts to me with horror or pity?

There is only one way to tell, came the canine response. Then, cheeky bastard that he was, he added, *what does it matter if you don't care for her anyway?*

Cheeky bastard. Finally, he nodded. "Step away. At times the beast is startled if there is someone too near when I complete the shift."

When Alice did as he asked, Donovan sighed. Anxiety twisted through his gut. No one, not even his sister, had known him thusly, let alone seen him, as the wolf. Rogue had on occasion, for they were both creatures of the night, but no one human had. It was a personal choice, and it was frightening as hell. But for one brunette beauty with big eyes and a bigger heart, he would break his own rule.

Then he called the shift.

Agony descended. Bones snapped and broke as they formed into a canine. Internal organs re-ordered themselves to fit the new, smaller body. Networks of blood vessels and nerves reformed, spreading out through growing limbs. His nose elongated. Teeth were ripped out and grew again to fit the new lengthened jawline. A tail sprouted where there was none. Fur populated and pushed through skin until the new canine form was covered with brownish ruddy hairs. Ears and eyes resituated on a new skull until finally, painfully, he became the wolf.

A low, warning growl echoed through the room as he shook his head and trained his wolfish eyes on Alice. Donovan ruffled his fur, his hackles raised at finding himself inside a house, which was not the place for a wild animal. The sense of being trapped filled him and he took a few steps toward her—the woman who'd insisted he become the beast. He bared his teeth. Did she wish him harm?

"Hush now," she whispered, her eyes wide with fear and a hand outstretched. To give her credit, she held her ground, but her hand shook.

He paused, waiting, his eyes narrowed, his muscles tensed to run or attack as the whim took him. It was odd, this pausing to gauge her reaction. If she ran, would he give chase?

Want her to run with us.

Donovan snorted, and Alice started. She came forward another step, nearly touching him now. *How the devil do you think she could do that? We'd outpace her soon after the chase began. She is human and will be for the rest of her life.* While he only had a chance of the same, depending on her love and a full moon and an ancient gypsy witch's will.

She is good, will save us, his wolf insisted.

Donovan huffed, narrowed his eyes further. *From what, the curse? If so, you will cease to exist.*

Then Alice kneeled on the ground until she was at eye level with him. She brought her face close to his, apparently not caring about his growl or his teeth, and she cupped the side of his wolfish face. "Oh, Donovan, you poor thing. The shift, it hurt you, I could hear it... feel it."

His wolf, in control, answered with a whine. But then he snapped at her fingers, growled again in warning, for no one dared to touch him as the wolf.

"None of that," she quietly instructed with a tap to his snout that had him uttering a whine and dipping his front half down slightly in submission.

What the hell? I do not bow to anyone as the wolf. What had the woman done to him?

"That's better. No need to get ugly because you're afraid." Tears sparkled in her expressive eyes. The silver flecks danced within the irises. "I had no idea. What you've dealt with your whole life staggers me." Just as she had when he'd been in human form, she explored his wolf body with her hands and fingertips. "I knew when you saved me that first morning of our meeting it wasn't a dog that pushed into me."

Her fingers riffling through his fur gave him pause. A novel sensation to be sure. Donovan cocked his head, his gaze still connected to hers. What did she think about, seeing her husband reduced to an animal—a beast? His heart lurched. Did she think less of him?

"This is..." She traced his snout, his ears, his wolfish eyebrows. "*You* are amazing." Awe hung on her words and mirrored in her eyes.

He sat on his haunches as a numbed sort of shock filled him. His wolf, on the other hand, yipped in the beginning stages of excitement.

"It's remarkable, this change," she continued as she examined him: paws, tail, teeth, snout, ears. Everywhere she touched she left tingles of awareness behind as if her fingers revitalized him somehow. "It is unreal, and I would never believe it if I wasn't seeing it myself." A little laugh escaped her. "Well, not exactly seeing in the traditional way."

When she held out a hand, Donovan placed a front paw into her palm. *She is not afraid.* He couldn't wrap his brain around the evidence of his own eyes.

She is our mate. There is no fear in one fated for us.

It wasn't fate that brought her to us. I manipulated the situation. I played a game with her, used her so her love will free me at the full moon. The knowledge tightened his chest, and even in wolf form, he hated himself.

You wouldn't have found her if not for fate, the wolf continued, adamant something beyond himself was at play.

Then Alice leaned forward and pressed her lips to the fur between his eyes. She sat back on her heels with a wobbly smile and released his paw. "You are truly a wolf. Incredible." Then she gasped and lowered her voice. "If the *ton* discovers your secret... If society knows, you will be captured, locked in an institution. That is worse than the curse."

Donovan shook his head. His wolf whined. How could he make her understand that the legends and rumors made certain no one of consequence

Devil Take the Duke (Lords of the Night #1)

socialized with him enough to delve deeper into the truth? He wished it to remain that way, and in essence keep everyone safe.

She glanced at him again and tears shimmered in her eyes. "Please be careful. I cannot lose you due to this." A few of the crystalline drops fell to her cheeks.

He crept closer until his front paws touched the skirts of her night dress pooled on the floor. How the devil could he comfort her as the beast?

I know how, his wolf replied. He surged to his feet, almost giddy at the prospect.

Before Donovan could protest, the wolf moved. He put his front paws on Alice's shoulders, and then he licked her face, lapping the tears away, his tail wagging, much to Donovan's eternal mortification.

What in the bloody hell are you doing? We look like nodcocks. Such indignity!

"Oh, you sweet little wolfie," she crooned and giggled as she wrapped her arms around his canine neck to hug him close.

Dear heaven above, I shall die of embarrassment, Donovan vowed, but his wolf didn't pay the slightest attention to him. He tried again while ignoring the sense of safety and comfort cycling through him to feel her arms about him… loving him while he was the wolf. *Has she forgotten I am still a duke and a bloody wolf to boot? I should be feared.*

Then she scratched behind his ears.

What the devil is happening?

Do shut up, human.

He uttered a half-sigh, half-whine, for the scratching felt so damn good. His tongue lolled out of his slightly open jaws, and when she laughed and kissed his nose, he bumped her chin with the top of his head.

I want her, he told his wolf. Never had he given a woman such access to his private life before, and never had anyone ever accepted him—all of him—with such enthusiasm.

You know what to do, his wolf reminded him with a new level of cheek he hadn't shown before. He licked Alice's face again and with a push, she tumbled backward onto the Oriental rug. She laughed as he lay on top of her, stretching out so he covered her like a thick, furry blanket. And through it all, she kept hold of him, petting him, soothing him, loving him like no other person had ever done before.

He couldn't wait any longer. Donovan called the shift, and when it concluded and exhaustion seeped into his limbs, he didn't care. He held his wife in his arms and joined in on her laughter. How long had it been since he unbent and allowed such carefree behavior reign? It removed the fear and confusion from the transformation, made the pain and tiredness fade. His heart squeezed, and he lost a piece of it to her in that moment.

"You, my lord, are quite magnificent," she whispered and held his face between her palms while staring into his eyes.

With his forehead pressed to hers, he grinned. "As the animal or as the man?" His length tightened insistently against her belly.

"Both." The huskiness of her laugh worked to undo him. "While I prefer the man for obvious reasons, I must say I'm not certain what you'd be like without your other half. It's quite a unique problem to have."

Another wave of shock moved through him, and her sparkling eyes had him tumbling down, down, down into the depths of that gaze. "You aren't disgusted or fearful of him?"

"Not at all." Alice slipped a hand about his nape and pulled him to her for a kiss. "Make no mistake, it's bizarre. But I'm willing to acclimate myself to it because, at the heart of the matter, the wolf is you and you are him. Now that I've seen you transform, there is no delineation."

Donovan stared at her as if seeing her for the first time. There were no words he could utter equal to what she'd just given him, didn't know what to think, so he did what he excelled at: he proceeded to kiss his wife senseless.

Tonight, he'd make love to her without expectations, lies, or barriers. Tonight, it was only him and her.

CHAPTER SEVENTEEN

October 2, 1815
Night of ball and first night of the full moon

I can hardly believe it.

"I cannot believe this night is finally here," Alice whispered to Elizabeth and her maid, Mary, as they helped put the finishing touches of her ensemble for the evening.

The knowledge that the full moon was upon them made her both giddy with excitement and had tears climbing her throat from the implications. Once the night was through, there would be no turning back—from anything. When the curse was lifted and Donovan became fully human, she couldn't imagine what would happen between them, for it had never been spoken.

"You will certainly make a splash through the *ton* this evening," Elizabeth said with encouragement in her voice. The blob that represented her came colored in deepest navy that sparkled each time she moved.

"It is not society I hope to impress tonight." Nerves bedeviled her belly. The night was important in so many ways. But if she failed to set him free? *Merciful heavens, I cannot worry about that now.*

"The duke won't know what to think of you," Mary whispered as she fussed with the hem of Alice's ball gown. The lavender satin flowed over like water around her. A fine overskirt of sheer white tulle fell from a heavily embroidered bodice. Swaths of white lace embroidered with tiny flowers lined her décolletage and draped over the shoulders. It shimmered in the light. "Love will surely be in his eyes tonight, my lady," the maid breathed with the awe of romance in her tone.

Alice applied herself to the task of drawing on white, elbow-length gloves while anxiety knotted in her stomach. "If only," she whispered to herself.

After he'd shifted into wolf form for her, she'd come to a better understanding of what drove her husband. It had a been a fearsomely wonderful act to witness, but when she'd stared into the eyes of the beast, she'd seen Donovan deep in those amber depths, and if that humanity could still shine forth through the animal, there was hope.

They'd made love on the floor when he transformed back into the form of a man, and the laughter they'd shared warmed her heart, brought them closer, and it gave her hope that perhaps he could indeed come to care for her.

She'd spent yesterday exclusively in his company. He'd taken her on a tour of London, where they visited typical sites of tourist interest. They'd strolled Hyde Park while talking on a variety of topics that had nothing to do with love or his cursed status. During tea, she'd gone over tentative plans for her school, and he'd tweaked them with encouragement and enthusiasm that had warmed her heart. Following dinner, they'd removed to her rooms where they spent the night together, doing what newly married couples did.

It had been a wonderful interlude she hadn't wished to end, but as with everything in life, of course it did. Such devotion from him was naught but an act, a final effort to ensure that she'd fallen so deeply in love with him that there'd be no doubt the curse would lift after the ball.

Alice's chin quivered with the want to cry in frustration and despair. Was his former existence so coveted that he'd throw her over once he was free in order to resume that carefree bachelor's life?

"Don't give into tears so early in the evening," Elizabeth cautioned with the stroke of her fingertips along Alice's cheek. "It'll mottle your complexion and the moisture will stain your gown." She put her face close so that Alice could see. "It'll come out right in the end. You have to believe."

"What if—"

"Hush." Her sister-in-law laid her hands on Alice's shoulders. "Enjoy the moment and the ball. Promise me you won't worry. Otherwise, it's simply too much to take in." With a few soft-spoken words, she dismissed the maid. When she'd gone and the door closed behind her, Elizabeth said, "I know what it's like to think about the bloody curse until you'll go mad. But you mustn't let that prohibit delight in life right now."

"It grows more difficult, for Donovan's actions are confusing." Why did he show such kindness and near-affection if it was all an act?

"He is conflicted, no doubt by his own feelings." Elizabeth smiled and briefly hugged her. "You have done all he has asked. And you've fallen in love with him; he cannot fault you for any of it."

Yes, she was irrevocably in love with the duke. He'd been the first man to look past her blindness and accept her as she was, let her test her wings and her abilities without stifling her. "He has moments when I think he might return those feelings, but then he speaks of the curse and how much he wants it gone, and I'm plunged again into indecision."

"He is a man, and men, for all their other wonderful qualities, do not often think with their hearts. Do keep that in mind." Elizabeth shrugged and then stepped away. "I want a happy life for you and my brother. Everyone deserves love."

"I believe that too." Even Donovan's wolf, for if the curse wasn't broken, the beast would still remain.

"What happens now is out of your hands, so you might as well have a nice time this evening."

"I shall try." She grasped Elizabeth's hand. "Thank you for what you've done for me. You have helped calm my fears, for jumping into a duchess' role as well as that of a newly married wife and a lifter of a curse is rather daunting."

"I don't know how you've managed it all without completely taking to your bed." Elizabeth squeezed her fingers. "You are a stronger woman than I." She paused and let her hand slide from Alice's. "If I were in your position, loving a man who labored beneath a curse, I'm quite certain I couldn't go the distance. As much as I adore my brother, that life… it's too much to contemplate."

A moment of clarity speared through Alice's worry-clouded mind. "You speak about the Earl of Devon."

"Yes." That one-word whisper sounded pulled from her companion. She cleared her throat. "But that is a tale of another time. Rafe is in my past, and he must stay there for my own sanity, for if I let him in—"

A knock on the door interrupted whatever Alice might say in response. Donovan came into her dressing room, his spicy citrus scent preceding him.

"You don't look half bad, brother," Elizabeth said by of way of greeting. "You might just be deemed respectable yet."

"Ah, that is the hope." Nothing in his voice gave away his mindset.

She touched Alice's shoulder. "I must go and make certain everything is as it should be by the time you and Donovan come downstairs."

"Thank you." The smart *tap tap* of her heels signaled her departure, and then the soft *click* of the door closing left Alice alone with her husband. "I assume you are as handsome this night as you always are," she said by way of introducing light conversation.

"That is for you and our guests to judge." He drifted close to her as a black blob. "However, yes, I look quite fine, and will provide the perfect foil for your beauty."

Tingles of pleasure tripped down her spine. "Silver-tongued devil." He might not love her like she desperately wished he would, but he had shown his affection for her in many ways over the course of their short marriage. Perhaps it was enough.

"Not a devil, love, a wolf." He clasped her hand and drew her into the middle of the room, away from her vanity table and mirror. "You are exquisite, though. All eyes will be on you. I will fade away." There was no mistaking the admiration in his voice.

Warmth filled her. "Will *your* eyes remain on me?" After tonight, would he stray once he had everything he'd dreamed of?

"How could I not look only upon you? Ah, Alice, you are beauty personified, and you still embody my sweet country flower." He tugged her into his arms, caressed his finger along the side of her face, for he'd yet to don gloves. "I brought you a bouquet of roses before I came in. They're on the table in your sitting room."

"You are sweet, Donovan. Thank you." She pressed herself against him and placed a kiss on his chin. "Shall I wear a bloom in my hair as I did on our wedding day?"

"It would be most appropriate." As she looked up into his eyes, his brandy depths darkened, but from what emotion? "First, I wish to give you a gift."

"You have already given me so much," she protested, but he silenced her with the fleeting touch of a finger to her lips.

"You are my duchess, and it is my prerogative to give you baubles." Donovan urged her to turn so that her back was to him. "You need adornment tonight, and pearls are just the thing."

Alice trembled as the coolness of the gems fell against her collarbones when he slipped a strand about her neck. "I've never had pearls." She touched the piece, surprised to feel a pendant at the front. "What is this?" It had the shape of a flower, not more than an inch in circumference.

"A flower that matches your ring. It was also part of my mother's trousseau jewels. I want you to have it, for it speaks your name." He put another strand of pearls into her hand the same time that he kissed the skin where her neck joined her shoulder. "There is also a bracelet, but it is merely pearls without a flower."

Her heart fluttered. She held out her wrist and he took the bauble from her. Then he fitted the pearls around her right wrist, quickly doing up the clasp. "It's too much." He would spoil her if she wasn't careful.

"There are times when I'm certain what I've given you isn't nearly enough." His voice was graveled, and since she couldn't see his face or touch it, she had no idea what emotion gripped him. He let his fingers linger at her nape, her shoulders, and his touch sent awareness skittering through her body. "Shall we go down and greet our guests? I want all of society to know what a wonderful duchess you're becoming."

"Oh, Donovan." Alice turned so quickly her skirts swirled about her ankles. She looped her arms about his neck and swiftly pressed a kiss to his lips. "Whatever happens tonight, know that I love you."

"I do know it." But that was all he said. Instead, he claimed her lips, treated her to long, drugging kisses that made her dizzy and weakened her knees. After a few minutes, he wrenched away and fitted his forehead to hers in an intimate gesture she was beginning to associate with him. "If only things were different..." He tightened his hold at her waist.

"There is no reason circumstances cannot change," she gently reminded him while peering into his eyes. Emotions she couldn't read clouded those depths, emotions he struggled with, kept to himself, and then his lids drifted closed, and she sighed. Cut off from those windows to his soul, she contented herself with fussing over the folds of his cravat, finger-combing strands of his chestnut locks from his forehead. His hair was unruly as ever, falling in waves to his collar, and she liked that he hadn't had it cut to suit convention. Finally, she closed her eyes as well and stood within the circle of his arms.

Why couldn't they remain here for the rest of the night?

Donovan stirred. He slipped from her hold, and she bit her bottom lip to keep from mourning the loss of his closeness. "I'll just nab a rose before we join the festivities."

Alice nodded. Despite the nerves that still fluttered in her belly, she couldn't help but give in to the cold shivers of apprehension trailing up her spine. When he returned and fit the bloom into her upswept tresses over her ear, she sighed. "What color is it?"

"White, for innocence and purity. But when I asked Elizabeth the color of your gown a few days before, I had the florist dye one of these lavender." He fit his lips to her ear and said, "There are also red ones mixed within the arrangement, for passion."

She couldn't help but smile as he threaded her hand through his crooked elbow. A mix of red and white roses also signified unity. Perhaps unconsciously he thought of them together as a force within the *ton*. There might be hope for them yet after the full moon.

Later that hour, Donovan pulled her to the top of ballroom and called the room to attention.

Alice waited with bated breath as she felt the weight of many pairs of eyes focus upon her. Loads of black and colorful blobs representing couples present stood before her. Pinpricks of candlelight danced through the white fuzziness that was her vision and the heat of so many bodies rolled through the room. Scents of perfume, talc, candle wax, and perspiration filled the air. The buzz of conversation trickled off and did nothing to calm the flutter of nerves.

"Thank you all for coming this evening. I'm pleased to see my ballroom filled with friends and acquaintances for what has been a culmination of an astonishing couple of weeks in my life." After a wave of polite acknowledgement swept through the assembly, her husband continued. "It brings me great pleasure to formally introduce you to my wife Alice, the Duchess of Manchester." He squeezed her hand. "She has been a singular bright spot in my life these days, and I look forward to how else she'll transform my life."

On the surface, the words were romantic enough, but only a few of the attending guests knew to what Donovan referred, and Alice quickly fell out of the charm that had poured over her since dressing for the event.

As the clapping and well-wishes faded, Donovan asked, "Shall we open the ball with a waltz?"

"Only if you lead your pretty wife out first," someone called and Alice thought she recognized the speaker as his best friend, Rogue.

Then she swiftly inhaled. Her heartbeat accelerated in panic. *No, no, no! He knows I'm not confident in these steps.*

"Done and done," Donovan responded, and with an arm about her waist, he propelled her over the marble floor until they gained the center of the dancing area. When he encouraged her into the correct posture and the opening strains of a popular waltz emanated from the five-piece orchestra, he flashed a grin. "Remember that night in the mill. Concentrate on me and you'll carry the dance off as if you've been doing it all your life."

He moved and she was swept into the dance, conscious of everyone in the room watching her—watching them. But when he pulled her closer to him and his face came somewhat into view and the earnestness and pride in his brandy depths registered, she relaxed and gave herself into his care.

Here, in the steps of the waltz, with him holding her steady and their bodies flowing as if cut from the same, liquid cloth, she forgot what else the night meant, let herself dream that he might return her love, consider her as more than a way to lift a curse.

Around and around, he whisked her over the floor. Her skirts swished and flared about her ankles. The heady scent of the flower nestled in her hair wafted to her nose. The faint grin flirting with his sensuous lips captivated her; he'd looked devastating when he allowed himself to fully smile as he had two nights ago when he'd shown her his wolfish side. The tiny dimple in his left cheek made itself known, and he winked at her as they took yet another turn about the room.

Other couples joined them on the floor. Soon laughter and conversation flowed, echoing off the walls. Everything passed by in a dizzying blur, but Alice kept her focus on the man holding her, and he reeled her a tiny bit closer in what was quickly becoming a scandalous position.

She didn't care. In this moment, he was completely hers and they moved together as if made exclusively for each other. The sure grip of his hand at the small of her back had her feeling protected. His hand holding hers imparted strength. Her skirts flowed about her legs and his. Each step caused her lower body, her legs to brush against his. That delicate friction sent heat through her and further ignited the fires that had begun when he kissed her after slipping the pearls about her neck.

In short, magic streamed about them and she wished the night would never end. In that tiny bubble, they were perfect for each other.

All too soon, the orchestra ceased playing and the waltz ended. Polite clapping broke out around them, and then Donovan offered his arm and he led her to the sidelines while a new set prepared to engage.

"I must circulate for a bit, but when I return, we'll make full use of the gardens," he whispered into her ear.

And then he was gone.

"Has there ever been a more beautiful duchess than you?" She turned her head toward the sound of a male's voice, and when she frowned, he tentatively touched her hand. "Forgive me. I'm Viscount Mountgarret, a friend of your husband's, but you may call me Valentine." His blob of black came closer and she discerned red hair that tended to curl.

"Is that your given name or an endearment?" The salty scent of the sea merged with the more calming smell of plant life emanated from him. How... odd.

"Sadly, my given name, but most call me Mountgarret, if you'd rather." He held out a gloved hand. "Would you care to dance?"

It would pass the time until Donovan came back, and the beginning of the end of their relationship began. "I would adore that, but you must remember I cannot see, and some of the dances require steps that are beyond me. I'd rather not be left open for gossip fodder."

"Ah, I am not so heartless as to invite the tabbies. Allow me to escort you to the refreshments table," he said in a smooth voice as he guided her hand into the crook of his elbow. "I'll regale you with tales of your husband from earlier in his life."

"Thank you for the kindness." And she smiled. Perhaps life as a duchess wouldn't be such an insurmountable obstacle as she'd thought.

Not long after midnight, Donovan returned to her side as she chatted with Elizabeth and some of Elizabeth's friends.

"Fancy taking in the outside air with me?" he asked as he snaked an arm about her waist. The faint scent of brandy on his breath wafted to her. Had he been playing cards with his friends in the intervening hour or so? But then the aroma of a floral perfume not her own teased her nostrils. Had he danced with other ladies as the host, or had he indulged in a dalliance? "My apologies, ladies, for taking the duchess from you. I only need her for a short time."

"Behave yourself, brother," Elizabeth said, and a warning wove through her voice even though she strove to keep the statement light.

Alice smiled up at him even while twisted through her stomach. His words were telling, and she forced a hard swallow into her suddenly dry throat. "That sounds lovely." *Please, please, please realize we can have a good life together no matter what happens tonight.*

"Capital." He led her about the perimeter of the ballroom, pausing here and there to return greetings. Three sets of garden doors had been thrown open to encourage the cool, autumn air into the room, and he guided her through one of them and onto the balcony beyond. "The moon is the second most beautiful sight tonight," he whispered, and then he ushered her over the stone flooring. "There are three steps," he warned, guiding her until soft grass crushed beneath the thin soles of her slippers, and the sharp crackle of an occasional dried leaf marked their passage.

While the noise of merriment faded into the background the deeper they went into the garden, Alice's heart raced. She clutched at his arm, her thoughts scattered.

"Ah, here we are." The tinkle of moving water gave away a fountain's position and the heavy scent of roses, not yet dead from the cold, filtered to her nose. "Elizabeth tends to a few flowers out here. Gardeners look after the rest, but these around a fountain depicting Aphrodite are my sister's favorites. I think working with her hands keeps her calm."

Alice lifted her face to the moon's glow. The chill in the air cooled her overheated skin and she burrowed into his side. "No doubt it's quite lovely with the moonlight." The whole of their married life came down to these handful of moments. Both excitement and dread mixed in her veins.

"It is. Think of the most wonderful garden frosted with silvery light." He pulled her closer. "I wish you could see it."

"So do I." But she couldn't, and never would. In other circumstances, such a spot would prove romantic, and she'd enjoy it immensely, but now, with her nerves crawling and worry gnawing at her insides, she merely wanted him to get on with it. "Donovan, please. Do not draw this out. I must know…" She swallowed. "…what will happen."

"As do I." He led her a little away from the fountain. "Ah, here. The moonlight is not obstructed with trees, and it pours down upon you." He took her into his arms with a low carol of smug, triumphant laughter. "That lunar power calls to me, Alice. Demands to let my wolf out and run."

She gave into a shiver that didn't come from the autumn chill. "Will you, as a last homage to your beast?"

"No." He layered his forehead against hers and stared into her eyes. "I'm most anxious to send him on his way. Are you ready for your part in this?" Anticipation wove through his voice and sparkled in the brandy depths of his eyes.

My part. All the events leading up to this moment crowded into her mind as well as his motivation in them. Her heart twinged. "Yes."

Devil Take the Duke (Lords of the Night #1)

Even if she wasn't. Everything would change. Her stomach knotted. "I want you to find happiness, and if this gives you that—"

He stopped her words with a kiss so sweet and gentle it brought tears to her eyes. When he pulled away, she wanted to hold her breath, but she had to know.

"Did it work? Can you still hear your wolf?"

"Yes, damn it." Annoyance flashed in his eyes as he stared at her. "Let's try again." He resettled her into his arms. Then he lifted his face to the heavens. "Hear me, gypsy witch, wherever you are. I have met your terms this night. Release your curse." Donovan framed her in his hands and when he kissed her this time, it was a savage meeting of mouths. He took from her, left his undeniable stamp upon her, set her head reeling from the passion in the embrace, but he thrust her from him so hard she stumbled back a few steps in order to regain her balance. "Bloody hell. Why isn't this working?"

"Are you certain you don't need to say anything else?" A trace of fear slid down her spine, for with every passing second, his mood changed into something ugly, primal, untamed.

"The curse clearly states *beneath the light of that one full moon when the kiss of unselfish, pure love crosses your lips...*" He shoved a hand through his hair. "We have done that. Met the requirements perfectly." A growl moved through his voice.

Her eyes widened. "It needs to be you."

"Beg pardon?" It came out around a snarl.

"*You* are the one who needs to be in love during the kiss." Foreboding crawled over her skin. He most certainly wasn't in love with her. He'd spent the whole of their time together making sure she'd fallen, yet the curse didn't have anything to do with her.

"No! I've had years to study the curse, to understand it. That's not true." He grabbed her shoulders, thrust his face close to hers. His eyes roiled with horror and anger. "You've been having me on this whole time, haven't you?"

"I haven't. I swear it." She clutched at his arms, but he wrenched from her hold. "I'm not lying when I tell you I love you. Despite everything, Donovan, you've won me. I've never felt like this before, and I…" She cleared her throat. "I cannot love you with anything more than what I am." A sob escaped. "I've given you my heart."

"It's not enough." When he growled, Alice retreated another few steps. Her back connected with the lip of the fountain. "Do you accept my wolf, too?"

"I…" She didn't like him in this volatile persona. "I am learning to, but it's a process. Seeing you in that form the other night helped draw me closer."

"Damn you, Alice." He paced before her, his heels grinding against the pebbles on the path. "Because you don't accept all of me, the curse won't break. You have wasted my time."

"There is one more opportunity this year." Elizabeth had confirmed what he'd already told her regarding the four chances this year. Her words tumbled on top of each other as all of her dreams crashed like glass around her. "Now that you know what's required of you, spend time with me, truly be my husband, and if you come to love me, you can try again."

His harsh bark of laughter rang with bitterness. "Did you think I wanted you for more than breaking the curse?" Pregnant silence brewed between them as tears sprang into her eyes. "I married you to prevent scandal so that I could bed you properly. I had no intentions of ever fostering a relationship with you; that was never the life I wished for."

Every sentence that fell from his lips plowed into her midsection like a punch. Alice cried out, not able to stifle her sob of helpless horror this time. "I had hoped we'd made progress. All this time when we got on together—"

"Lies, carefully crafted to make certain you were firmly in love with me." He growled again. "I chose the wrong woman, obviously, and now we're both trapped."

Alice gulped in a shuddering breath. Tears fell to her cheeks. What had started as a romantic, hopeful night had turned into a nightmare. She took a few steps toward him, a hand outstretched. "Give us a chance. Try for the future. I love—"

"Don't. Touch. Me." The words were graveled, full of loathing. "You cannot stand what I truly am and that has somehow tainted the love you claim to hold for me." He shook his head. "I don't need you, Alice, never wanted you past what you could do this night, but bravo for playing your part to the hilt. You had me on and all the while, you knew you'd reject me for my affliction, the same as all of them. I'll give you the protection of my name, but we are done."

Hot anger rushed through her to temporarily disrupt the sorrow flooding her. She curled her hands into fists. "Devil take you, Donovan. I gave you my body. I gave you my heart." Her chin quivered as the urge to cry rolled over her. "How can you be so cruel?"

With a string of vulgarity, Donovan apparently called forth the shift. Not being able to see the transformation happen, the sounds of agony he made chilled her to the bone. Then a commanding snarl and growl split the night air. Before she could attempt to soothe him, his paws ground upon the gravel path and he darted from the area, leaving her standing alone in the darkness, her heart breaking into thousands of jagged shards.

She covered her face with her hands and cried so hard her chest heaved. *What do I do now?*

CHAPTER EIGHTEEN

October 4, 1815

Donovan maintained a rotten temper for two days following the ball. He spent most of that time as the wolf, giving the beast control, terrorizing the countryside, not caring what happened to him.

And he'd not gone home, he couldn't.

Alice's last words to him rang in his ears. *Devil take you, Donovan.* He cringed as he skulked about the streets of Mayfair toward the direction of his club. *How can you be so cruel?* The disappointment in her voice, every word she'd hurled, pierced his chest like the sharpest of arrows. But what haunted him the most was the fading joy in her eyes, the love he'd always glimpsed there dimming.

I deserve her ire and her wrath. He'd shamelessly used her in the basest of ways, manipulated her feelings so she'd fall for him, pretended he'd cared when he'd had no intentions of keeping her in his life beyond that damn full moon.

You deserve a slap in the face, human. However, I am glad the curse wasn't broken, for I still retain life.

Donovan refused to answer his animal. At least that failed moment had prevented a murder of sorts. Quickly, he padded through the near-empty streets, and when he gained his club, he transformed into a human in an alley at the rear then slipped inside from a servant's door.

A half hour later, he'd taken a bath and then dressed in the rooms set aside for his use. Then he gained the common room and threw himself into a chair at his favorite table. Even at this hour, attendance surged, and ordinarily it would have uplifted his mood, for that helped fill coffers, but in his current frame of mind, he wished every one of those people gone. All the better to sulk in silence. When a serving woman brought his customary brandy bottle and a crystal tumbler, he snarled his thanks and poured a healthy dose of the amber liquid into the glass.

Mountgarret spied him. He approached the table with wariness in his eyes but sat when bid. "I must say that I'm shocked to see you here." The viscount declined a drink and the server sauntered away, hips swishing. "After the way you danced and flirted with your wife at the ball, I assumed you'd have business in someone's perfumed arms now that the curse is lifted."

Donovan grunted. Damn his friend for knowing his life so well. "Where's Rogue?"

The viscount shrugged. "Upstairs taking nourishment." His eyes gleamed nearly turquoise. "You're troubled, more than usual. What has occurred?"

"Much." Donovan emptied the contents of his tumbler in one, large gulp. His eyes watered as the sting of alcohol hit the back of his throat. Restless, he drummed the fingers of his free hand on his thigh. When his wolf tried to punch into his thoughts, Donovan shut him out. He needed to talk to Alice, hear her voice of reason, know that she still loved him despite his behavior, feel the touch of her hand, perhaps listen to her play the harp and soothe his ragged feelings, but after how he'd acted, after the words he'd hurled at her in anger and confusion, how could he even present himself to her?

Hot shame surged through him, and he poured another measure of brandy into his glass. "Dear God, Mountgarret, I have mucked up everything."

That was the single most honest thing he'd uttered in the last fortnight.

Mountgarret eyed him with speculation. He sat back in his chair and rested an ankle on a knee. "Perhaps you should narrow that term. It could refer to a host of subjects."

"With Alice." Again, he downed the drink, only this time he didn't pour out more. He set the tumbler on the tabletop with a thump.

"Ah." The viscount nodded. "I happened to talk with your lovely wife while you were busy doing the pretty at the ball. She's knowledgeable on a myriad of subjects, and a shocking one in particular." His gaze bore into Donovan's. "She confessed that she'd seen you shift."

He shrugged, not even summoning caring to utter a verbal response.

"How did she react?"

Why wouldn't the damned viscount leave him alone to nurse his disappointments and sorrows? When the man raised his eyebrows in expectation, Donovan sighed. "She stood her ground, petted me like I was a deuced hound, and she…" *Bloody, bloody hell.* "She accepted that the beast was a part of me." And he'd made love to her afterward, slow gentle intercourse that had him giving up another piece of his heart to her.

"I see." Mountgarret frowned. "This should be cause for celebration."

"It's not."

"Let's change subjects. What happened after you took Alice into the garden beneath the full moon?" Interest hung on the question. "Did the curse break? Are you fully human?"

"I am not." Bitterness hung on the confirmation. He ignored the whine of his wolf in his mind. "The beast still lives inside me."

Surprise lined the viscount's expression while his eyes rounded. "I must say, I'm shocked, Manchester. You seemed so sure." He peered at Donovan. "She does love you, does she not?"

Memories of his time with Alice flitted through his mind like horses on a loop. Her twinkling eyes with the silver flecks when under high emotion. The tinkle of her laughter when he'd managed to amuse her. The way she'd embodied music as she'd played her harp. Her childlike delight when given sorbet. Her gentle teaching of his staff and everyone she met regarding her handicap and the bravery therein. The dreams she carried.

"Yes, she loves me." Strain graveled his voice. He shoved a hand through his hair, still damp from his bath. "Or, she did." *I took that love and smashed it beneath my heel as if it was nothing.* More of his words came back to haunt him. *I never wanted you, Alice... I chose the wrong woman...* A sob built, but he swallowed down the urge to vocalize his torment.

The viscount cleared his throat. "She returned to the ballroom in tears, looking as if she'd just lost her best friend."

His chest tightened. He poured out another measure of brandy and this time his hand shook. Crystal clinked against crystal. He'd seen her face with every word he'd uttered; he knew how destroyed she'd been. "What happened to her after that? I shifted and left London."

"Running away from problems of your own making." Amusement lit the other man's gaze.

Donovan narrowed his eyes. The question bore repeating. "What happened to her?"

Mountgarret sobered. "Your sister ushered her from the room. Neither of them reappeared at the ball, and without you in attendance either, guests left directly after dinner. It was a rather maudlin end to a promising evening." He peered at Donovan. "What did you do?" He planted both feet on the floor. "In your infinite arrogance, what the hell did you do?" The viscount leaned closer and dropped his voice to a whisper. "She loved you, man. Does that mean nothing? Do you know how rare that is in this world—our world?"

"Do you think I don't know that?" he shot back and followed the outburst with a sip of brandy. The drink no longer took the edge off the feelings pressing in on him. In a ragged voice, he related the incident that took place in the garden, told of all the terrible words he'd hurled at her. "There is no excuse for what I said." He shook his head. "I was disappointed, wounded, angry. I lashed out at her, wished to hurt her as I was."

You are a nodcock, human. His wolf huffed into his mind, clearly annoyed.

"I shouldn't have said those things. She deserved none of them, for she is everything good, where I am everything horrid." He swallowed the remainder of his drink, wincing at the burn. "But when the curse didn't lift and my wolf rejoiced, I... snapped." His rage having finally been spent during the two-day run, the only thing he felt now was shame and sorrow... and fear.

"In light of all you've told me, I must ask you this." Mountgarret leaned back, his eyes once more full of speculation. "Do you love her?"

Obviously I do not if the curse is based on what she said, that it's on me. "It's complicated."

There were many things he adored about his wife, that he'd discovered after they'd married, but love? They'd shared intimate moments where things had shifted for him and he regarded her in new lights each time, but did that constitute love? If he had, he wouldn't have hurled such insulting things at her.

Mountgarret's laughter brought him out of the moment. "Nothing is truly complicated. We make it that way because we cannot crawl out of our own heads."

"Don't talk to me about love if you haven't gone through that gauntlet." The reply was more harsh than he intended.

"Haven't I? Haven't we all and have known disappointment because of the curse?" The viscount glared and then sighed when Donovan failed to rise to the bait. "Still licking your wounds, I see," the other man said in good humor. When Donovan didn't reply, he sighed. "Still cursed and hurting, not because of that, but because you have failed to gain something else entirely."

How to even answer that when he marinated in a morass of confusion? "Everything I've hoped for is for naught."

"You have your wife. It'll be a good life between you if you let it."

"How?" Donovan eyed the brandy bottle with its remaining third of the amber drink. Perhaps if he got himself good in his cups, he could forget Alice's expressive eyes and the hurt therein. "I'm not a full human. Any male children we might have will suffer the curse." Bloody hell, she could even now be increasing. "And…"

"And?" The viscount lifted an eyebrow.

"I married her to bed her, so she'd break the curse."

"But the woman loves you anyway. After everything you've done to her over the course of your relationship, she cares for you despite it."

"Yes." The word was yanked from his tight throat. "She never wavered. How is that possible, Valentine?" He lifted his gaze to his friend's. "I used her, and she loved me anyway." Donovan raked his hands through his hair and then laid his head on the tabletop. "I don't deserve her." Alice should belong with a man enamored of her, a fellow who'd care for her as if she was the most valuable treasure on earth.

"No, you don't, but she's yours regardless. You have to face life as it stands now." The viscount remained silent for a few seconds. "Honestly, you wouldn't be as wretched as you are now if you didn't feel something for her."

Was that true? "I cannot face her. What would I say?" The table muffled his question.

"Try honesty. Apologize. It might help."

Donovan raised his head. "I rather doubt it. What I said was too egregious."

"Well, you cannot keep running from your problems. Neither can you hide from them."

"I can if I make a concentrated effort, Mountgarret." He fairly snarled the response.

The viscount rolled his eyes. "You made those messes; you clean them up." The viscount slammed a hand down onto the tabletop and Donovan jumped. "Don't become your father. Don't make the same mistakes he did."

"Why? It's inevitable now, don't you think?" He rubbed his eyes. "The curse revolved around Father's life until he became it; mine will too, since I cannot avoid it."

"Listen to yourself." Mountgarret grabbed a handful of Donovan's shirt and brought him close. "An arrogant prick like you, drinking himself into his cups and drowning in pity. Where is the pride in yourself? This is not you. You decide where you go in this life. Make certain it's somewhere that will bring you happiness. Patch things up with your wife."

Donovan reached for the brandy bottle, but the viscount moved it out of the way. Then he sighed. "I shall try." He owed her a wealth of apologies but feared those words would come too late. Hadn't she always told him actions over words meant everything? *I've failed her.*

"I'm glad to hear that." Mountgarret released his shirt. "Alice is good for you. And once you pull your head out of your arse, you'll be good for her. You have been all along, but you've been too blind to see it."

It struck him as funny, and a snort escaped him. "She's the one who is blind."

"It doesn't seem so." The viscount shoved at his shoulder. "Call for some coffee and sober up. Then go home to your duchess."

My duchess. He grunted. *The woman who hates me.*

It wasn't until after sunrise that he worked up enough courage to arrive at his townhouse.

As soon as he strode through the door, Griggs scrambled to meet him. To give the older man credit, despite the early hour, he was well turned out. "Where is my wife?" he demanded of the butler.

"I believe she's still abed, Your Grace. She hasn't slept well since you left." He swept his faded gaze over Donovan's attire: crumpled jacked, loosened cravat, unbuttoned waistcoat, and not at all the clothing he'd worn to the ball. His eyes widened. "Where have you been? The duchess has walked about worried to the point of not eating. I've never seen such a haunted visage."

Guilt washed through Donovan in a heated tide. "I was on business." He cleared his throat. "I shall go up to her." He strode down the hall toward the staircase.

"Very well, Your Grace." He was wise enough not to question Donovan further. "However, before you do, there is a Lady Cecily in the Gold Parlor."

Damnation. "So early? Calling hours are not upon us."

"I told her that, but she refuses to leave without speaking to you. She is quite agitated."

"Fine." He was restless and distracted by what he'd say to Alice. "Now is as good a time as any to formally break it off with the woman." When she'd left after a major squabble they'd had and he hadn't heard from her, he'd assumed their association was over. Apparently not. *Botheration*. Changing directions, he headed toward the parlor. He should have done it weeks ago, but Alice had occupied the whole of his attention, just as she did now.

As soon as he entered the parlor, Lady Cecily rose from a gold brocade settee. For the early hour, the woman had chosen to wear a gown more suited to an evening function, and it was rather more scandalous for even that, with a bodice that dipped low enough to show half of her voluptuous, pale breasts. Those were the very assets that had drawn him to her in the first place, but he barely spared a glance to them at the moment.

"What is the meaning of this, entering my home when I've made it clear you and I are through?" he hissed, uncaring that all of his ire and displeasure from the last few days had found its mark in her.

She rolled her blue eyes as she minced over the Aubusson carpet to meet him in the middle of the room. "Don't come the crab with me, Donovan. You know what we are to each other, and I don't believe you wish to break our association merely due to the fact you married some country nobody."

When she slid her hands up his chest to lock about his neck, he disengaged her hold. "I'm adamant, woman. We are through and have been for some time. My silence regarding not inviting you back should have been enough for you to figure out." Should he throw himself upon his knees before Alice once he rid the house of this pest? Perhaps Mountgarret was correct, and he should pour out the truth to her, hoping for forgiveness.

Lady Cecily pouted, and the gesture didn't affect him quite like when Alice frowned. The lips of the woman before him no longer held sway, for his wife's cradled his with tender perfection. "You don't mean that. Nothing should change what's between us."

"Oh, but it has." An unexpected grin took hold of him, for *he'd* changed since he'd met Alice. Never once had he thought about taking another female to bed since beginning his relationship with his sweet country flower.

"Pish posh." The blonde once more attached herself to him and this time he had the devil's own time extricating himself from her hold. "You were the best lover I ever had, Donovan. Don't you remember how we were together?" A whine had set up in her voice. "Now that you're being accepted throughout the *ton* more readily, I wouldn't mind being with you again. The things we fought about are forgotten."

"Ah, except you are more grasping than ever." He snorted and leveled a glare upon her. How had he ever thought lush curves and light blue eyes were more attractive than a laughing silvery gaze and the slender form Alice possessed? He'd explored every inch of his wife's body, knew all of her secrets, and lived to make her come undone—to make her smile. Donovan reeled with the knowledge. "Ah, so then you only wish to be with me in an effort to further your own agenda and reach." It had been the lady who'd thrown him over for another, vowing she couldn't be seen with one as sullied and as consumed in darkness as him, which had been the crux of their last disagreement.

Alice made you respectable. It is your wife's doing you are accepted, his wolf inserted with a grin that bared all his teeth.

Of course he couldn't ignore that fact. Alice had accomplished in two weeks what he'd not been able to in a lifetime.

Yet you've tossed it all away in a tantrum best suited for a nursery, his wolf tacked on.

Shut up. I'll go to her, but I must clean up this mess first. His chest tightened, and still his grasping, former mistress wouldn't suddenly vanish into thin air.

"Well, yes, this is true, because every woman in the *ton* wishes to elevate her standing," Lady Cecily replied with the bat of her long eyelashes. "You cannot fault me for it."

Not all of them. Alice didn't wish for anything... except my love. And he'd let her down.

She wrapped a hand about his nape. "We were good together, made quite the sensation when we went out." The lady walked the fingers of her other hand up his chest as she peered into his face, her color slightly overblown and garish for the time of day. "We were perfectly matched in the bedroom, or have you forgotten me so quickly?"

Donovan once more detached himself from her grip. Her scent of musk and Oriental lilies was all wrong, not sweet or innocent enough.

She's not Alice; not our mate. His wolf's whine echoed through the chamber of his mind. *Alice likes me. She scratches my ears, and she kissed my nose.* He wagged his tail. *This one doesn't know me.*

He gritted his teeth. *Don't remind me.* To the obnoxious lady before him, he said, "What was once between us is no more. Please understand this." Then he threw out a barb sure to cement his statement. "I am more than satisfied with my wife." Another grin surfaced, for it was true enough. Alice rubbed along well in every aspect of his life, and his respect for her knew no bounds. She'd embraced the position of duchess with elegance and grace from the start. In her, there would be no scandal or gossip.

He sucked in a breath. In her he'd found everything he'd ever wanted, and quite by accident.

Lady Cecily narrowed her eyes. Perhaps finally she understood. "I want the things I left here." She crossed her arms beneath her breasts and caused those charms to push dangerously tight against her bodice.

Briefly, he dropped his gaze to her bosom, and when he attended her face once more, a knowing light gleamed in her eyes. "My sister tossed them out with the rubbish days ago." He advanced upon her, hoping she'd retreat toward the door. "You refused to accept me for who—and what—I am, so I have nothing more to say. You made your choice; I'm making mine."

A trace of panic flitted into her expression. In a flurry of yellow satin, Lady Cecily flung herself into his arms, and this time she clung tight. "I can be your secret. Your wife need never know. Remember how I made you feel." Her whispered pleas fell fast and furious into his ear. Then she mashed her mouth to his, kissed him with a veracity he couldn't quite slow. "Remember how I touched you?" The lady slipped a hand between them and dared to cup his member through his trousers, rubbed her hand up and down his growing length.

An involuntary moan escaped him. Despite thoughts of Alice, he held the woman in his arms tighter. He returned her embrace before common sense came pouring in with loathing, guilt and a hefty dose of anger at himself.

"You're back. I was so worried…" The sound of rustling fabric at the door not two feet away brought his gaze snapping to that position.

Alice! He thrust Lady Cecily away from him so hard that she stumbled. "Enough. Do you hear me? Enough. We are done."

Alice stood within the frame, the robin's egg blue of her dress and her curly, brown hair held back with a ribbon a stark contrast to the overblown female before him. Her eyes rounded with shock and dismay as she stared at both of them, and even though she couldn't see, she'd no doubt heard enough that the exchange was damning. Moisture pooled in those gray depths, and when the tears fell to her cheeks, he shoved a shaking hand through his hair.

"Alice, please, it's not what you assume." He took a step toward her, but she backed into the corridor beyond.

"Donovan, why?" And then she fled, a hand to the wall as her guide.

Go after her!

He ignored the demand of his wolf as he took refuge in his ire. What was the point? She'd obviously come to her own conclusions and would think what she wanted. Once again, he wasn't good enough... More annoyed than ever, for these problems, this damned ache in his chest were of his own making, he grabbed Lady Cecily's wrist in a grip harder than he liked. "Get out of this house, and if I ever see you here again, I cannot be held responsible for what might happen to you." He growled to shore up the claim. "Do remember there are beasts that prowl the night—I am one of them—so run as far away from me as you can." As anger and self-loathing mixed within him, he half-pulled half-dragged his former mistress through the halls to the foyer, where he all but pushed her into his butler's care. "Put her out, Griggs. I have another disaster to attend."

Then he turned his attention to tracking Alice.

CHAPTER NINETEEN

Alice's heart beat so quickly she feared it would burst from her chest as she fled up the stairs and through corridors to the music room.

When Griggs had come to her earlier and told her Donovan had returned and would be up soon, she'd been elated and a bit fearful. He'd been absent for two days, left her heartbroken after the ball, but she'd thought perhaps they could work through the obstacles facing them. He'd uttered the words he had in anger and frustration and fear, she was sure of it.

So she'd dressed with Mary's assistance. Alice had made her way down to the main level, intent to catch him, and when she'd caught his voice in the Gold Parlor, she drifted toward that location.

She'd overheard what could only have been an embrace between her husband and his former mistress, for there was no doubt that's what those sounds of pleasure had meant. Then when he'd sprang from the woman, the actions had more or less proclaimed his guilt. In the home they shared, with an open parlor door where anyone could have seen them.

He had cracked the remaining pieces of her heart with the blatant disrespect.

Quietly, she closed the music room door behind her, and as the tears continued to fall, she stumbled over the floor and collapsed onto the stool at her harp. She didn't care that the rising sun glimmered off the gilt paint of the instrument or made the strings seem made of spun silk. Needing refuge, a solace from the unrelenting pain she'd known since the night of the ball, Alice began to play. The act of plucking at the strings, concentrating on the music stilled her thoughts, but no matter how sweet or angelic the notes were, they couldn't bind her shattered heart back together.

What did one do with a husband who didn't love her and wished to be with a mistress over her?

A soft click of the opening door alerted her to *his* presence, for it could only be Donovan. "Alice." The panel closed behind him, and he didn't advance fully into the room.

She ignored him; she had to protect herself, but her fingers slowed on the strings and her pulse quickened knowing he was so near.

The heels of his boots thudded against the hardwood as he approached. "Please let me explain. What you heard wasn't what truly was happening." Strain growled through his low-pitched voice, and it tugged at her. "I didn't…"

Alice stood. She came down the few steps to the floor and faced him. Oh, how she wanted to comfort him, soothe the pain he must battle with, but she couldn't. Not now, not when he'd essentially betrayed their vows and had hurt her terribly. Not after the horrible words he'd hurled at her the night of the ball. They echoed in her ears, and with every damning syllable, her world rocked once more. "Why did you do it? I can understand the annoyance at not having the curse broken, but this? Taking up with a mistress in our home, before God and everyone?" Her voice cracked and she hated that show of emotion.

"I didn't…" Donovan blew out a heavy breath. "She arrived while I was out. When Griggs told me of her presence, I met her for the express purpose of formally ending it with her." He edged forward a few more steps. His spicy citrus scent assaulted her, and as waves of memories washed over her, she whimpered. "My relationship with Lady Cecily has been over for some time now. Truly."

She bit her bottom lip while she stared past his shoulder, at the green blob that represented his jacket. As the sun continued to rise, his blob grew brighter. "Is that where you've been for the past two days? With her?" A sob climbed her throat and she swallowed it. "Working out your frustrations in her bed?" Did he truly prefer the woman with the shrill voice over her?

"No. That's not true." Honesty rang in his voice, his tone graveled with emotion he didn't reveal. "Since the night of the ball, I've been the wolf, acted as the beast. I gave the animal his head, let him run where he would, do what he liked. I cared not for my human life any longer."

Her eyebrows rose. That was quite the turnabout for him, since he'd previously refused to allow his animal full control. "You ran off like a child in a temper because you weren't handed what you wanted, what you thought you were entitled to."

"Perhaps." Silence brewed between them. Then he huffed out a breath. "I was disappointed in the outcome of that night and my conduct was unbecoming of a duke."

It wasn't an apology, nor did he claim responsibility. *Does he even realize how I feel, that he thrust me into this morass?* "You've previously lived your life in the hopes you would someday be free of the beast. However, what happened after such a letdown rests entirely on your shoulders. The mettle of a man is shown in how he faces adversity."

"I had just cause for my actions." He crept toward her another step.

Why couldn't he see the truth? "You let anger dictate your response."

"My reaction was warranted!"

Oh, Donovan, you have much maturing yet to do. "Perhaps but becoming the beast for so long and neglecting your duties was not." Alice wrapped her arms about her waist. He needed to understand his actions had consequences. That he was a duke and he couldn't carry on as if he were a thwarted youth. "Life, Donovan, is sometimes not fair. That doesn't mean it's not worth living or striving for happiness. You must attempt to find balance to all aspects of your existence."

"What do you know of it?" A growl threaded through his voice, but he didn't put space between them. "It's so easy for you to hand me those words when you have no idea what sort of strain I labor under."

"Every one of us has a struggle. Some accept it with more grace than you have shown." She flung out her arms as annoyance crawled over her skin and built through her chest in a hot wave. "Do you think I asked God for the blindness that leaves me ostracized from everyone? Do you think I would have chosen to lose my parents to fever at a young age, which thrust me onto the not so tender mercies of others?" She shook from the anger she'd not let herself show before. Then she modulated her voice, dropped it low. "Do you think I aspired to marry a man who is half beast, who doesn't return my love, who cannot wait to rid himself of my presence, who thinks of me as a mistake?" Despite her resolve to remain calm, tears spilled onto her cheeks. Two weeks ago she was blissfully naïve of how life would treat her as a duke's wife. Now that she knew better, she hurt as much as he, but she refused to wound him further or sink to his level.

Yes, he was at fault and yes, he'd brought them both to this pass, but the rift could mend if they came together in compassion.

Silence reigned between them for long moments. What did he think about and why wouldn't he voice those thoughts so they could talk about them?

"Please tell me how you carry on despite everything against you. I need to know." Pain wove through his tone, a pain that throbbed through his words, cut so deep she wasn't sure if even she could pull him out of it. He battled within himself, not just with the immediate problems their marriage faced.

She wilted while empathy for him crowded out the annoyance. "To give up is being a disappointment to myself." Alice took a deep breath and let it ease out. "Life is difficult enough without constantly berating myself, second guessing my choices." Her voice wavered. "I still have plenty of good left to fight for in my life, things I consider worthwhile despite being broken." She lapsed into silence, and finally asked, "Do you? Do you carry the will to fight for what you truly want?"

Fight for me, Donovan.

"At this moment, I am not certain."

The glimmer of hope she'd carried, faded. She turned away from him. "Then I cannot help you." Had she truly lost him?

"Alice, please, look at me." Donovan laid a hand on her shoulder and turned her about.

"Do not touch me." She shook off his hold even as need for him sent tingles through her lower belly. "You do not have the right any longer." Until he took responsibility for his actions, there could be no future for them. "Not after what you did in that parlor."

He blew out a breath but didn't step away. "I've told the truth. I haven't been with her for some time now. Not since you came into my life."

Her heart squeezed at the sincerity in his voice. "Words only," she said instead of the forgiveness she wanted to give right now. He wouldn't learn the lesson so soon. "Remember when I told you actions spoke louder? It is no less true now, and you have acted, quite frankly, like an arse since the ball."

He didn't reply.

Alice forged ahead, determined to lay everything to rest. "Did you return that woman's kiss?"

Another large swath of silence, then the word, "Yes," was pulled from him.

Tears filled her eyes once more. "Did you enjoy it?" Her heart broke all over again. They could move past everything except his willingness to betray their marriage vows.

"I won't lie to you. Not anymore because I want to repair the damage I've wrought..."

Those words warmed her heart, and it was a start, but she had to know. "Please answer my question." She swiped at the moisture on her cheeks.

"Yes, but—"

"Enough." Alice nearly went into hysterics when he touched her arm. She darted away from him. "You want her in a way you never wanted me."

"Once I met you, everything changed. Alice, please listen to me." Desperation wove through his tone. "That woman means nothing anymore."

"Except, you kissed her. That means something and solidifies that everything you've ever said to me has been a lie."

"No."

"Do you care about me at all, above and beyond the game you've played with me? Do I mean anything to you now that I've failed at lifting the curse?"

Please say you're coming to love me. If you do, there is hope.

His silence served as his answer.

She unsuccessfully stifled a sob. "Love is not a game, Your Grace. I gave you my heart and you threw it back at me in a million pieces. How can we overcome that?" Alice stumbled past him, ignoring the glance of his fingers along her arm, and she gained the door, gasping for breath, struggling to breathe past the pain. "I'm sorry I ever met you; that I ever fell for you."

"What we share is still good." His cry speared through her chest. "I saw that the moment Lady Cecily touched me."

"But you kissed her anyway." She shook her head. "I must get away and think but know this." She jerked open the door. "If you cannot love and accept yourself, you will never love anyone else, neither will you understand what it is to be human, cursed or not. And that is the crux of your current angst."

And once more, she fled from her husband.

She went as far as the private parlor set aside for family use when she ran fully into the hard chest of a man who smelled of cedarwood and cinnamon—the Earl of Devon.

"Pardon me, my lord. I'm somewhat distraught and not myself."

Devil Take the Duke (Lords of the Night #1)

"I know. Elizabeth told me, sent me an immediate summons." Instead of sending her on her way, he wrapped an arm about her waist and ushered her into the parlor. A growl sounded behind them—Donovan. Then the earl said, "Give her time. Find yourself before you make things worse."

"She is my wife," the duke protested on a shout.

"Then treat her as such. I refuse to let you destroy the one good thing you've ever done like your father did. You might not care, but I do." The hard edge to his voice surprised her, for she'd never heard the earl speak in anger. "Elizabeth, please take your brother in hand while I speak with the duchess."

"Thank you for being here, Rafe. It is… pleasant when you concentrate on Donovan instead of me." Elizabeth's soft tones promoted calm.

His sigh was barely audible. "Perhaps, one day…" The words were so quiet Alice hardly caught them.

Then the brush of skirting against hers made Alice aware of Elizabeth's brief presence before the parlor door closed and the earl guided her to a settee. He gently pushed her onto the piece of furniture and then sat beside her.

"Here." He pressed a cup of tepid tea into her hand. "Elizabeth and I had a meeting this morning to discuss how to help when we heard of Donovan's return and subsequent landing in the drink."

Alice appreciated the beverage as much as the support. "Thank you. I... I must look a fright." She wanted to concentrate on why his voice sounded so sad and resigned, but her husband occupied her thoughts. "It has been a trying few days."

He chuckled. "You look as one would expect in such circumstances. I apologize for Donovan. I had hoped... well, it is neither here nor there."

"I should forgive him. I know this, but he isn't sorry for what he did. He doesn't love me, so what good will it do?" She sipped at the lukewarm tea.

"Give you peace while he works through his feelings enough to pull his head from his arse." The earl patted her free hand. "He's conflicted. I've never seen him like that before, and that, my dear, is a good sign."

Alice laid the teacup onto the low table before her. "I'd like to believe that, but my heart hurts too much."

"What can I do?"

"Nothing, except talking sense into your friend."

"I'll do what I can, but he is still your husband." His voice was kind and there was a smile in the tone.

"Yes." And she was bound to him for the rest of her life. Without love. Such was her lot. "Do you think he is finished with the mistress?"

"I believe he is. Duchess, you must understand your husband has changed from the man I once knew. Even if you can't—or won't—see it."

Her chin quivered. Now that Donovan's friend vouched for him, she felt doubly bad she hadn't

Devil Take the Duke (Lords of the Night #1)

given him the chance to talk when he asked for it. "He doesn't love me, my lord. I doubt he ever will."

"You're wrong." He took her hand and held it between both of hers.

A tear splashed to her cheek. "He wouldn't have kissed that woman if he did." With her free hand she wiped at the moisture. "Never has he said he loved me. That is telling, is it not?"

The earl snorted. "Donovan's afraid. It has always made him retreat into himself." He sighed. "I'm not saying it's right, but he must learn a different way of living and it's undoubtedly thrown him into confusion and fear."

"Mayhap. I am feeling all of those things, too. I need him, now more than ever, but if he doesn't feel the same…" A shuddering sigh escaped her and she willed away any more tears. "I must move forward, as I always have. But I am adamant I cannot stay here."

"That's understandable. What will you do?" He squeezed her fingers.

"I suppose I'll go to his country estate."

The earl inhaled sharply. "Kimbolton Castle in Cambridgeshire?"

"If that is where the duke's estate is, then yes." It was yet another thing he hadn't discussed with her. "From there, I'll re-tie the threads of my life. Perhaps I'll make plans for my school." Despite her personal vow of no more tears, a sob raced through her and escaped. "I'll learn to live without him… just the way he wished it."

"There, there." The earl wrapped an arm about her shoulders, and when she turned into him, he let her cry into his cravat. "I wish you luck, and if at any time you need me, please write. I will do what I can to ease you into this next stage of your life."

She nodded. "Thank you. Please don't let Donovan destroy himself. There's still good inside him, even if he doesn't believe it."

And mayhap that tiny kernel, if coaxed out, could blossom into something more with time.

CHAPTER TWENTY

October 5, 1815

Donovan's whole life was falling apart. Every breath he took brought him pain, and not from any physical wound. No, he suffered from internal injuries brought about by his own stupidity and arrogance. His wife was leaving, and there was nothing he could do to stop it.

That's a lie. You can tell her how you feel, his wolf said with a healthy dose of disappointment in the response.

Easy for the beast to say. *I don't know how I feel!*

Another lie. His wolf snorted. *You tell so many you don't know what's truth. Haven't you pitied yourself enough? Stop using me as an excuse to hide from life.*

Perhaps human beings are not as strong or wise as wolves. I am failing miserably.

His wolf kept his own counsel.

Would that he could hide as he stood outside Alice's suite of rooms. The corridor was full of activity with servants running to and fro between the suite and a staging area in the downstairs entry hall. His chest tightened and the ache about his heart intensified. Elizabeth was angry with him, if the glares she sent his way from the sitting room were any indication. His wolf was disappointment and annoyance personified—if he were a human. Rogue had proverbially washed his hands of him after a failed conversation yesterday. Alice was hurt and broken, all because he couldn't work through the tangled knots of his emotions and core beliefs. He had wronged everyone he cared for in his life, and there'd been no excuse for it. He saw that now. Plus, he was still connected to his damned beast.

Yet, was it the horrible situation he once thought? Since the advent of Alice, he'd somehow become more respectable, more accepted in some aspects of society.

Why can she not accept me too, flaws and all?

Absently, he rubbed the skin over his heart through his clothing. Why the devil was that organ acting finicky as of late? Surely he was too young to have it attack him.

You are a bacon-brained idiot, human. His wolf snuffled. *You are in love with your wife. Admit it.*

Bah! Love for someone like me is folly. Donovan pushed off from the wall. As he entered the sitting room, Elizabeth stood up from her position on a settee. She held a leather folio in her hand, but her eyes narrowed.

"I hope you're pleased, you selfish bastard," she said by way of greeting while she strode over the floor. When she reached him, she drilled a forefinger into his chest. "She is the best thing you ever managed to do for yourself, and you've destroyed her like you do everything—everyone—else."

"But I—"

"No." She shook her head. "You have forfeited your right to explain. Because I refuse to lose a sister, I'll accompany her to the castle. You manage your bloody social life alone. I'm fairly certain you don't appreciate me either."

"Elizabeth, don't be like that. You know how it is."

"That doesn't mean it *always* has to be so. You *men*!" She uttered a sound of annoyed rage. "Every misstep or mistake cannot be placed on the curse. Every vile thing you men do isn't because of it. Take responsibility for you own actions, for beneath it all, you are human. Own that if you cannot do anything else. Yes, you've failed, but being human also means making amends and starting again. It means asking for and receiving forgiveness and learning there is more than one way to do things." Without another word, she swept from the room. The angry *tap-tap* of her heels echoed long after she was gone.

You're right, Elizabeth. Dear Lord, I need help. Yet why wasn't he strong enough to ask for it?

Griggs and a footman gathering luggage both eyed him askance before departing the room, and he sank further into the morass of his own creation. Alice had made a lasting impression on every person in his household, brought life back to the townhouse. Now, with her defection, would all of that go with her? A lonely future stretched out before him, and it terrified him.

His feet felt made of stone as he moved toward the adjoining bedroom door. With the veriest incline of his chin, he sent the maid scurrying from the room, her eyes wide and fearful. Finally, he was alone with his wife, the woman he'd wronged in so many ways, the only person to completely upend his world with a glance, a laugh, a kiss—her steadfast love.

Oh, God.

Alice glanced up from a trunk she knelt before. Mid-afternoon sunlight streamed around her, making her ethereal than ever before. She said nothing. After all, hadn't she said everything she could yesterday?

Words danced on the tip of his tongue, but pride and arrogance kept him from uttering any of them. Why should he? She was rejecting him anyway, just as every woman did. He wasn't good enough, *human* enough, so why should he unbend enough to appear vulnerable—to let her wound him further?

To let her help him?

Yet he raked his gaze over her person as she rose to her feet as stately as any duchess born to the role could be. Again, she wore the gown of silver satin and he couldn't help but think she was unconsciously on her way to donning mourning colors. But her expression was wan and pale. Faint purple smudges marred the skin beneath her eyes and her curly chestnut hair didn't gleam as it once had.

I did that to her. His chest ached. It was much like seeing an abandoned, crushed flower on an empty country lane.

Finally, he cleared his throat and moistened his lips. "Have you finished packing?" Damn, what a stupid thing to ask.

"Almost." Her shrug pulled her bodice across the soft swell of her breasts. How had he never seen it before how delicate yet strong she was, how perfectly she fit against him when they came together, how she'd tried to guide him? "Have you come to say goodbye?" The dulcet tones, once so lively and full of excitement for the world around her, now rang flat and tired. She'd given up.

Goodbye was such a final thing... and it scared him. His life had already seen too many of them. "I came to..." What? Why exactly had he come after what he'd done, what he'd said?

Tell her the truth. Bare your soul before it's too late, his wolf urged.

Perhaps it is already too late. There was no sparkle in her eyes. "You are truly leaving?"

"I am." She folded a shawl—the same garment she'd loaned him all those days ago—and then put it into the trunk. "At the moment, it's for the best."

For who? The rejection stung. How could it not? Out of all of them in his circle, he never thought she'd turn from him, yet they all had because he'd pushed them away. He gritted his teeth against the growing ache around his heart. Not even Alice, with her love, could save him.

Please try one more time.

"I hope the trip is pleasant. No rain expected." The pain of imminent loss throbbed through his veins, and he searched about for something more erudite to say. There was nothing except the horrible need for her. *I am a duke, damn it. Why can I not find the words she's desperate to hear?*

Because words aren't actions, his wolf mocked.

"How fortunate." She cast her gaze down. "If there's nothing else, I should return to final preparations. I would like to arrive before nightfall."

"Of course." Donovan's heart lurched. Inside his head, his wolf whined. The beast's sadness was palpable and only increased his own. "Alice, please reconsider." His voice rasped harsh with emotion. *Please don't leave.* How could he survive without her when he'd come to depend on her unwavering support that made him better?

"You know I cannot." She edged around the trunk but then halted her forward movement. "And you know why."

He reeled as if she'd struck him. Guilt plowed through his gut in a cold wave. "I don't want you to go." It was as truthful as he'd ever been. "I need you to save me," he added in a whisper.

A tiny smile curved her kissable lips, fading as soon as she gave it life. "For my benefit, or for yours?" When he remained silent, grappling with foreign emotions he couldn't speak aloud, she continued. "Save yourself, Donovan." Alice shook her head, her eyes reflecting grief. "Love yourself, for you cannot do the same for anyone else unless you square with who you really are, and I know it's someone beyond the broken man you are now."

There was a certain truth to her words. Why couldn't she see that her love was what he needed to glue his pieces back together? The unexpected prickle of tears at the backs of his eyelids surprised him. Never had he been brought low with so much emotion. Never had he met a woman capable of putting him at such sixes and sevens. Never had he respected, appreciated—loved—any female more.

And he was losing her because he didn't know how to live this new way.

"Alice…" He was falling and she wouldn't be there to catch him.

His wolf was quick to argue. *Isn't that what you wanted? A wife to pack off to the country, out of sight, so you could continue your previous life?*

Self-loathing, guilt and regret worked together to beat him bloody on the inside as he stared at her, his tongue tangled. *I don't want that life anymore.* Donovan tried again to stave off the inevitable. "The man you are disgusted by, the man you are disappointed in, I am, too." He rubbed a hand along his jaw. "Because of you, I've changed. I'm not that man any longer, and I'm grateful for it."

"I'm glad to hear that."

"But this new man, he's fragile and vulnerable like a baby bird, and I'm afraid."

"You will learn." She took a few steps toward him. "Do you love me?"

Tell her you do! His wolf strained at the edges of his mind, anxious to have the matter settled.

If he uttered those words, would she believe him? "I am quite fond of you and adore spending time with you." What the deuce was he doing? That wasn't what he wanted—needed—to say to her. *Yes, damn it, I think I'm tip over tail in love with you, but you're leaving as if I don't matter...* And he'd lose face once he said those words.

Confliction clouded her eyes, but she shook her head again. "You haven't changed that much if you won't speak from the heart regardless of how it makes you appear."

Damnation, she'd always had the ability to see into his mind.

"Donovan." She smiled, and it was a sad affair that tugged at him. "You have to want the change for you too. Find your peace. Love yourself," she said as she closed the distance and pressed herself close to him, her arms about his shoulders as she held his gaze with hers. "Once you do, come find me. I still want you, but not if you cannot know contentment with who—and what—you truly are. We all suffer hurts and setbacks, but only you can choose to use them as steppingstones for growth or let them weigh you down." She kissed him, moved her lips over his, and the innocent finality of that gesture shredded his soul. Before he could wrap his arms about her, she pulled away.

Donovan nearly threw himself at her feet, wanted to beg her to stay and be his duchess in truth because he loved her, wanted her in all the ways that mattered, but his damn pride flared and he kept quiet, much to the annoyance of his wolf, who howled long and mournfully in his head. If he said those magic words to her now and she still rejected him, how could he live with himself? His wolf would remain and she would leave.

I cannot survive with only the beast any longer.

"Very well then." He stepped away, out of her reach, and as a single tear slid down the slope of her pale cheek, he willed himself not to react. Her actions spoke loud as well. She would leave because she didn't love him enough—for himself. "No matter our differences, we both gaze at the same moon every night, Alice. I'll remember you when I have no choice but to become the beast. I hope you'll do the same."

Coward. His wolf turned his back on him.

I might be exactly that, but this hurt is infinitely better than handing her my heart and having her trample it.

Yet he didn't know how it could hurt more.

"I will." Another tear fell, and that singular drop had the power to make him come undone. "You are so loved," she whispered in a ragged breath that broke on the last word. "Why can you not allow yourself to see this?"

He straightened his spine. "Safe travels." With an aching heart that felt as if it had been splayed asunder, Donovan quit the room.

Moisture blurred his vision as he tore through the halls. Griggs attempted to waylay him, but he ignored the butler. Nothing could take this terrible pain from his chest, the agony that went so deep his soul cried out from the destruction worse than what he experienced while transforming into the wolf.

Not caring that it neared midday or that the streets of Mayfair were busy with carriages and foot traffic, he burst from the townhouse and ran until he found a halfway sheltered spot. Then, he called the shift, welcomed the pain but even that didn't soothe his breaking heart or fill the place that Alice had occupied.

His breath coming in short pants, Donovan ran and he kept running until his leg muscles ached and his lungs burned. He didn't stop until he'd reached Shalford an hour or so later, and even then he kept moving, for if he stopped, he'd think about *her* and remember... and feel.

Oh God, I love her, and I've lost her.

Thankfully, his wolf didn't answer, and still he kept running, for over an hour or more. He visited the villages far beyond Shalford's borders and then, in a bout of melancholy, he returned to the exact place where he'd first met Alice, where he'd rescued her from the runaway curricle. He darted into the thicket and down the embankment, swore he smelled her lingering apricot scent.

How could I have been so stupid?

Over and over their life together played through his mind until he feared he'd go mad from it. Donovan howled. He followed the river for a time and then ran into the thick tree line, wanting to return to London, to her, pour out his heart and say the words of love they both needed to hear, the words that would heal the rift between them and in him. Through every interaction since he'd told her of his beastly side, she'd done nothing but accept him—love him though he'd tried to deny it—and he needed her in his life because she was wonderful.

For no other reason than he loved her for her, loved and accepted himself now that he saw everything through her eyes. The weight about his shoulders lifted. He hadn't realized how heavy hating himself had become.

That was the lesson I had to learn. Now he understood everything, and the scattered pieces of his life clicked into place like a puzzle suddenly coming together.

He turned, changed his direction toward London, jumping over a fallen tree, skirting around dense shrubbery, his mind wholly absorbed on Alice, the light of his life. Every beat of his heart spoke her name. The terrible pressure in his chest eased. *I'm coming, Alice. Please wait for me. I can fix this.*

The sharp lance of acute pain shot up his rear right leg. Something pulled at that limb and halted his movement. With a yelp, Donovan writhed on the forest floor. He glanced over his wolfish shoulder, stunned that his foot was caught in one of the damn metal traps laid throughout the area.

Well and truly stuck, but thankfully, the ankle wasn't broken, only mangled, but if he thrashed, it would make matters worse.

Annoyed, and needing to return to Alice, he shifted into human form. Perhaps he could pry the metal jaws from his ankle and continue on his way. As he feverishly worked, three men came out of the undergrowth, one carrying a shovel, another a pistol. The third, Joe the blacksmith, had no weapons except his fists.

Damn and blast.

"Look what we've caught," Joe taunted with a grin that revealed a missing canine tooth. "That fancy duke who stole Miss Morrowe away from me."

"Naked bastard," another man said and spit in his direction. "Thinking you can do whatever you want. Hoping to lure another woman to your bed?"

The blacksmith smirked. "She didn't choose him for the size of his prick, did she, boys?"

Ribald laughter cycled through the group of hoodlums while Donovan glared. There was nothing wrong with the size of his member.

The third man frowned. "I swore we'd trapped a wolf. Saw him there."

Joe stepped forward, yanked Donovan upward with a fist in his hair. Pain streaked through his leg and scalp. "Oh, he's the wolf all right. Mayhap a demon. I saw him transform with nothing but dark magic."

"Unhand me this instant," Donovan demanded. He threw a punch, but the beefy man easily avoided it, and he retaliated by clipping Donovan on the chin with a blow of his own. Pain exploded through his face. He couldn't stand fully upright with his ankle caught and preventing leverage.

"You have no power here." With a hand still in his hair, Joe brought him so close that the blacksmith's garlic-scented breath infiltrated his nostrils. "I'll let you go on one condition."

"That would be?" This unnecessary delay might cost him Alice.

The other's man's grin chilled Donovan's blood. "You give me Miss Morrowe and I'll let you live, even though you deserve put down like the devil dog you are. We are good folks here and don't practice your witchcraft."

"Absolutely not. She's mine, and most definitely not a miss any longer." He couldn't keep the smugness from his tone. "She is my duchess." He'd tear this man apart for his insolence, relish sinking his teeth into his flesh. "You will not touch my wife." A certain amount of pride moved through him because she was indeed his, and once he was free, he'd tell her exactly how that made him feel. Never would he part from her again.

Go carefully, human. This man will hurt our mate, his wolf cautioned.

Joe snorted. "You think she's safe tucked away in London, bearing your name?" He shared a laugh with his cohorts. "Not with you and your evil."

"She is under my protection, and I will kill you if you touch her." Donovan snarled as his wolf strained for action despite the nagging pain in his ankle.

"Miss Morrowe—

"Lady Manchester," Donovan interrupted with a certain amount of cheek.

The blacksmith continued as if he'd not spoken. "Will come to me soon enough with you as bait. She's confused and thinks herself in love with the likes of you, the man who ruined her." He shoved, and Donovan stumbled then fell on his naked arse, jarring his ankle, the chains rattling, the coolness of the ground sinking into his skin. "Once she does, I'll exchange her for you, and even though she's been sullied by your dark magic, I'll still take her to wife. She was mine long before you came along."

"Like hell you will." Rage such as he'd never experienced before slammed into him in a white-hot wall. He summoned the shift, already imagining the forest floor littered with bloody body parts, but before the transformation could take effect, one of the other men slammed the flat of his shovel into the back of Donovan's head. White stars burst into his vision as a cloud of pain enveloped him.

As darkness claimed him, he cried out in frustration and agony. *Alice, I love you. Please don't leave me.*

CHAPTER TWENTY-ONE

Alice delayed her final preparations for as long as she could, hoping against hope that Donovan would run in and tell her the words she desperately needed to hear.

When he hadn't, she gave herself over to the numbing pain. Besides, she wished to tell every member of his staff goodbye, and that would take some time, for she knew what it was like to work for little or no recognition. The servants in the townhouse had been everything kind and considerate to her from the moment she'd arrived.

With Elizabeth's assistance, Alice sought out each and every member of Donovan's—her—staff. Some openly shed tears at her parting, some remained stoic but grew visibly upset when she touched their hands or traced their faces with her fingertips. Certainly, it wasn't what an ordinary duchess would do, but then she wasn't in the usual style. She never had been what anyone expected, and that was how she'd live the remainder of her life. There was a certain strength in the knowing, but that confidence did nothing to quell the ache in her heart. Donovan had given her many wonderful things, shown her even more, but he'd also made her wary and untrusting. She hated that about herself, but it was another part of growth. The key was in not letting it color everything else.

Bitterness had no place in her world. It served no defining purpose.

By the time she'd met with every person the townhouse contained, the purpling shadows of twilight had descended. She could delay no longer. Donovan wasn't coming for her. It was time to go. Her heart broke anew for them both. Yes, she'd married him knowing he hadn't loved her, and when she'd fallen headlong into that glorious state, she'd carried hope about her shoulders like a mantle. Perhaps there was still hope, but it rested on him alone. She couldn't work through his problems for him.

"We should gain the road before it grows too dark," Elizabeth murmured as she took Alice's arm and led her through the corridors to the entry hall.

"You're right." The suspicious sniffling from Griggs as he rushed to pull open the door for her further added to the torment storming about her heart. "I did so enjoy my time in London, though, when Donovan forgot himself enough to be human."

"The irony of it is that he is failing as only a human can," Elizabeth murmured as she led Alice down the short walkway, through the gate and then to the street where the dark blob of a traveling coach awaited. "I hope he finds peace. It's all I've ever wished for him." Tears lingered in her voice, and she squeezed Alice's arm. "He deserves that. I've tried to help him discover it long before you arrived. But if he's unwilling…"

"Yes."

"There's a step up here, Your Grace," a footman murmured, and she clutched at his gloved hand as he assisted her into the luxurious coach. "Safe journey." Griggs, who'd followed them, mumbled the same.

"Thank you." No sooner had Alice settled onto the squabs than Elizabeth joined her, sitting on the opposite bench. "I am glad you're coming. I don't know if I could manage the trip by myself, let alone pick up the pieces of my life."

"I want to come. At the moment, I'm out of sorts with my brother." Her companion heaved a sigh. "And things with Rafe are... awkward. I'm not certain how to navigate suddenly complicated waters with him, so it's best to remain out of arm's reach. It isn't something I'm interested in exploring at this time." A note of firm closure hung on her tone.

Alice kept her own counsel, but if fate worked to put Elizabeth and Donovan's best friend together, it would happen in its own time.

The pounding rhythm of galloping hooves shattered the silence. Alice craned her neck the better to listen while Elizabeth stood. "Who is that?" Could it be Donovan coming after all? Her heartbeat kicked up as hope glimmered once more.

"Griggs, what occurs?" Elizabeth inquired of the butler who still stood waiting at the open coach door.

"A courier, Lady Elizabeth. One moment." He stepped away, exchanged a few words with the man. Agitation filtered through both of their voices, and then the butler directed the other man to rest his horse and find sustenance in the kitchens. Seconds later, Griggs reappeared at the coach door.

"Is it regarding Donovan?" Alice asked as icy foreboding circled through her insides.

"Yes, Your Grace, and there is a missive."

Elizabeth sat heavily upon her bench. "Let me see." Paper rustled and scratched as her sister-in-law freed a note from an envelope. She gasped. "Oh, dear Lord."

Anxiety clawed at Alice's throat. "Read it, please." What had happened to her husband? Had he run from the townhouse in wolf form? His mindset had certainly not been sound when they'd parted. "Elizabeth?" She thrust out a hand, and it was Griggs who clutched her fingers in his gloved hand.

"It is but a short note, yet powerful if written somewhat crudely, so I will fill in the blanks," she breathed. "'If you wish to see the duke again, come to Shalford or else we will kill the beast he truly is and then spread the tale of his evilness far and wide.'" A sob left Elizabeth's throat. "Someone in Shalford has taken my brother hostage, and for whatever reason, they know of his true nature." The fear in her voice fed Alice's. Silence fell over them.

"How did they figure out his secret?" Alice asked and hated the quake in her tone.

"Perhaps he accidentally called forth the shift and someone saw."

Oh, no. "Or he was challenged, and gripped with high emotion, he couldn't help it. Perhaps he is in more peril than the note indicates." She clung to Griggs' hand. "I cannot lose him, Elizabeth. Not now, not like this." The two of them were still broken, hadn't had the chance to heal, and some of the people in Shalford were superstitious and ignorant. They could easily put him down if he still retained his wolfish form. "I have to go."

"But, Your Grace, it will soon be dark," the butler protested as he released her hand. "The roads are dangerous."

"No more dangerous than my ire knowing that the people I lived among for so many years have committed such a trespass against my husband." Strength infused her voice, and she straightened her spine. Feeling every inch the duchess she was, Alice said, "I need Thomas. Go fetch him. He's coming with me. Then send a message to the Earl of Devon. He'll want to help. After that, Griggs, I need you to prepare for any contingency." Power and a new look at life coursed through her veins. "I *will* bring the duke home. I swear it."

Griggs gasped. "Is there nothing you cannot do, my lady?"

Despite the horror of the circumstances, she laughed, and the sound dispelled some of the tension riding her shoulders. "I suppose we shall find out together." As the butler departed, Alice leaned across the aisle and grabbed one of Elizabeth's hands. "You can come or stay here, but I intend to rescue Donovan."

"Oh, Alice, you are a jewel." Elizabeth launched herself at Alice and hugged her. "I will come, of course, and then I'll tell everyone in the *ton* how brave and heroic you are." She loosed a shuddering sigh as she returned to her seat. "So much more courageous than I."

Alice allowed a tiny smile. "You simply haven't reached a place in your life where you are willing to risk everything you are for another person."

"You've not only changed my brother, but you are urging me into a better person as well." There was no doubting the smile in the other woman's voice.

Nothing else was said, for Thomas arrived at the coach's door. "I'm in your service, Your Grace."

"Good. Come. Share the coach with me and Lady Elizabeth. We must plan." She scooted over on her bench.

"My lady, it isn't done," he protested.

She uttered something that sounded suspiciously like one of Donovan's growls, and then unsuccessfully stifled a giggle. "There is no time for class separation or proper manners at the moment, Thomas. We must go."

Once the young man came inside and swung the door closed, Alice gave an amended address to the driver, and they were off.

Only then did fear creep in on her, almost paralyzing in its coldness. She had no plan. In fact, she didn't know what she'd do once they arrived in Shalford. For all her earlier bravado, she was blind, and it would be nightfall, and if the men who had Donovan were armed… Alice swallowed down the urge to cry. If this was to be her last stand, her final effort to win back her husband, then so be it. And if he truly didn't love her, she would wish him well—and perhaps to the devil—for his foolishness, but this was something she must do.

For them.

Once in Shalford, Alice's nerves crawled. The light of the new moon didn't lend much illumination. For the moment, Elizabeth and Thomas remained in the coach, which had been parked in the woods and hopefully not prematurely announce their arrival. They would spring out when or if negotiations turned dire.

Alice, in the meanwhile, had directed the driver to let her out on the public road in front of the mill. She would mount her attack from that direction and hopefully throw off the oafs who'd taken her husband. Nearly sick with fear, she followed the hard-packed dirt road toward what appeared to be flickering torches but resembled orange and yellow dancing blobs to her. The closer she drew to the meeting place—near the woods and river where Donovan had saved her from the blacksmith's embrace seemingly so long ago—the buzz of angry voices led her onward.

The flare of a bonfire near the tree stand confused her and burst upon her compromised vision with a brightness that stole her breath. She would make her stand here until she could take stock of the full situation. In a voice that shook, she demanded, "What is the meaning of this?"

A warning cry went out, followed by shouts from a few other men, and then Joe stepped forward out of the clinging darkness.

"Always so dutiful, Alice. Coming when called."

She narrowed her eyes as another man with a torch joined them. "And you are as repugnant as I expected. How dare you perpetrate something of this magnitude?"

"Fancy words won't reunite you with your devil duke any quicker," he warned and exchanged a laugh with his fellow.

"I want to see my husband."

Joe snorted. "Stupid girl. You can't see anything."

Alice curled one hand into a fist. She'd removed her gloves in the coach, wishing for practical over proper. "I refuse to talk further with you until you take me to the duke, so if it's me that you want, you'd best do what I ask." Fear careened down her spine as did sweat, which plastered her shift and petticoat to her back despite the autumnal chill in the air.

The blacksmith snorted. "Fine. So many airs from a woman who is nothing."

The other man grabbed her upper arm and roughly marched her toward the wooded area, skirting the bonfire. Out of the vast darkness, a lighter blob came into her compromised vision, and she held her breath. "I'll give you two minutes. No more, and even that's too good for the likes of 'im." The man shoved her in the blob's direction.

She stumbled, tripping over her skirts, and as her heartbeat raced a frantic tattoo, Alice approached what she now saw as her husband against the wide trunk of a tree. "Donovan?" She didn't stop until she laid hands on him. Once more he was as naked as the day she'd met him. The metallic scent of blood invaded her nostrils as did the wild, primal smell of him that she'd come to associate as his wolf. "You're hurt."

He roused himself once she traced her fingertips over his face, his shoulders, his chest. "Alice." Wonder infused that one-word response. "You came."

"I did." She pressed herself against him enough to discern his hands tied behind his back and ropes across his chest that bound him to the tree. "Are you in pain?" Bruises and a few shallow cuts decorated his once proud face. A trickle of dried blood marred his chin.

"My ankle was caught in one of their metal traps as I ran as the wolf," he said in a low voice, his brown eyes clouded with pain and anger. "They took me unawares; I was distracted, lost in my thoughts, attempting to return to... you."

"What?" He'd wished to come back? Her heart trembled with renewed hope.

When she finger-combed his disheveled hair away from his brow, he snarled at her, making her doubt the sincerity of his hint. "You shouldn't have come. Return home immediately. Get far away." Emotion graveled his voice, but he didn't expand his command.

Still as stubborn as ever. Oh, how she loved him. "I refuse, and since you obviously cannot take care of yourself, I'll have to rescue you." She softened the chastisement with a smile. "It's the least I can do, for you did the same to me at our first meeting."

"Alice," he hissed but there was no anger in his eyes. "This isn't a game. I want you protected."

"Of course it's not a game, Your Grace. It is my life—our life—and I must take it in hand." No matter that she'd been wronged, she intended to fight for what she wanted, especially if he truly had experienced a change.

"Enough." Joe barged into their space. He slid a beefy hand around her upper arm and tore her away from Donovan. "Why would you do anything for this nob? He used you, or were the rumors wrong?"

The ache around her heart throbbed. "The rumors are not wrong." She hated that her name and the duke's had been bandied about by gossips all the way out here in Shalford. Did the whole of England know of their torrid marriage? Then she shrugged, her gaze still on her husband even though he'd become lost in the fuzzy whiteness of her vision. "I love him. Nothing else matters."

"Ha!" Joe spit on the ground. "He is a monster, sent from the devil himself. There is something evil about a man who isn't fully human, who possesses dark magic to change into a beast."

She refused to rise to his challenge. "Whatever Donovan is, whatever he has done, he is still mine, and he *is* human, with the same rights that you enjoy, except you are acting the animal at present time. I'm honoring my vows to him, and nothing except death can part us." Standing stiff in Joe's crushing grip, she dared him to contradict her.

"That can be arranged." Hatred wove through the reply, and it sent icy terror rushing through her veins. He waved his free hand. "Time to try him by fire, boys. Make him shift so we can send him back to the demons he serves. Men like him are not natural."

"No!" Alice screamed. Her heartbeat pounded. "Donovan, shift! Show them why you are not to be trifled with." Surely if he called upon his beast, the strength of the animal could burst from the ropes that bound him. Easily he could take out these men who didn't wish to understand, who threatened them both. "Give the beast control."

"What you ask is too much." Donovan shook his head. "If I assume the wolf, he won't discern between you and them. He will attack everyone who is here."

"No. He knows me." She was sure of it.

"I cannot chance it." There was a decided growl in his tone, rage barely held in check. "I refuse to risk your safety in order to give these ruffians what they want most, for they won't hesitate to put me down in my beastly form, and it will be warranted, for I would kill them."

"But—" Would he not fight for them?

"I am not that man anymore." His voice had softened. "Because of you, because I wish not to be—for me."

Oh, Donovan! As much as it made sense, she didn't like it by half. When she attempted to wrench free from Joe's hold, he tightened his grip to the point of pain. Tears sprang into her eyes. "I hope you rot in hell for what you're doing. My husband is a duke. Threatening him, attempting his murder is a crime punishable by hanging."

"Who will tell once this night is over?" Joe laughed her in face. "And since you'll be with me, I'll have no problem keeping you quiet."

A handful of men swarmed around them, all facing the tree where Donovan was tied. Accusations flew, ranging from him killing their sheep and cows, to him destroying barns and fences, to defiling their daughters. Others claimed to have seen him murder a man in cold blood after he'd shifted from the wolf. Some of the men threw rocks at him. And though all the charges were damning, Alice believed none of them, with the exception of the slaughter of livestock. He was a wolf, after all, and even beasts must eat, but he'd told her he'd never killed or violated humans. It was enough and didn't sway her own thoughts. After everything they'd been through, if he had done what they said, her husband would have confessed it to her with everything else.

Through it all, Donovan remained silent though he growled and pulled at his bonds. Did he struggle with his wolf? Did it pain him to keep that tight control? Did blood trickle from his wounds? No doubt he glared at them all with arrogance and anger flashing in his eyes. Oh, how she would have loved to see such a sight, but her respect for him grew, for he didn't once bow to their level nor respond to their taunts. Like the duke he was, he kept his own counsel, bred to withstand torment from the masses.

Or he had truly found peace with what he was at last.

His very reticence sent Joe into a fury. The bigger man yelled, hurled insults at him, never releasing his hold on Alice. And then he apparently found Donovan's weakness. "What will you do when your whore gets with child, and she bears you a beast? Perhaps she's now as filled with darkness as you, has your devil's spawn in her belly, and the only way to stop the spread of such evil through England is to kill her, too."

Gooseflesh popped on Alice's skin. "No." She struggled in his hold, certain the man was mad.

"Let her go." Donovan's ducal command rang in the night air before she could say anything else. "I will do whatever you ask, submit to any of your insane demands, but you must let Alice go. She deserves none of this and is only here because of me. I want her to live the beautiful life she deserves. The world needs her light."

"Liar. All of London knows you only wanted her for your game of fate, and since it's failed, you have no more use for her. She's but a plaything, nothing more." Joe's taunting words stabbed through Alice's chest as if he'd wielded a physical knife.

"No. You were not given correct information. But then how could you know when I've just figured out the puzzle for myself?" Donovan grunted. A rasping sound filled the void as if he chafed against his bonds. "I would gladly give up my life to save hers, for that is what a man in love does."

...a man in love... Alice gaped. She went slack in Joe's hold. *Does he truly mean those words, or did he say them due to the situation?* "Oh, Donovan," she whispered, and when she would have gone to him, the blacksmith yanked her back so that she crashed into his chest. "Is that true?"

"Alice is not leaving Shalford again, but you might if you forsake all rights to your wife, *Your Grace.*" He spat after he mentioned the duke's address. "She'll remain alive, and I won't give her back to you. She's mine."

Heaven save me from overly possessive and stubborn men. "Enough!" Tired of males dictating her life, Alice uttered a garbled cry. She yanked her arm from Joe's hold, and then determined to guide her own fate, she rushed at her captor, flinging herself into his solid body with enough force that they both fell to the cold grass in a jumbled heap. "When will you understand my life is my own, and always has been?" With each word, she kicked and punched him as they rolled upon the ground. If she wanted a chance with Donovan, she'd have to take it herself.

A shout of warning went through the remainder of men assembled, and Alice prayed that Thomas and Elizabeth had chosen that moment to come to her aid. Sounds of skirmishes reached her ears, but she couldn't spare a second to listen or worry.

Devil Take the Duke (Lords of the Night #1)

She continued to fight against Joe. Scratched at his face with her fingernails, kicked his shins, drove a knee into the soft tissue between his legs, bit his earlobe when he surged against her and pressed her into the dirt. With everything that she was, she would fight until he was either bested or she was. "Being his duchess is my life now. I can help others with that title." She panted between blows. "No one has the right to take it from me."

"He is not for you." Joe got off a slap, and her ears rang from it. "You were content enough here with me."

"I was never with you! You assumed like everyone else in this village. I'm blind, not an idiot. Why can you not believe I don't feel for you in that way?" She levered a foot against his belly and shoved. When he fell off her, she scrambled to her feet. "I will say when this portion of my life ends, and damn it all, I have much to keep fighting for."

"You're wrong, Alice. He's cursed."

"I know." Perhaps she'd given up on Donovan too soon. No longer would she run to his country estate, not when things had turned a corner. "I want him anyway. Love changes everything." And it did. It blurred the edges, and like a watercolor painting, it made the harshness softer, more acceptable. She renewed her fight against her captor.

"Remember, you made me do this." Joe had gained his feet. He came close, and though she attempted to duck around him, he fisted his hand in her hair and wrenched her into forward motion with him, around the fire with its crackling flames and toward the river. "You're dull, Alice, and in league with dark forces. He's ruined you."

"No." As pain skittered along her scalp, she continued to struggle. "He has, in fact, saved me, perhaps from myself, from a life where I wasn't fully appreciated." No amount of clawing at his hand released his hold. "You think a woman is only on this earth to be bedded. I have much to offer beyond that."

He snorted and continued his relentless stride. "You're blind. I'm doing you a kindness by offering for you."

"So that I'd become little more than your slave, reminded every day how you extended charity, like everyone in this village?" Alice snorted. "That is no life."

The closer they came to the river, the louder the splash of its current grew. Her fear expanded. Joe tightened his grip. "What does the duke have that I don't?"

She smiled through the fear choking her. "A wolf." That was the truth. The beast was part of Donovan, and she accepted all of him.

"You're too far gone to save. I see it now."

"You see nothing; never have, you great lout."

"Bitch." With an enraged cry, he wrapped a beefy arm about her waist and lifted her off her feet. "If I can't have you, no one will." Then, with a mighty heave, he threw her from him and she went airborne.

For the space of a few terrifying heartbeats, Alice was weightless. She screamed into the night, and then she crashed into the cold embrace of the river.

Panic surged as the dark water came over her head and she sank beneath the surface. Wet skirts worked to further pull her downward. She fought, but she'd never learned how to swim. There wasn't a need or an opportunity. Every movement she executed made the situation worse, but when her head broke the surface, she gulped in lungsful of air. From somewhere in the distance, Elizabeth screamed her name; there was only wet and cold and darkness following.

Then Donovan called to her, asked her to stay with him, but she slipped back under. No matter how hard she fought, she couldn't find her way back to the surface. How would he know she didn't wish to run if she couldn't tell him? The current tugged at her, the skirting twisted about her legs to immobilize them. Her lungs burned; her arms ached. The ever-present panic clogged her throat and the heaviness of the water pressed in on her. *So cold. I am so cold.* She couldn't discern the world around her, for everything was dark, even the fuzzy patch in her vision. Drowning was such a horrible way to die.

A disturbance hit the water near to her position. Fear slid down her spine. Perhaps it was Joe coming in to make certain she perished. She flailed in an effort to move away, but her arms and legs wouldn't work properly. The current was too strong. Alice cried out, forgetting where she was, and muddy water filled her mouth, snatching the remainder of the air she'd horded.

I don't want to die.

Then a pair of arms wrapped firmly about her waist, and she had no more strength to fight, but instead of keeping her down in the murk, the man attached to the arms dragged her up, up, up, and when her head broke the surface, she spat out the water and sucked in as much air as she could, great, gasping gulps mixed with coughing. She cried, so grateful for the ability to breathe, and as she came back to herself, she beat at the chest of the man moving with her toward the bank.

"Alice, hold. It's me." Donovan's tone rumbled in her ear. "How could I let my sweet country flower drown when I've only just discovered how much I need her?"

Relief washed over her in warming waves. Love swelled within her chest, and she cried for a different reason as she clung to his neck, this man of contrasts, the man who changed her life, rocked it to its very foundations, taught her how to survive, to grow through the greatest of life's storms.

At the bank, he lifted her up. Elizabeth and Thomas as well as the coach driver helped to pull her from the water and to safety. Once Donovan joined her and picked her up into his arms, he ordered them all back to the London townhouse.

"What will you do about the men who attempted to kill us?" Alice asked, so weary she laid her head on his shoulder as he followed Elizabeth to the coach. "I want them punished." But if they told of his secret, what would become of Donovan?

"Once young Thomas freed me, I beat Joe bloody, I told the blacksmith that never again would I step foot in Shalford, and if he never set foot out of it, I wouldn't level charges at him. The same threat was given to the others. And if they bandy about such incredible tales, who will believe them? It's highly likely they cannot tolerate their ale. Seeing men transform into wolves indeed."

Despite the gravity of the situation, Alice managed a weak laugh. "Let us pray this is so."

"I am a duke. It will be." He pressed his lips against her sopping hair. "Those men don't matter to me now that I have you."

With the remainder of her strength, she smiled. It was enough.

CHAPTER TWENTY-TWO

October 7, 1815

Two days had passed since the events of that terrible night when Donovan had feared he'd lose Alice to death's embrace. Two days since he realized he couldn't live without her, that he loved her.

Even now he still reeled with the knowledge.

She'd come after him, and that in itself was extraordinary. She'd fought for him no matter what he'd done or said, even when she'd intended to leave. And she'd brought help.

His heart ached and he rubbed the spot above it, though he'd become accustomed to the pain. How many women would have sacrificed all for him? How many would have stood by him, loved him, even after he'd mucked up his life so badly?

Alice would, and she did.

Damnation, but he loved her. She had more integrity and courage in her little finger than he had in his whole body, but he was learning from her. That was a start.

He'd held her in the coach that night during the trip to London, loath to let her go. Elizabeth had wrapped her in a shawl, but still she'd shivered, and her teeth chattered from the wet and cold. He'd worn naught but the carriage blanket bundled about his waist, and as they'd traveled, Thomas had dressed Donovan's shredded ankle with strips from his own livery. Gratitude for these people in his life had overcome him. He'd been an arse, but they'd stood by him regardless.

None of them had conversed during the journey. Elizabeth had apparently taken down two of the men, wielded a large stick from the fire with a rage he hadn't expected; Thomas incapacitated a third while Donovan had laid into Joe and didn't stop until the man had been beaten bloody and rendered unconscious. By sheer willpower alone, he'd kept the wolf from taking control. He'd meant every word he'd said to Alice. If he would have shifted, none of those men would have left camp alive, and his sanity, his very humanity, would have been lost.

That wasn't who he was anymore.

I could have fought well, and you know it, his wolf protested.

We are held to a higher standard, and you know that, he reminded his furry half. *If you and I are to co-exist, we do it on my terms. Period. No more mindless violence, no more bloody anger.*

His wolf whined but didn't comment.

Once in London, Griggs had taken over and acted out Alice's orders. He'd whisked Donovan upstairs for a warm bath and properly dressed his ankle, and then tea was administered, copious amounts, until his body temperature had come back up. Alice was sent to her room and given into the care of an army of servants who'd been only too glad to see her return to their loving fold. After, she was sent to bed with a pile of blankets while he'd been assigned to his with the caveat that he'd prop his ankle and not move for a at least two days.

He'd done exactly that, even left Alice alone due to embarrassment, shame, and fear that she'd leave once she was able to travel.

What the devil would he say to her anyway?

Give her your everything, his wolf urged. *There is nothing else.*

Donovan still didn't know as he stood outside the closed door to the music room while nerves beset him. His ankle throbbed, but since he'd only suffered torn flesh and bruised tendons, he was able to hobble about for short periods. The magic that belonged to his wolf would heal him soon enough.

"Tell her the truth," Elizabeth whispered as she touched his elbow, and he started from his thoughts. He met her brown gaze. "Pour out your heart. It's all you need."

That's what I said, human. But his wolf grinned, paced about in anticipation.

He knew this, but to actually put it into practice? He sighed. "I'm afraid, Elizabeth." He didn't mind admitting it, not anymore.

She patted his cheek, her eyes full of compassion and sibling fondness. All traces of anger had fled. "Everything you've ever wanted is on the other side of that fear, brother. Make the leap."

"I hope when—or if—you find yourself in this situation in the future, that you remember this time in my life."

"There is no need to worry about that. Love is not for me." She tugged on a lock of his hair. Infinite sorrow and regret reflected in her eyes, but before he could question it, she continued down the corridor, leaving him alone once more.

Finally, he summoned the last vestiges of his courage and entered the room. His wife sat at her harp, playing a song that evoked sadness but was no less ethereally beautiful than any other he'd heard her play. *She* was beautiful, and the green gown she'd worn once before set off her ivory skin and caused her eyes to gleam. He forced a hard swallow into his suddenly tight throat. "Alice." The ragged utterance of that word fairly exploded through the room.

She ceased her playing and turned her head, training her gaze upon him. "I am surprised to see you." A tiny laugh followed. "Not that I can truly see." But a tremulous smile curved her kissable lips. "Are you well?"

"Yes." Donovan limped to her location as she stood. "I am. I shall return to full health quickly." So many words tumbled through his mind, sat on the tip of his tongue. How could he choose which held the most importance when so many things needed said? He took her hand, guided her down the few steps, and then he began the task of securing himself in her life permanently. "You told me to come to you when I found my peace."

She arched an eyebrow, and he knew a strong desire to press a kiss there. "And?"

An answering grin tugged at his mouth. "I found it, and it's you. When you are with me, I'm at peace with myself and the world. I feel... complete."

Our mate. Tell her she is ours forever.

Donovan ignored his wolf. He refused to rush his fences.

"What of your beast?" The silver flecks surfaced in her remarkable eyes.

"I have accepted he is part of me, and I will strive to keep him happy." He squeezed her fingers. "I'll learn from him. He will learn from me. When the two halves of myself aren't fighting, I am stronger."

A tiny smile again curved her lips. "And any male children we might have? If they fall under the curse?" Her voice wavered slightly and that small tell went straight to his soul.

"I shall properly teach them and guide them. I have wolfish tendencies, but that does not mean I am cursed." It had been a long road, but finally he'd learned such a simple lesson. "In fact, such a thing makes me unique but doesn't define me."

"Oh, Donovan, that makes me happy to hear." She never moved her gaze from his.

He had to tell her, confess everything, and in many ways this was bigger than telling her about his beast. "There is something else." Even his wolf held his breath. When she looked at him with speculation in her expression, he continued onward before his courage gave out. Wanting her to see his face, his eyes, he came close, their noses almost touching. "I love you, Alice. I have since that night in this very room." When she remained silent, he rushed onward. "I don't know how it happened.

Perhaps it came over me bit by bit, but I cannot live without you. What I said while tied to that tree was the truth." His pulse pounded in his temples. Had he'd confessed too late? "You are the reason I breathe. Please stay with me."

"Of course I will." Her chin trembled. "But—"

No, no, no! She couldn't reject him after all of this. Frantic that he'd lose her anyway, Donovan kneeled at her feet, still holding onto her hand. "Alice Sinclair, I have been a complete and utter arse. I've made mistakes, and I apologize heartily for them, but I'm learning from them. Will you make me the happiest of men, truly this time, and remain married to me?"

"I will!" Alice's grin dazzled him, was bright enough to complete with the afternoon sun streaming in through the windows, and it enchanted him. "Oh, I've waited so long for you to say those words." She pulled at his hand until he stood. "Come."

"I'll follow wherever you wish to lead." And he meant every word, but his chest remained tight with worry.

Inside his head, his wolf danced on his hind legs with joy. *She is ours!*

Indeed. Donovan couldn't keep the smug grin from his face. He'd fought his circumstances, himself and her, but in the end, when he gave up that constant strife, peace had poured in.

Alice moved through the corridors and up the stairs, her grip on his hand strong. When they reached her suite, she drew him inside, dismissed her maid, and as the door closed behind the young woman, Alice pressed herself against his chest, twined her arms about his neck and kissed him so hard and so deep that the sensation of falling assailed him. When they parted, breathless, she whispered, "Make love to me. Let me finally see the man I married with no lies or secrets between us."

"Gladly." Relief rushed through him, cleansed him, left him giddy with happiness and anticipation. He'd finally won her, and now his marriage was fastened to solid ground. For the rest of his years, she would be at his side, and they would help each other—change everything around them for the better, manage the curse now that he—they—understood it.

The kisses they shared were interrupted only as long as it took for various layers of clothing to hit the floor. He caressed her body, worshipped at her temple with fingers, lips and tongue, and when she was sufficiently aroused and panting with need, he laid her down on the sumptuous four-poster bed, caught her between his elbows, tangled his fingers into her hair, and as he layered his forehead to hers, he penetrated her body ever so slowly.

His moan blended with hers, and he released a shuddering breath of gratitude. Inside his head, his wolf howled with pleasure, and he shoved the beast behind a barrier. He did *not* need a voyeur right now.

This time, claiming her body, joining with her, having love behind the action, was a nearly transcendent experience, and as he moved within her honeyed heat and she matched his rhythm, he paused in order to catch his breath and marvel at the realization. It was him all along. *Dear God, it had all been so simple!* "I had to love someone more than myself, unselfishly. I missed the chance to change, to break the curse because I couldn't grasp the concept."

Alice finger-combed his hair, her touch light as it had been when she'd petted him as the wolf. "There is one more full moon that would possibly work this year." She stared into his eyes, and those silver flecks danced. "We could try again. Imagine how romantic the gardens will look with the frost and snows of winter."

Ah, how much did he adore her? Donovan smiled. "I have you. That is all I need in this life, but if my sons wish to break the curse for themselves, I shall be sure to tell them that love is the key." He thrust into her warmth a couple more times, astonished at the shift in perspective and how it enhanced everything. Once more he paused, and she blew out a frustrated breath that had him grinning. "I wish I had met you earlier, Alice, so I could have loved you longer." He kissed her deeply, drank from her until his head swam. "I have wasted so much time. If only I saw the truth sooner."

"Hush, my love." Alice held him close, her arms looped about his shoulders, her ankles planted just beneath his bum. She kissed him, and it was the sweetest benediction of all. As she stared into his eyes, she said, "We are here now. It is enough to build forever on." She smiled. "No more delays." And she wriggled beneath him.

The movement sent a host of sensation through his length and stones. He tumbled tip over tail into the depths of her eyes. He made love to his wife intimately pressed against her body, holding her gaze. Deeper and deeper he stroked. Higher and higher he climbed the rise as release built. Pressure mounted and he continued to move into her, with her. Over and over, again and again, and when her breath quickened and she begged him to finish her, he stroked faster. She shattered with a low keening cry, and the flutters around his member tugged him into his own bliss.

His breathing labored as he sucked in breath, and as he came back to himself, he pressed a kiss into the side of her neck. "Ah, Alice, my sweet country flower." Donovan flopped onto his back and grinned when she snuggled into his side with a palm resting upon his chest. He wrapped an arm around her, loath to break their connection. "Thank you for believing in me. Even when I didn't."

"I knew you would find your way, but I must confess, I would rather not go through such emotional trauma again." Alice smiled and he was lost—completely, fully, irrevocably. He was in love with his wife. She ran her fingers through the mat of hair on his chest. Awareness sailed over his skin. "Love that comes after moonlight is the sweetest of all, wouldn't you say?"

Ah, such a clever woman, his Alice. For in their case, love had indeed hit him well after that all-important moon. He pressed a kiss into her hair and reveled in her apricot scent. "Truer words have never been spoken."

How splendid he needn't fear the future any longer, nor fight with his wolf. He'd been wrong. The right woman didn't make a man weak or vulnerable; she made him so much stronger.

And perhaps that was the most valuable lesson of all.

The End

If you enjoyed this book, please leave a review. To find out what happens next in the Lords of the Night series, read *Bitten by the Earl*.

Regency-era romances by Sandra Sookoo

Colors of Scandal series

Dressed in White
Draped in Green
Trimmed in Blue
Wrapped in Red
Graced in Scarlet
Adorned in Violet
Embellished in Mauve
Clad in Midnight
Garbed in Purple
Resplendent in Ruby
Cloaked in Shadows
Decorated in Christmas
Tangled in Lavender (coming January 2022)
Persuasive in Pink (coming February 2022)
Disguised in Tartan (coming April 2022)
Attired in Highland Gold (coming May 2022)
Hopeful in Yellow (coming September 2022)
Christmas in Claret (coming October 2022)

Storme Brothers series

The Soul of a Storme
The Heart of a Storme
The Look of a Storme
A Storme's Christmas Legacy (coming November 2021)
A Storme's First Noelle in the *Star of Light* antho
The Sting of a Storme (coming January 2022)
The Touch of a Storme (coming March 2022)
The Fury of a Storme (coming May 2022)

Home for the Holidays series

The Folly of Caroling
Three Mistletoe Kisses
Silver Bells Scandal
A Holly and Ivy Affair

Willful Winterbournes series

Romancing Miss Quill (coming June 2022)
Pursing Mr. Mattingly (coming August 2022)
Courting Lady Yeardly (coming October 2022)
Teasing Miss Atherby (coming late 2022)

Singular Sensations series

One Little Indiscretion (coming July 2022)
One Secret Wish (coming September 2022)
One Tiny On-Dit Later (coming February 2023)
One Accidental Night with an Improper Duke (coming May 2023)

Diamonds of London

My Dear Mr. Ridley (coming February 14, 2023)
The Merry Widow's Wager (coming April 23, 2023)
Catch Her if You Can (coming June 13, 2023)
Yours Respectfully, My Lord (coming August 15, 2023)

Thieves of the Ton series

Captivated by an Adventurous Lady
Engaged to a Scandalous Earl
Married on a Wicked Morning
Intrigued by an Ancient Pedigree
Beguiled on a Christmas Morning: Christmas novella
Caught with a Stolen Diamond
Tortured by a Horrible Secret
Delighted on a Summer's Evening
Trapped in the British Museum
Charmed at a Yuletide Ball
One Silent Night
Redeeming a Tarnished Lord

Lords of Happenstance series

What the Stubborn Viscount Desires
What a Wayward Lord Needs
What the Dashing Duke Deserves

Scandal in Surrey series

Lady Parker's Grand Affair

The Bride's Gambit
Misfortune's Lady
Miss Bennett's Naughty Secret

Standalone Regency romances

Lady Isabella's Splendid Folly
Wagering on Christmas
Magic in Mayflowers
Act of Pardon
Angel's Master
Storm Tossed Rogue
Claiming His Wife
Scoundrel's Trespass
On a Midnight Clear
A Fowl Christmastide
His Pretend Duchess
Visions of Christmastide
The Viscount's Bluestocking Vixen (coming December 2021)
Pistols at Dawn, Your Grace, as part of the *Shifting Hearts* boxed set (coming February 2022)
An Accidental Countess (coming March 2022)
A Rogue for Lady Peacock (coming July 2022)
How the Lady Landed Her Viscount (coming August 2022)
She's Got a Duke to Keep Her Warm (coming December 2022)

Author Bio

Sandra Sookoo is a *USA Today* bestselling author who firmly believes every person deserves acceptance and a happy ending. She's written for publication since 2008. Most days you can find her creating scandal and mischief in the Regency-era, serendipity and happenstance in the Victorian era, or historical romantic suspense complete with mystery and intrigue. Reading is a lot like eating chocolates—you can't just have one book. Good thing they don't have calories!

When she's not wearing out computer keyboards, Sandra spends time with her real-life Prince Charming in Central Indiana where she's been known to bake cookies and make moments count because the key to life is laughter. A Disney fan since the age of ten, when her soul gets bogged down and her imagination flags, a trip to Walt Disney World is in order. Nothing fuels her dreams more than the land of eternal happy endings, hope and love stories.

Stay in Touch

Sign up for Sandra's bi-monthly newsletter and you'll be given exclusive excerpts, cover reveals before the general public as well as opportunities to enter contests you won't find anywhere else.

Just send an email to sandrasookoo@yahoo.com with SUBSCRIBE in the subject line.

Or follow/friend her on social media:

Facebook: https://www.facebook.com/sandra.sookoo

Facebook Author Page:
https://www.facebook.com/sandrasookooauthor/

Pinterest: https://www.pinterest.com/sandrasookoo/

Instagram: https://www.instagram.com/sandrasookoo/

BookBub Page:
https://www.bookbub.com/authors/sandra-sookoo

Made in the USA
Monee, IL
04 February 2025